Finding Home

A Windsor Peak Novel

Book 3

Denise Latham

Copyright © 2024 Denise Latham

All rights reserved. No part of this publication may be reproduced, distributed, or transmitted in any form or by any means, including photocopying, recording, or other electronic or mechanical methods, without the prior written permission of the publisher, except in the case of brief quotations embodied in critical reviews and certain other noncommercial uses permitted by copyright law. For permission requests, please visit the website below.

Any references to historical events, real people, or real places are used fictitiously. Names, Characters, and places are products of the author's imagination.

ISBN: 979-8-9888952-4-4

Cover design by Book Designs by Shae.

www.deniselatham.com

Dedication

To all those who rescue animals and people or donate their time and money to help save them.

To my fellow bookworms who share their love of reading on BookTok, Bookstagram and in FB groups like my favorite, the PMBC – thank you. Your enthusiasm for books keeps me excited to write, and I fully appreciate the warnings about things to avoid (looking at you, "breath she didn't know she was holding").

Chapter 1

Somewhere over the middle of the country, Patrick Burrows realized he was sick. Not just sick, but the kind where knowing your own name is difficult and waves of nausea make you aware of every breath that you take. He knew he had a fever, despite the fact that his chattering teeth had a flight attendant getting him a blanket and shooting him a concerned look. Sweat was running down his temples and his back, even though he couldn't get warm.

"Are you alright, Mr. Burrows?" The flight attendant squatted down next to his seat in First Class, half in the empty seat next to him and half in the aisle.

"Yes, thank you." He managed to rasp out the words out of his throat, despite feeling as though he had swallowed swords recently. "Water, please."

She nodded and hurried to the front of the galley, returning a moment later with a glass of ice and a large bottle of water. Setting both down on the arm rest, she looked around before pulling a small pouch out of her pocket. He watched as she rifled through it and then quickly tucked two small packets next to the bottle of water before walking away.

Taking a sip of the drink was difficult with his hands shaking so terribly, but he managed. Squinting at the packets, he realized she had left him Tylenol and an over-the-counter medication for motion sickness. She probably thought he was hungover, but he didn't care as he swallowed them down. All he needed was to get through the next few hours, and then he would be home in his own bed to recover.

The assistant working at the studio had purchased two seats for him, so he occupied his whole row and wouldn't need to make small talk for six hours. He was in the first row of first class, so when he had stepped onto the plane and dropped into the window seat, very few people had spotted him. Frequent flyers were probably aware that the empty seats meant a celebrity was boarding, especially on a flight departing Los Angeles, but no one had tried to sneak into the empty row this time. Earlier in the flight he had noticed an abnormal number of passengers getting up to use the restroom, trying to catch a glimpse of his face on their way back. Fortunately, this wasn't his first rodeo, so he was well prepared. A hoodie was pulled low over his face, and he kept a book to hide behind when he couldn't turn his face toward the window in time to escape the looks. Now if he could manage to get home before this illness completely took over his body, he would consider that a win.

His day had started off fine. Waking in his Malibu home, he had managed a last run on the beach outside his house before grabbing his bags and being whisked to the airport in a private car. Once at the airport, a team had met him outside to bring him in through a quiet entrance, where he was quickly shuttled through TSA and escorted to the lounge to wait for his flight. Forty-five minutes later, a petite brunette in a short skirt had approached him as he read a book in the corner.

"Mr. Burrows," she said quietly. "I'd like to bring you to your flight now."

"Thank you," he had responded, quickly tucking the book away. He followed her to the busy hallway, where he was placed in a golf cart and whisked to the gate. As usual, he was the last person to board, and the flight attendant was ready to assist with anything he needed.

"I'm so thrilled to have you on board," she enthused. "If there is anything at all I can do for you, please just ring the bell. And I mean anything." Her look left no question as to what she had been offering, and he had busied himself with putting AirPods in his ears and taking his book out of his bag.

Some of his co-stars had told stories about joining the Mile High Club with willing members of the flight crews, but that wasn't his style. He had simply nodded and smiled at her, then buried his face in the book hoping she would get the message. She had not, and continued to come by regularly, using the empty seat next to him as a way to get even closer to him physically. When she came to ask for his meal choice, she had conveniently dropped a napkin by his foot, and her hand on his thigh left no question as to why it had happened.

Feigning sleep had been his latest attempt at escaping her seduction attempt, and he must have dozed off before the poison in his bloodstream had reared its ugly head. Whatever virus he had picked up along the way was not going to wait until he was in his new house in Vermont to appear. No, it had to surface when he still had a connecting flight to make in Boston and was at the mercy of the flight and ground crew to get him through it somehow.

***

Two days prior to this miserable flight, he had been lounging in his trailer with a couple of his co-stars when an assistant director stuck her head in the door. "You three," she said to them, pointing a finger as she spoke. "You have a few weeks off after tomorrow."

"What?" Liam asked, staring at her with a piece of sushi halfway to his mouth. "Since when?"

She shrugged and consulted her clipboard. "No idea. You know they don't tell me much. But they want to work on the CGI stuff and have you all still available for reshoots, and with Natalie's schedule, this is how they decided to do it. Finish all her scenes and work on CGI, give you guys a couple of weeks to rest. You've all been complaining nonstop about sore muscles. She shot everything with you three already, but she has a bunch of solo stuff to do with background actors who aren't complaining as much as you."

"That's them," Zane pointed at Patrick and Liam. "I'm younger and could keep going."

"You're six months older than me," Liam pointed out.

"Younger at heart. And in better shape."

"Not even a little," Patrick replied. "But I'll take it. I've been looking for a few days to sneak home."

"No way dude," Zane shook his head. "We are all headed to Fiji. Or Tahiti. Hawaii at the very least."

"I'm going home. I didn't get a chance to go between Georgia and LA, and I have stuff to do," Patrick told him. "I just finished a complete renovation on a new house, and I've only seen pictures of it. I have a niece and nephew who keep asking me when I'll be home again, so it will be nice to surprise them. Plus, both of my sisters-in-law are pregnant, and I haven't seen my family in months. You guys go."

"You know we could spend a couple weeks on the beach relaxing, with a different girl every night, right?" Zane prodded.

"I'm good," Patrick said. "You guys have fun."

"We knew your brothers got married but didn't know that means you can't have some fun," Liam teased. "Meet us there after you visit your family. We'll save you a few single girls."

"I'll try," he agreed. He had little intention of trying but knew it would appease his friends. They had been together nonstop for the last few months; it was time to go home and have some quiet.

"Maybe we should go to Vermont," Zane suggested. "See what this town has over him. Maybe he's got a girl stashed there he doesn't want us to know about."

"No girl," Patrick insisted. "But it's quiet and peaceful. I get so tired of this city, not being able to breathe the air. Being on the mountains with people who knew me before I got famous is an easier way to live."

"Alright," Zane held up his hands. "You go to Vermont; we go to Fiji. Or Hawaii. Someone should be figuring this out."

Liam held up his phone. "I just texted and asked for an assistant to get in here to book flights."

"We could probably manage on our own," Patrick groaned. "Why are we incapable of doing anything ourselves? It's embarrassing."

"I have no idea how they make it so we don't have to see anyone at an airport, but they have their magical ways," Zane insisted. "And this is someone's job. If we don't ask for help, they won't have a job tomorrow."

"You've been a celebrity since you were a kid," Liam pointed out. "We suffered through the months and years of auditions and being broke, and now it's time to enjoy the benefits of what we do."

"Not my fault Allison had the good sense to pluck me from the ski slope in Vermont and put me on her latest hit show," Patrick laughed. "It took about five minutes between the time she saw me, and I got my first paycheck. I still can't believe how fast it all happened, it's like a blur when I think about it. I had no intention of being an actor, the thought had never crossed my mind."

"Trust me, I don't enjoy hearing that." Zane popped another piece of sushi in his mouth. "As someone who had to wait tables and sleep on couches for years before I even got a commercial, knowing you walked onto the set of the season's biggest hit with zero experience is annoying."

"Imagine how my dad felt. He thought we were just flying out so people could have a look at me, figured it was a free vacation. Next thing he knew, I was on a set, surrounded by people I had been watching on screens for years." Patrick rubbed a hand over his face, flashing back in his mind to those days. "My dad was out of his element. He was a big shot in our small town, now suddenly he was stuck standing behind all these people just watching this all unfold. He couldn't escape L.A. fast enough."

"Did you emancipate?" Liam asked, referring to the practice young actors went through to live independently at a young age.

"No," he replied. "I was so green, there was no way I could have lived alone. And even with a housekeeper, I would have been lost. You guys know my oldest brother, Dan. Luckily, he had just graduated from college and agreed to do law school out here, at UCLA. That way we could live together, and he was my guardian. He stayed years longer than he needed to, just so I wouldn't be lonely."

"Of course we know Dan," Liam laughed. "He deals with all our legal stuff. I don't sign anything without him saying yes first."

Patrick laughed. "Imagine how he is with anything of mine."

"Must have been quite the bachelor pad, you two living together in California," Zane said.

"Not quite," Patrick replied. "Our brother Jake had lost his wife in a terrorist attack and almost immediately enlisted in the Army to avenge her. We were all shellshocked, I think the reason Dan stayed here after I turned eighteen was because he felt like we had to stick together. Jake was in some other country and we barely heard from him, I think Dan worried that if he let me out of his sight, I'd drop off the face of the earth too."

"Not like you at all," Liam said. "We can barely get rid of you, and we aren't family."

"Rude," Patrick said. "I thought I was just like a brother to you. And you were just complaining about me not going with you on vacation, but you want to be rid of me?"

"Maybe I can tolerate you a little," Liam laughed. "It won't be the same without you. It's always the three of us, plus Tyson and Nat when we can drag them along."

"You'll have to make do without me this time," Patrick said.

He turned as the assistant knocked on the trailer and came in, laptop under her arm. She looked a little nervous to be alone with the three of them, so he sent her a quick smile before turning back to his lunch. Sometimes it was best to just act as though all of this was normal, like everyone around the world was eating sushi while travel was booked for them, and outside their door, paparazzi were hiding to try and get pictures of them at work. The less he acknowledged the weirdness of it all and pretended this was what he wanted, the less awkward it was for people who had to do trivial things for him. As much as he wanted to be treated like everyone else, sometimes he had to act like a movie star to make people more comfortable. They came in expecting him to act a certain way, and it only threw a wrench in the situation when he was nice, so he was constantly telling himself to keep himself in check.

An hour later, Liam and Zane had flights booked to Hawaii and Patrick was booked on a connecting flight to Vermont. They left his trailer bickering over the hotel options while Patrick debated texting his brothers before arriving, ultimately deciding to surprise his family. Instead, he sent a few texts to make sure things were ready for him when he arrived in Windsor Peak, and went back to the set with a smile on his face.

***

Now he found himself in the back of a Town Car, flying down the highway to Windsor Peak. He had no idea how he had managed to hold it together for the rest of the flight to Boston, or on the short connection. Somehow, he had found the driver in the small Burlington airport, who had retrieved his luggage for him and folded him into the back seat of this car. The driver looked in the mirror often, clearly concerned that his passenger was on drugs or about to vomit, but Patrick could only focus on making it to his house before he passed out.

The driver unloaded his luggage and then, realizing Patrick wasn't in any shape to carry it, dragged the bags to the porch and left them by his side. He sagged against the wall, trying to pat his pockets for the keys. After what seemed like hours, he felt the driver help him approach the door and take the keys from his hand. The door swung open and he sighed in relief, so happy to have made it, and disappointed his first look at his new home was through feverish eyes. He had yet to see it and had been looking forward to this moment for days, but all he could manage was to take the twenty steps from the door to a sofa before he fell down. He would look tomorrow if he was still alive.

Just before his eyes closed, he became aware that he wasn't alone. A figure seemed to glow across the room, standing in the open doorway. It wasn't moving and he didn't have the energy to fight even if one of the aliens from his movie had appeared in his new house. He muttered something that sounded like a threat to his brain but didn't sound like English when the words hit his ears. When the figure still didn't move, the black around his vision closed in and everything faded away into peaceful silence.

Chapter 2

Emma Martin eyed the still figure on the couch, unsure what she should do. She had been shocked when the car had pulled into the driveway, since the house had been empty for months. Her fight or flight response had apparently been to freeze, which disappointed her to no end. She had considered herself tough once upon a time, ready to defend herself, and yet she had stood locked in place as the car unloaded its passenger, dumped the luggage in the snow and peeled back out again. The man had stood, wavering unsteadily on his feet, before trying to make his way toward the door. Watching him stumble and nearly fall had her rushing forward to help, praying he wasn't a drunk on a bender.

She had slipped under his arm and was relieved when he didn't smell of booze, but had a pasty white sheen to his skin that didn't look good. He had felt hot to the touch, and his glazed eyes looked at her, but he didn't say anything. She saw the keys clutched in his hand and after successfully getting him to the doorway, waited to see if he would insert one into the lock.

"Can I just—" Without waiting for an answer, she had grabbed the keys and found the correct one for the lock. When the door swung open, he had lurched forward, dropping his coat to the floor as he took large steps towards the couch. She had waited several minutes to see if he would move, if it was a trick of some kind, even as the cold air swirled in from the open door at her back. Finally deciding he wasn't faking, she had gone back out and dragged all his luggage inside.

Creeping forward on tiptoes, she determined that he was not awake or likely to be faking it. His skin was pale, and there was sweat on his brow. He had fallen on the couch so his feet were still on the floor, and one arm was flung to the side and hung at an awkward angle. She debated whether to try and help him or take the time to escape. Deciding that he was too big to fight off if he were to wake up, or be faking, she started towards the kitchen door. It wasn't until her hand started to push down on the handle that she found she was frozen again. She couldn't possibly leave him like this. Even if she just made him more comfortable and made sure the door was locked behind him, she would feel better. Maybe she could even call for help before she took off, so a professional could come in case he was very sick.

Turning back from the door, she took a deep breath and quietly walked back to the base of the couch. He was exactly as before, still and pale, and didn't move when she reached forward with a finger and poked him. Content that he was soundly unconscious, she lugged his legs onto the couch and then pulled off his sneakers. Gingerly lifting his arm, she laid it across his chest before taking a quick step back. He continued to sleep, apparently unaware of her presence. She grabbed a blanket off the shelf next to the fireplace and draped it over him, realizing how cold it felt in the room as she did. Her fault, of course, for leaving the door open for so long.

Chewing on her thumbnail she debated her options. Lighting a fire would keep him warm, but if she did that, she couldn't leave in fear of the house burning down while he slept. The thermostat was set low, and even if she cranked it up, it could be hours before it warmed enough. Besides, if she left, there really was no way to figure out how to get him help, and she would be worried that he was dying on the couch while she made her getaway. Helping him seemed like the only logical answer, and she could figure out her excuse for being there if he woke up. Or if she started to see him come around, maybe she would have time to run off before he could grab her.

Decisively, she grabbed a small pile of kindling and a log from the stand next to the fireplace. For someone who was never at this house, it was well equipped, with everything he could possibly need. She couldn't help but wonder what it would be like to have all this and not even use it but pushed the thought aside. It wasn't her place to judge him, maybe he was serving in the Peace Corps or doing charity work somewhere. Just because he looked like a model didn't mean that he wasn't off doing good deeds while this huge house sat empty.

The fire flickered to life, so she made sure to open the flue and watched the smoke disappear up the stone chimney. Glancing back at the prone body on the couch, she tiptoed back to the kitchen and pulled the door of the refrigerator, stunned to see that it was full. Turning to the pantry, she found fresh snacks and fruits lining the shelves. She took two steps back from the food before thinking about what it meant. Clearly, someone knew that he was coming here, and must have brought all this in earlier in the day. Surely that person would come back and check on him, so she would have to remain alert to any noise from outside the house.

Finding a large, insulated cup in the pantry, she filled it with ice and water, adding some fresh lemon that was sliced in the refrigerator. Placing it down on the coffee table close to where he slept, she took a minute to study his face. He did look familiar, although she couldn't quite place how she would recognize him. Dark hair hung down over his forehead, making her want to push it back with her hand. His eyelashes were long and dark, dramatic against the paleness of his cheeks. He was big, almost too tall for the couch and clearly kept in good shape.

Windsor Peak was new to her, so she couldn't know him from the town. She definitely would have remembered if she saw someone like him at one of the places she frequented. It would be easier if his eyes were open, but then again, if they were she would need to be fifteen feet away from the back door before he could react to her sitting in his living room. Between the length of his legs and how fit he looked, she didn't think she could outrun him if he was healthy. Maybe in his current state, she decided, forcing herself to stay put.

Perching on the edge of the fireplace, she felt the warmth seep through her thin sweatshirt to her skin. It was rare that she felt warm these days, or in any days she could remember, if she were being honest. The last few years had been hard, every day being a unique struggle that she couldn't seem to break free of. Every time she thought maybe she was about to catch a break, something happened to make it all fall apart again. Her current circumstances were less than ideal, and she knew it was illegal, but the empty property had been too tempting. Not that she had dared to step inside the house, or touch anything other than the occasional shower that she allowed herself in the small stable bathroom. Even then, she took it cold so she wasn't using hot water she couldn't afford to pay for, but it was still wrong.

She had hitched a ride to this little town a few weeks back, hearing through her limited grapevine that she might have a family member here. Then the fear had kicked in, and she hadn't been able to push through to see if the rumor was true. Instead, she had discovered this empty stable, full of blankets and fresh hay for horses that didn't live there, and decided it was a better option than anything else she had. Rationing her small pile of food and refilling water bottles had helped extend her even smaller pocket of cash, but she needed to find a way to start earning money again. Unfortunately, the best possibility to find work was the exact place she didn't want to go.

The man groaned and she nearly jumped out of her skin, having been so lost in thought she almost forgot he was there. He started to roll over, and the exertion of it seemed too much, so he flopped back where he was and groaned again. Creeping forward, she grabbed the water and brought the straw to his lips gently.

"Try to take a drink," she whispered.

His eyes tried to flutter open, but stayed closed while his lips wrapped around the straw and took a small sip. He sighed again, as if that one movement had used up all his energy. She dared to brush the hair back off his forehead finally, feeling the heat from his skin as she did. Darting to the bathroom off the kitchen, she grabbed a small towel and soaked it in water, running back to place it across his forehead. When he didn't move, she went back to the bathroom and looked through the cabinet above the sink, finding a bottle of medicine that would help with his fever.

Pouring the two tablets into her hand she took a deep breath as she knelt down next to him. "Hey," she whispered, poking his side. "I need you to take these pills."

He groaned in response, which sounded like a no.

"It's just some Tylenol," she pushed. "You're really sick. Try to take one."

Putting her fingers on his lips, she pressed one tablet in. Grabbing the water, she pushed the straw against his lips and was relieved when he took a sip and swallowed. "One more," she encouraged, repeating the process. When he swallowed the second, she sat back, feeling relief.

She hadn't had someone take care of her when she was sick for a long, long time. Vague memories of her mother pressing a cool cloth to her head surfaced, and her mom holding her hair as she launched herself at a toilet. Somewhere along the line she had learned the basics of reducing a fever, and the need to drink water, but that was about the extent of her caretaking skills. If he didn't wake up soon, she would probably need to call for help, but that meant she would also need to leave.

Glancing out the window, she saw fresh snow falling heavily, and knew she couldn't go anywhere tonight. Better to do the best she could taking care of him and slip away in the morning. With the storm, it was unlikely that anyone would come up this mountain road to check on him anyway, so she could allow herself the luxury of curling up on the couch across from where he lay. Telling herself it was more for him than for her, she moved to the edge of a cushion, still debating the comfort of the sofa to sleeping on the floor so she wouldn't damage his beautiful furniture. Even the pillows looked brand new and expensive, way out of her reach.

Easing herself back on the couch, she couldn't help the sigh that escaped her lips. This was pure, decadent comfort. Her fingers traced patterns on the soft material, which was probably some kind of fancy leather she wouldn't recognize even if someone said what it was called. The pillow beckoned, encouraging her to lie down, so she gave in, allowing her whole body to relax on the couch. Just as she drifted off to sleep, luxurious on the soft cushions and warm from the fire, she had the thought that this was the greatest night of her life.

***

The colder air woke her up just before the fire went out, so she jumped off the couch to put more wood in. It robbed her of the opportunity to soak in the comfort for a few extra minutes, but that was probably a good thing. If she had taken the time to really appreciate where she had slept, she probably would have spent the whole day lying there. As the flames grew in the fireplace she turned to the man on the couch, taking stock. His eyes were still closed but his coloring looked better in the pale morning light, and he seemed to be breathing easier. Moving closer, she tugged the blanket up so it covered his torso before reaching out to brush a hand across his forehead, relieved that it felt cooler.

It wasn't until she went to take a step back that his hand reached out from under the blanket and grabbed her wrist, his bright blue eyes meeting her own.

"Who are you?"

Chapter 3

His vision was blurry, and it hurt to fully open his eyes, so he could only see a shadow of the person he held on to. It almost appeared as if she was glowing, and he questioned if he was about to die. The feel of warm skin under his fingers proved him wrong, that this person was alive and not a ghost. She was small, and he registered light hair before his eyes had to close again. He felt her slip from his grip and struggled to reach out again, but she was gone.

He could hear sounds as she moved around, but she remained silent. The crackle of the fire as another log was added, water running in the kitchen, and then the weight of a cold compress across his eyes. The struggle between sleep and figuring out where he was and who was with him was a losing battle, as his eyes refused to stay open. As his eyes drifted closed, he couldn't help but think that if he had to be miserable, at least he was in Windsor Peak. This was far better than his last night out in Hollywood, which had ended up decorating every entertainment magazine and talk show for weeks after.

***

He fiddled with the lapel of his tux as he flirted with the host of an entertainment show on the red carpet, knowing exactly what was expected at him when he attended a movie premiere. It was the type of event he both loved and hated, as he enjoyed seeing their work come to life, but hated the feeling that he was performing in his real life. Smiling at cameras and answering scripted questions into microphones was never his strong suit, he did much better connecting with people individually, but he went where the studio asked him to.

"Did no one think to bring us drinks?" Liam asked out of the side of his mouth as they took a cast picture on the red carpet.

"We're almost inside," Natalie soothed. "Then we can have fun."

A particularly clingy host, who Patrick usually tried to avoid, grabbed him with one hand and Natalie with the other, pulling them closer to her. "You two look delightful this evening," she gushed. "Any interest in discussing the rumor that there is as much chemistry between you off screen as there is on?"

Natalie draped herself on him, smiling with lowered eyes at the camera. "You know we don't discuss our love life with the press." She tucked her face into his chest briefly before turning back to the host. "Whoops, I mean our love lives."

Patrick turned, pulling her along with him for the rest of the red carpet. That one picture is what would be on the front of every tabloid and entertainment magazine for the next week, and all the work he had done prior to that was tossed aside. Nat, poured into a low-cut emerald gown that left little to the imagination, draped across his tuxedoed self would grace every magazine cover and TV screen. The time he had spent talking up his upcoming projects and smiling for pictures alone and with other costars would be left on the cutting room floor, all to showcase his supposed romance with his on-screen love.

"You know I hate when you do that," he whispered to her. "Liam eats it up, do it with him."

"I would, but it's so much more fun with you." She turned to wink at the cameras as he opened the door for her. "Besides, the world knows Liam is a total manwhore. No one would believe anything was happening between us, or that it wasn't a one-night thing. But you, everyone is obsessed with your chronic single status, and the quickest way to get on a cover is to fuel the rumor that we've been in a relationship for years."

"But we haven't been," Patrick sighed.

"No one needs to know that," she chided. "Besides, put yourself in my shoes. Everyone in the world thinks I've slept with all of you. The best thing for my reputation is to be tied to you, not jumping between you all. And it keeps people off your back, because no one is going to try and get with you when they think I'm in the way. It's a win-win for both of us."

"Why does everything have to be so complicated?" Patrick accepted a glass of champagne from a waiter, who was so busy staring at Natalie he almost dropped the whole tray. "You should wear more clothes."

She laughed, then took a long sip of the champagne. "That wouldn't fly in Hollywood, we both know that."

"Well, that dress should be illegal."

"Why do you think I wore it?" She smiled over her shoulder as she started across the room towards the producers, walking in her trademark slow glide that somehow drew eyes to all her assets. Patrick turned away, seeing his best options were to join Liam and Zane at the bar or his agent who was talking to the director.

"What's up?" He grabbed the glass Liam held towards him, knowing it would hold a fine whiskey.

"Just talking about you and Nat," Zane said.

"Nothing to talk about."

"You know she's turned us all down, right? Just try, for our sake," Liam suggested.

"No thanks," Patrick responded.

"Men across the country would trade places with you in a heartbeat," Zane groaned.

"Across the world," Liam corrected. "Honestly, at this point I believe the magazines. You guys have to be doing it and lying to us about it."

"I'm never alone," Patrick pointed out. "One of you is almost always staying at my place, and we're always together on set. When exactly would I be in bed with Nat?"

"Who said anything about a bed?" Zane winked. "I can think of ten other places I'd like to—"

"Enough," Patrick cut him off. "She's our friend. Let's try to be a little respectful."

"Dude," Liam said. "She loves it. Look at her."

They all watched as she threw her head back and laughed, and the men around her nearly fawned at her feet. Patrick could tell which man had made her laugh by the utter joy on his face. When she sipped her drink and caught his eye, she stared long enough for everyone around her to see who she was looking at. Patrick could feel the heat of hundreds of jealous men, and a few women, as she made her way to where he stood.

"Want to head into the theater?" She slipped her arm through his in a possessive way, nestling her breasts against his arm. He could practically hear clicks from the iPhone cameras across the room.

"Zane was hoping you would sit with him this time," Patrick said.

"He chews with his mouth open," she retorted. "I'm not listening to him eat popcorn for the next three hours."

"I do not," Zane objected.

"If this is really bothering you tonight," Natalie whispered. "I can lay off."

"No, it's fine. I'm just in a mood."

"There are scientific facts that if you—"

"Please don't finish that sentence," Patrick cut Zane off. "Let's go inside."

The four of them crossed the lobby to meet up with the rest of the cast, the director and producers, so they could all walk in together. One last set of photos as a group, once again with Natalie practically attached to him, and they were inside sinking into luxurious leather recliners. Natalie sat between him and the director, Zane and Liam sat on his other side. Snacks and cocktails were delivered to the small tables between the seats, and he allowed himself to relax as the lights dimmed.

***

His throat was so dry, and he couldn't reach the drink that was placed next to the popcorn. Trying to even lift his arm was hard, every muscle seemed to hurt. What had he done to cause himself this much pain? Suddenly he felt a straw on his lips and he drank quickly, then as he fell back, he realized he wasn't in the movie theater. He was lying on a soft surface, and he tried to open his eyes to see if the same woman was the one helping him.

"Nat?"

"Umm, no. Can you swallow a couple of pills?" A soft, unfamiliar voice came from next to him, where she must be crouched down. "I'm going to put them in your mouth, but you have to swallow them, okay?"

He may have nodded, but either way, he felt the capsules enter his mouth. Panicking at the last second because he didn't know what they were, he tried to spit them out.

"It's just some Tylenol," she said. "I promise."

He had no reason to trust her, but his current state required some kind of medical intervention, so he swallowed them down. Grabbing onto her again and managing to half open one eye, he was met with a look of terror in blue eyes. He quickly dropped his hand, not wanting to scare someone who appeared to be helping him.

"Who are you?" he managed to whisper.

"My name is Emma," her soft voice replied. "I'm just trying to help you, and then I'll leave."

"Don't," he whispered. "Don't leave."

Chapter 4

Emma went back to perch on the hearth in front of the fire, unsure of what to do. His firm grip had startled her, and there was no doubt he could overpower her. The alternative, to leave him here on his own, just wasn't a possibility in her mind. No one should ever be that alone and vulnerable, at least if she could help it.

She stood to pace back and forth, debating her options. *Call for help?* She could do that, simply call 911 as she darted out the back door and hope that whoever responded would take care of him. And what if they didn't come, or they left thinking the house was empty? She would never know, and he would be alone. *What about his phone?* She glanced at where the iPhone was lying on the floor next to him, screen facing the floor. She hadn't dared touch it, even when it rang and dinged all night. It was probably dead now, but she never knew someone could get that many phone calls and text messages. Surely, someone had to be looking for him?

It would be just her luck if she stuck around trying to help him, and he woke up and murdered her. Or if he was on the run for some heinous crime, and she would get arrested right along with him. Studying his face again, she weighed the possibility of him being a violent criminal and decided against it. Not that her better judgement had ever worked in her favor before, but he was just too good looking to be evil. And there was something in how he had said "please" that told her that he was a decent person.

Staying was the only option. With that decided, she went back to the kitchen. If she was going to be arrested or murdered, she might as well make some soup first. Homemade chicken noodle soup and some fresh bread would probably wake him, or at least be a welcome meal when he finally did wake up.

***

Lost in the task of cleaning the tools she had used to make the soup and loaf of bread, she jumped what felt like a mile when the body on the couch sat up suddenly. Dropping the cutting board she held, she winced when it clashed in the sink, causing him to turn his head.

"Hi," she said softly. "I'm glad to see you're feeling better."

"Who are you?" He rubbed a hand across his pale face, still looking off. "What's happening?"

"I'm Emma," she said as she dried her hands on a towel and then started edging toward the door. "I was just trying to make sure you were okay. You were pretty sick. But now that you're feeling better, I'll get out of your way."

"Please don't."

That please hung in the air and tugged at her heart, wanting to believe things would be okay, but still feeling the temptation to make a run for it.

"I don't know who you are, Emma, but please don't leave yet. If you wanted to kill me, you would have already. I'm not worried about you being in my house."

"I uhm—" She glanced around, trying to think of a convincing story. Why hadn't she spent the last twenty-four hours thinking up an excuse? "I don't want to kill you."

"Well, that's a relief." He sent a small smile her way before he stood up, pausing as if he was dizzy when he was standing.

"Are you okay?"

"I am, thank you. Just a little woozy, it's passing." He stood still for another minute before starting to walk in the opposite direction of where she stood. "I'm going to use the bathroom, and I hope you'll be here when I come out."

She paced back and forth, unsure if she should make a run for it or trust him. It wouldn't take her long to gather her meager belongings and get off his property, and it wasn't like he could move quickly. But she also had nowhere to go, and it was snowing heavily. She had taken advantage of his unknowing hospitality for weeks, the least she could do was face him. Hearing the water run in the bathroom, she steeled herself for the anger that was sure to come.

He walked slowly from the bathroom towards the barstools on the opposite side of the island than where she stood. Sliding one out, he sat heavily, sighing as he did so.

"Sorry, I'm really not feeling good." He closed his eyes, and she was sure he would fall asleep where he sat, but then they snapped open suddenly. "Emma."

"Hi," she whispered.

"Thank you for taking care of me."

"I couldn't just leave you like that," she replied.

"Did you drive me here from the airport?"

Her head snapped up. "You don't remember anything?"

"Nothing," he shook his head. "The last thing I remember is connecting to a flight in Boston. I knew I was sick at that point, but just wanted to get home."

"You looked awful." Her head was spinning, trying to decide the best option. Going along with what he thought might be the easiest option, but it felt dishonest. He was being too nice to lie to. "But I didn't drive you here, I was here when you arrived."

He looked confused, staring at her. "Were you bringing the groceries I had ordered?"

"No," she said as she studied the granite of the island.

"It might be easier if you told me, instead of me trying to guess," he said. "After all, I'm in a fragile state right now, I shouldn't be straining my brain."

"I umm—" She cleared her throat before continuing. "I was kind of staying in your stable, and I was on my way there when the car pulled in. He just dropped you and your stuff and left, and you didn't look like you could get inside on your own, so I helped."

"You've been living in my stable?" He didn't sound angry, just confused.

"Yes." She hung her head, feeling her cheeks burn while she waited for him to respond.

"Why are you living in a stable?"

"I didn't have anywhere else to go. And I don't have much money. And it was so cold, I couldn't stay outside. There aren't any shelters or anything around here, the closest one is miles away," she said quickly. The words had probably run over each other in her haste to get them out, but it was done. He could throw her out now.

He rubbed a hand over his face before meeting her eyes again. "I don't know if I'm dreaming or if this is really happening. I'm having a hard time following."

"Do you want some soup?" At his nod, she moved quickly to find a bowl and fill it, then sliced a large piece of bread to put on a napkin. Hesitating slightly, she opted to slide it all to him rather than come within arm's reach of where he sat.

He studied her some more as he took a spoonful of the soup. "This is really good. Thank you."

"You're welcome." She watched as he ate some more, unsure of what to do or say. "I'm sorry."

"I don't think you really have anything to be sorry about," he said. "You didn't kill me, so that's a good thing. The rest we can work out when I don't feel like I might have been better off if you did."

"I can go." She pointed to the door.

"No," he shook his head as he spoke. "Please don't. I'm going to eat this and then I'm going to find my bedroom and sleep for a lot longer. Then maybe we can talk, and this will all make sense. Promise me you won't disappear while I do that."

She met his gaze, only seeing kindness in his eyes. If he had wanted to call the police, he probably would have by now. But then again, keeping her here while he went to another room and called would be the smart thing to do.

"I won't hurt you or do anything, I swear." He pushed the empty bowl back. "I wouldn't do that to someone who helped me, and that's not who I am anyway. Whatever it is you think I'm going to do, I won't. I'm going to sleep, and I want you to stay inside where it's warm, and then we will talk. Okay?"

She nodded slowly, watching as he stood and moved toward the stairs. "Can I ask one thing?"

"Of course." He adjusted the thermostat as he answered.

"What's your name?"

He frowned at her, looking more confused before he responded. "Patrick."

"Nice to meet you, Patrick."

"You too, Emma. Please make yourself at home, I'll be down when I feel a little more like a human. If you'd be more comfortable in a bedroom, there are plenty, just pick one. They should all have doors that lock, which might make you feel more comfortable." He disappeared up the stairs, leaving her standing stunned in the kitchen.

Rinsing his bowl, she debated her options. The sun had set outside, but the last time she had checked, it was still snowing. Getting to the stable would soak the clothes she was wearing and leave her feeling cold all night. Sleeping in an actual bed would be heaven, and even though she had the comfort of his sofa the night before, it was too tempting to walk away from. Cleaning the kitchen quickly, she stored the soup in the refrigerator and the bread in a bag and dimmed the lights.

She crossed to the bottom of the stairs, peeking up to see an empty hallway with a light glowing from somewhere. Making her way up, she found the light was from a bathroom in the hall, the door open. All the doors were open other than one, at the far end of the hall, so she went in the opposite direction and chose the room furthest from where she assumed he slept. Closing the door softly behind her, she hesitated before turning the lock, feeling badly that she didn't trust him, but too often the people who seemed nice had ulterior motives. Turning, she stared at the giant bed in front of her, covered in pillows. It was beautiful and like nothing she had ever seen before, and she sighed when she pressed her hand to the top, feeling the plush comforter and the softness of the mattress beneath.

The open door in the room led to a bathroom, which she used quickly before shedding most of her clothes. The downside of her situation was that the little clothing she had was all in the stable, and she hadn't braved the storm to go get more. She had slept in her clothes the night before on the couch, but in the privacy of this room, she was happy to leave them folded neatly on the chair next to the bed.

Glancing around quickly to reassure herself she was alone, she giggled as she jumped toward the bed, bouncing in the middle and feeling a pillow bump into her head. Resisting the urge to stand and jump on it, instead she rolled back and forth as she smiled, feeling more like a child than she had in her life. Finally sliding between the sheets, she felt luxury as her skin met the material. Sleep tugged at her, but she resisted for a few extra moments, wanting to savor the feeling before drifting off.

Chapter 5

The smell of coffee brewing woke him from a sound sleep, and it took Patrick a minute to figure out where he was. The sun was just starting to rise, based on the scant amount of pink he could see around the curtains in the bedroom. The room was large and warm, and the bed comfortable under him. He propped himself up, testing his head and stomach, and was relieved when neither objected to movement. Swinging his legs over the edge, he surveyed the room.

The king size bed stood prominently in the room, covered in a dark blue comforter and way too many pillows. A large, plush looking chair and ottoman sat in a corner with a lamp and small table next to it, and on the opposite wall, a small writing desk was set up. A large bureau with a TV mounted over it was directly across from his bed. He guessed the walk-in closet was filled with clothes, and all the items he preferred were in the attached bathroom. Someone had done a good job of decorating the room to his preferences, and he sent a silent thank you to his stepmother, Stella, who he assumed had led the charge.

The bathroom mirror revealed what the sudden illness had done to him, and he was thankful for the lack of paparazzi in Vermont. His hair stood at all ends, and his stubble had turned nearly into a beard. Opting to skip the shave, he took a fast and hot shower before pulling on clean clothes, feeling like a new man. A ravenously hungry new man, he realized as his stomach growled.

When he got to the bottom of the stairs, he saw Emma jump from the seat she had been settled into, sipping on a cup of coffee. The startled look in her eye told him she still wasn't sure what to make of him, and the feeling was mutual.

"Morning, Emma." He crossed the kitchen and found a coffee mug, pouring himself a steaming cup while he studied her. It appeared she was in the same clothes as the previous night, but she had neatened her blond hair and her skin glowed as though she had just washed her face.

"Good morning," she replied. "How are you feeling?"

"Much better. Thank you for everything you did for me. I'm not even sure I know how long I was out for."

"Almost thirty-six hours, if you include last night."

"Wow." He was stunned at how much time had passed, when the last solid thought he had was of being on the plane from Los Angeles to Boston.

"I was worried that I should call for help, but I didn't know if they could get here in the storm. And I didn't want to leave when I wasn't sure you were okay."

"I appreciate you not leaving me alone." He caught her gaze before her eyes darted back to the counter in front of her. "I'm starving. Want some breakfast?"

"I can make you something," she offered.

"No, you sit and relax. Breakfast is the one meal that I am halfway good at." He gathered ingredients and bowls, before turning back to her. "Anything you won't eat? Dairy, meat, anything?"

She shook her head, so he went back to the task. Lining a tray, he placed raw bacon on it before sticking it in the oven he had already turned on. As he started cracking eggs, he gestured to the speaker on the counter. "Do you want to sync your phone, put some music on?"

"I don't have a phone," she responded quietly.

"You what?" He stopped and stared at her.

"No phone." She shrugged, not meeting his eyes. "They're expensive, and I don't need one."

"Ok, we can use mine." He grabbed his off the counter and found it to be dead. "On second thought, we can use Alexa. Just tell her what you like to listen to."

"Could you?"

"Sure," he replied, more perplexed than before. "Alexa, play some country music."

The sounds of Luke Bryan came through the speakers, and he could see Emma relax slightly. "I've never done that."

"Listened to country music?" he asked as he whisked.

"No, told her to do something." She nodded toward the speaker.

"Really? I use it all the time. It's much easier than googling the answer half the time." He put the pan on the burner before opening the oven to check on the bacon, and then putting slices of bread into the toaster. "Is this music okay?"

"It's great." She watched him as he moved, without allowing him to make eye contact. He paused when she cleared her throat and looked as though she had something important to say. "This is your house, right?"

He laughed, looking around the space. "It is. It's the first time I've been here though. I bought it a few months ago, and it had to be renovated. This is the first time I'm seeing it."

"Why weren't you here for the renovations?"

"I was working. My brother was in charge, so I had confidence in him."

"Must be weird, though. Having this big house and never seeing it," she said, looking around in awe.

He considered his words carefully as he poured eggs into the hot skillet. "I guess you could say that."

"What do you do for work?"

He turned to face her, unsure if she was serious or not. It had been many years since he could go out in public without everyone knowing who he was or had met someone who didn't recognize him. The TV show he had been on as a teenager had been hugely popular, and the movies he was in now had made him even more famous. He was sick of his own face, it was in so many places.

"Enough about me for a second," he said as he plated their breakfast. "Let's eat, and maybe you can tell me how you came to live in my stable."

She took the plate he held out to her after a moment's hesitation, and then leaned her face in and took a sniff before meeting his eyes and flushing. "Sorry, it smells delicious."

"No need to be sorry when you're complimenting my cooking," he laughed. "Or complimenting me in general. I tend to like that, just ask my family."

"Do they live nearby?" she asked, glancing toward the window. "You mentioned your brother was doing the renovations."

He nodded as he took a bite of his toast. "Yes, just on the other side of the trees here." He pointed in the direction of his father's house. "That's where I grew up. My dad and stepmom live there, although she's more like a mom than a stepmom. My brother Jake, who oversaw this, is also living there with his new wife while they wait until spring to build a house on the other side of my dad's. My oldest brother, Dan, lives in town with his new wife and stepdaughter, but I think he'll move into my dad's house when Jake moves out. Lots of moving going on."

"They both have new wives, that's exciting."

"Got married on the same day, as corny as that sounds. Dan lacks any patience, and when Kendra finally gave him another chance, he wasn't wasting any time. But it worked out great, and everyone was happy." He sipped his coffee and glanced toward her, seeing her more relaxed as he talked and didn't push her. "Dan and Kendra were high school sweethearts, and he had a lot of work to do to win her back."

"What about Jake and his wife?"

"Jake lost his first wife Jenna in a terrorist attack when their son was a few months old," he explained.

"That's terrible. I'm so sorry," her voice cracked as she said the words, as if she was fighting off tears.

"Thank you. It was terrible, still is." Patrick thought of Jenna's smiling face as she held her newborn son. "Jake enlisted in the Army and was gone for years, but Shea wrote to him the whole time. When he came home last fall after being injured, they started dating."

"They got married quickly," she pointed out.

"When Jake decides something, it tends to happen quickly," he said. "Actually, I guess people would say that about all three of us."

"No sisters for you?"

"Just the three of us. Our mom passed away after having me," he told her.

"Oh, no. I'm sorry, I seem to keep bringing up sad things." She had paled at the words, and he felt badly.

"I never knew her, it's different for me than for my dad or brothers. Stella, my dad's wife, has always been there for us. She raised us, we all think of her as our mom. No disrespect to our actual mom, she sounds like she was incredible. But we didn't have a chance to know her, and Stella did her best to honor her while also loving us like we were her own."

"That's wonderful." Her voice contained a note of sadness and she played with her fork as she spoke, her plate empty.

"Do you want more to eat?"

"No, thank you. I'm full." She stood and collected her plate, then hesitated before walking toward him to take his. "Are you done?"

"Yes, but I can wash that." He watched as she placed the dishes in the sink and turned the water on.

"You cook, I clean. It's only fair."

"Do you have family around here?" He saw her flinch briefly, even though she had her eyes on the sink. She seemed to shrink into herself, and he regretted having asked the question. "You don't have to answer that."

She sent him a small smile. "I'm taking advantage of your home and your kindness. You can ask me anything." She carefully placed the plate into the dishwasher before picking up the next one. "I don't know for sure, but I heard that I might. That's why I came here."

"Want to tell me about it?"

Chapter 6

His words hung in the air, and she scrubbed at the pan he had used to make the eggs with extra vigor as she considered her answer. "I'm not big on sharing," she said quietly. "But I've intruded on you, so I should."

"I don't want to force you to tell me anything," he said kindly.

"I came here from New York," she said in a rush. "I was born in upstate and bounced around for most of my childhood. I don't have a family like you do."

"That might be a good thing," he said with a smile.

"I appreciate you trying to lighten the mood, but don't take them for granted. They sound like good people, and you must be close to them to want to live right next door."

"You're right, I shouldn't joke. I know I hit the lottery with them." He glanced toward the window where he indicated they lived, and she could see the love on his face as he did.

"Whatever the opposite of that is, that's what I had. At least from twelve on. Before that, I had an amazing mom." She dried her hands and then looked around, hoping for something else she could do as they talked.

He stood suddenly, gesturing to the couches by the fire. "Let's sit over here. I need to add more logs to the fire, and it's more comfortable."

"I should really get going." She glanced toward the back door, seeing the piles of snow between where she stood and the stable and knowing it would be tough.

"That doesn't sound like the best idea," he replied. "It's still snowing, and there's at least three feet out there already, if not more. I've got a fire, I have food, and I haven't done anything to make you scared, I hope."

"No, you've been very nice. I just hate that I'm in your space and I wasn't invited."

"Well, I'm inviting you now. Please let that go."

"Are you always so nice?" She blurted it out without thinking.

"No," he shook his head. "But I am always nice to people who are nice to me. People who take advantage or look at me as a means to an end, I treat differently. You took care of me when I was sick, and I appreciate that. Plus, I really want to know how you are living in a stable, and what I can do to help fix that."

"Oh, no," she objected. "I don't need charity."

His head tilted to the side as he studied her. "I didn't say anything about charity. Sit, please."

She perched on the edge of the couch she had slept on two nights before, resisting the urge to drape herself across the silky cushions. The lights flickered and then went out, after a moment of silence she heard the refrigerator kick on at the same time Patrick stood up. He walked around the room, trying lamps until one turned on.

"Generator," he explained. "It doesn't power the overhead lights, but some of the plugs and the appliances. Plus, the hot water, so we can still have showers, luckily."

"You should probably charge your phone," she told him. "It was making noises constantly when you were sick, and then it must have died. But people must be worried about you."

"Good idea." He grabbed the phone from the island and looked around before pulling a cord from a drawer in the kitchen and plugging the phone in, leaving it on the counter as he came to sit back down. "All I know so far is that you're from New York, it sounds like your mom may have died, and you don't need charity, but you live in my stable. Also, that you aren't a murderer. Let's fill in some blanks."

"Yes, my mom died when I was twelve. She was the only family that I had, really. My father was a no show for my entire life, and if he knew that she died, he wasn't going to help. I worked really hard and saved as much as I could, and started moving around to try and find the one person I knew I could count on, but it's expensive to move around like that," she explained. "I don't have much money left. I was going to get a job in town, save a little and find a room to rent, but it hasn't happened yet. The closest shelter is in Burlington, and I couldn't get back and forth." The words came out in a rush, surprising even her.

"You think the person you're looking for is in Windsor Peak," he replied.

"Yes," she nodded with certainty. She had confirmed it on the first day she arrived, but something that felt like fear had stopped her from reaching out. If this went badly, she would have not only no one to rely on, but no hope. And that was her worst fear.

"And you'd rather not share who it is."

She nodded, avoiding his gaze.

"But it has nothing to do with me."

"What would it have to do with you?" Confusion ran through her as she looked up to meet his eyes, seeing a look she didn't understand on his face.

"Never mind, I believe you." His phone started making noises and he sighed, looking weary suddenly. "You need a place to stay while you figure out your mystery, right?"

"I do. I can find somewhere else, maybe the church can help—"

"No need. You're fine here."

"Thank you. I don't make a mess out there, I promise." The sudden relief made her feel weak; she didn't have to find a new place to sleep or store her few belongings.

"I didn't mean the stable."

Her head snapped up to look at him. "What?"

"You can't live in the stable."

"But you just said—"

"Look around, Emma." He waited while her eyes swept the room. "It's just me, and it's a big house. But I know that seems weird, so my suggestion is that when the snow stops, we check out the caretaker cottage out back. It should be in halfway decent shape, although the renovations hadn't reached there yet. But it's safe, it's warm, and if you can handle the décor from the seventies, I'm fine with you staying there."

"Why would you do that for me? I've been intruding on your property for weeks. You should be mad."

For a minute, she didn't think he would answer. He was staring into the fire, making her think he hadn't even heard her. Then he cleared his throat and looked at her. "I don't know that I deserve any of this, but I try to be a decent person to feel like I do. Helping you, or anyone who's in a situation where I feel like I could help, makes me feel less guilty about all I have."

"You shouldn't feel guilty," she blurted out.

"Maybe guilty is the wrong word," he said slowly. "Unworthy? I don't know. All I know is that my life is a little crazy, and I fell into it with very little effort on my part. But without going into all of that, I hope you'll agree. I can't have you sleeping in my stable when it's below zero most nights."

"I could leave?" she whispered.

"And go where?" His eyes wouldn't release her no matter where she tried to look.

"I don't know." She chewed on her thumbnail again, before realizing what she was doing and pulling it from her mouth. "I can pay you back. I'll pay you rent, as soon as I get a job, I promise."

"Then it's settled." He stood again, ignoring what she had said about rent. "I'm going to text my brother, ask him to get someone out to check to make sure the electrical and plumbing are working and safe."

"I don't need anything," she objected. "Don't bother him."

"It's not a bother," he explained. "I'll feel better knowing it won't burn down, and that everything works as it should."

"Do they know that you're here?"

"No," he laughed. "This will be the double whammy. I'm home, and I need a favor."

"Honestly, I'm fine," she said. "No need to call him if you'd rather wait."

"No, I had planned to tell them right away when I got home. The flu didn't factor into my plans, I thought I would have been showing up for breakfast the morning after I flew in," he explained. "Now with all this snow, I need to call to have someone come plow. Obviously not a priority when they think I'm a few thousand miles away, but now I need one of them to get over here."

Emma watched as he picked up the phone, unsure of how to stop him. Her plan to fly under the radar until she decided what to do with her life was coming to a crashing halt. Although, that plan had her living in a cold stable with dwindling money and food, so maybe that wasn't a bad thing. She stopped her spiraling thoughts as Patrick began speaking to his brother, shamelessly listening in on his half of the conversation.

"Jake," Patrick said into the phone. "How are you? Yeah, I'm good. I'm home. Yes, in Windsor Peak. I'm next door. It's beautiful, I can't believe how much you got done. I know, I'm sorry, I should have waited for you to show me, but I was sick when I landed. No, I'm okay now. Don't tell Stella. Don't. Ugh. Well, now you have to plow the way here for her, and I'll tell you why I was calling when you get here." He tossed the phone onto the counter and sighed.

"That didn't go as planned?" she asked with a laugh.

"No," he grinned at her. "It's fine, but you should prepare yourself. In about twenty minutes, there are going to be way more people here. And don't even think about making a run for it."

"You probably want to be alone with your family," she suggested. "I could just hide out somewhere, no one has to see me."

"They'll sniff you out, trust me," he said.

"I don't know why, but I do," she replied softly.

He stared at her for a long minute, and then smiled at her. "Ditto."

***

She snuck upstairs, clutching the clean clothes he had offered her to put on after a hot shower. They were way too big for her, but it would beat putting her dirty clothes back on until she could get to her bag in the stable. His family was on their way, so she appreciated him giving her an easy excuse to hide. She stepped into the hot shower with a sigh, realizing how often she had enjoyed this small luxury without fully appreciating it. Using supplies that were abundantly stocked in the bathroom, she felt like a new woman by the time she was done.

The clothes were even bigger than she thought, so she tied the waistband on the sweatpants before folding it over several times. The sweatshirt he had given her to wear over a clean t-shirt hung to almost her knees, the arms comically hanging well below her fingertips. She rolled the sleeves and laughed at her image in the mirror, she looked like a toddler playing dress up in adult clothing. Combing her blonde hair with the comb she had found next to the razor, she allowed herself a small smile in the mirror. A comfortable bed, a big breakfast and a warm shower was apparently all she needed to be put in a good mood.

Opening the bathroom door, she heard excited voices from the floor below. Knowing his family must have just arrived, she lingered in the hall for an extra minute. His low voice was easy to distinguish among all the others, although it sounded as though half the town had arrived.

"Why didn't you tell us you were coming?" A woman's voice demanded.

"I thought I could sneak in and surprise you all, but then I got sick."

"Sick? What's wrong?" The woman's voice had taken on a gentler tone, and she could picture a hand pressed to his forehead.

"I'm better now but it must have been some kind of flu."

"All the more reason to call us," she insisted. "I would have come over and taken care of you. You shouldn't be alone when you're sick like that."

"I wasn't," he replied.

"Who's here? Did your friends come?" A man's voice joined in.

"No," he said. "A new friend. No one freak out or make a big fuss when she comes down, okay?"

"A new woman friend? I'm intrigued." A laughing man's voice this time.

"Seriously, you guys are a lot, and she seems shy. Take it easy and don't freak her out, okay? And no questions, I'll answer them all later."

"This is all very mysterious," the woman replied.

Emma crept forward, forcing herself to move down the stairs. She could see Patrick just below the open staircase, a crowd of people surrounding him still wearing their coats. An older couple, a couple about their own age and a teenage boy were all looking at him with curious expressions on their faces. When the floorboard creaked under her foot, all those faces swung in her direction, and she felt her cheeks heat.

"Everyone, this is Emma. Emma, this is my family. Please excuse any embarrassing behavior they demonstrate; they can't help themselves." Patrick grinned at her as he extended his arms to indicate the crowd around him.

"When did you get to be so fresh?" The older woman scolded him as she stepped toward Emma. "I'm Stella, it's so nice to meet you."

"Nice to meet you," she replied quietly.

"This is my dad, Ben." Patrick pointed at the older gentleman. "My brother Jake and his wife Shea, and my nephew Charlie. Thankfully Dan couldn't make it up the mountain, but I would guess as soon as Shea finishes texting Dan's wife, they'll find a plow and make it."

Emma stifled a laugh as Shea shot a guilty look at Patrick and slid the phone back into her pocket. "I didn't want them to be left out. This is a big deal, you bringing a woman home with you."

"No-"

"I didn't," Patrick said at the same time Emma responded. "Emma is a friend, so all of you, please hold it together."

"That's what we do best," said the man Patrick had introduced as his brother.

"Take off your coats, let's make some coffee." Patrick collected jackets and shot Emma a small smile as he did.

"I'll get it started," Stella said. "Ben, come help me."

"You need help to put on coffee? Since when," Ben grumbled, a smile on his face.

"Since I got married and have a second set of hands to keep me company in the kitchen," she replied.

"And in the—"

"Do not finish that sentence," the teenager yelled, covering his ears. "Ever since they got married, it's brutal."

"Charlie, want to get my Xbox set up for me? I don't think anyone did that," Patrick pointed to the shelves next to the large TV.

"On it." He clapped his hands together as he headed toward the large entertainment center.

"Mind if we leave you two for a minute? I just need to talk to Jake," Patrick looked between Emma and Shea.

"Go," Shea waved her hand. "I'll get to know Emma."

Emma followed the other woman, watching as Patrick smiled at her before heading off and leaving her in a room full of strangers. She didn't know whether to hope that his brother talked him out of her living in the guest house, or if he said it was safe, because for someone used to being alone, there were suddenly a lot of people around her.

Chapter 7

Patrick watched Emma as she smiled hesitantly at Shea, and felt guilty leaving her behind, but knew he needed to catch up with his brother. They made their way into his office, tucked down the short hall to the garage, just behind the living room. Jake had kept much of the structure in the old house but had opened up the main area so the large kitchen and living room were all one open space. The pantry, bathroom and office were between the kitchen and garage, and on the other side of the stairs sat a large room that was presently empty. At some point he would figure out what he wanted to do with it, but that was a problem for another day.

"Nice to have you home," Jake said as he closed the door. "Filming wrap early?"

"No, I have to go back. They were a little behind schedule on some scenes, and Natalie has a commitment she has to be wrapped for. It was easier to finalize her stuff and give the rest of us a break, so here I am." Patrick dropped into the large chair behind the desk while his brother settled into an armchair by the door. "How are things here? How's married life?"

"It's amazing," Jake said, sounding excited for once. "I'm so lucky."

"She's feeling alright? When is baby Patrick due?"

"She feels great, only a little morning sickness but that's just about gone now. Baby will be here in late August," Jake laughed. "Trying to get my sleep now while I can, but with a teenager at home, that's a challenge."

"Things good with Charlie?" Jake had recently reconnected with his son after being injured in Afghanistan, and their relationship was finally healthy after years of strife.

"Great," Jake nodded. "Just finishing up his first season of varsity hockey, he's loving life. Helps that you were here for so long, the cheerleaders won't leave him alone."

"Want me to talk to him, tell him to be careful?"

"No, he's good. We talked about it," Jake leaned forward. "What's with the secret talk here, Patrick? And who's Emma?"

"Well, that's what I wanted to talk to you about," Patrick said slowly. "How much time have you spent checking out the guest house?"

"Not much," Jake frowned. "We did the electrical and plumbing inspection for all the buildings and made sure the whole property was safe. But it needs a full renovation if you want it to be modern and clean."

"I do, but maybe that can wait a bit. I offered to let Emma stay there."

"Let me ask again," Jake stared at him. "Who is Emma?"

"I wish I could answer that," Patrick started. "All I know is that she helped me when I was sick. And she's been living in my stable."

"I'm sorry, what?" Jake started to stand before Patrick waved him back into his seat. "She's been what?"

"I think she's homeless—"

"I'm calling the sheriff," Jake pulled his phone out of his pocket. "JJ will take care of this."

"Knock it off, Jake. Honestly, I don't need you to be big-brothering me right now."

"You think I'm bad? Wait until Dan hears about this. Actually, let's call Dan."

"No, we aren't calling anyone," Patrick glared until his brother put his phone away. "Don't you think if she was a danger to me or the house, she would have already done something? She was in here for almost two full days while I was basically unconscious, and she took care of me and didn't steal anything. She doesn't even know who I am."

"That's bull," Jake snorted. "There isn't a woman alive under ninety who doesn't know who you are."

Patrick shook his head. "I really don't think she does. She asked me what I do for work."

"She's playing you, Patty. Don't fall for this."

"Why can't it be possible that someone was nice to me for the sake of being nice, not for who I am?" Patrick realized his voice had gotten louder, his indignation at his brothers and frustration over their inability to trust his judgement coming out in his voice.

"It is possible," Jake softened. "I'm sorry, I hate that you feel like that. But it's also a very real possibility that this woman is unbalanced and knows exactly who you are."

"I'm trusting my gut here," Patrick said stubbornly. "I'll find out more. All I know right now is that she came to town to find someone, not me, and she was living in my stable. She's skittish and nervous, but I don't think it's because she wants to kill me. Or marry me for my money."

"What do you want from me?"

"Help me make the guest house useable so she's not living in the stable, or in here with me."

"Patrick, is this a romantic thing?" Jake asked, leaning forward. "She's very pretty, but you could have anyone. You don't need to save this girl."

"I'm not trying to save her," Patrick said quietly. "I'm just trying to help someone who needs it. I've done it plenty of times without an issue."

"I know," Jake said. "And we appreciate it. You paid for basically our entire wedding and flew in that crazy band, and the dresses, and we are so grateful."

"That stuff you guys get for being family," Patrick laughed. "I replaced the roof on the library last year when the tree went through it and no one had a problem with that. If I can help fix a problem I do, especially when it's just money."

"And you see her as a problem?" Jake prodded.

"No," Patrick groaned. "You make me sound like an ass. I see her as someone who needs a break in life. Who maybe deserves a little kindness. And I can give her that."

"And you think she's pretty?"

"Are you twelve?" Patrick stared at his brother, somewhat shocked that Jake of all people had asked. Jake, who had spent years in war zones and up until a few months ago, had seemed oblivious to things like other people's feelings.

"Just admit it," Jake pushed.

"Fine, she's very pretty. Happy?"

"No, now I'm nervous to leave you alone with her. Don't get anyone pregnant."

"Pot, meet kettle."

"Shea is my wife," Jake laughed. "I'm supposed to knock her up."

"Save your speeches for your teenager," Patrick said as he stood. "I'm very capable of protecting myself. Now can we go look at the guest house?"

"With Dad and Stella here? You want to open that can of worms?"

"They're already going to have a million questions," Patrick pointed out. "Might as well give them and you the peace of mind knowing that the big bad girl is not in the same house as me."

Jake laughed as they went out to join the family by the fire, where Charlie was happily engrossed in an Xbox game. "Hey, Charlie, I need your help," he called out.

"Can I finish this?" The teen asked, not taking his eyes off the screen.

"Sure," Jake agreed. "There are a couple shovels outside in the garage, I'll go grab them and Charlie and I can make a path."

"Path to what?" Ben asked. "I can help."

"No, you sit and enjoy your coffee. We don't need any management help while shoveling," Jake laughed. "Patrick will explain."

"I asked Jake to take a look at the guest house, see what we can do to make it livable," Patrick said to the group.

"Is someone coming to visit?" Stella asked. "Your friends might be more comfortable in the main house."

"It's for Emma," he nodded in her direction. "She needs a place to stay, and I offered it to her."

The silence descended, and Patrick saw the red creeping up Emma's cheeks even though she ducked her head down. She seemed to shrivel as the attention turned to her before everyone's eyes swung back in his direction.

"That was very nice of you," Shea murmured, smiling at him.

"Thanks," he responded. "I'll explain it all later, but that's what's happening."

"How do you two know each other?" Ben demanded, his gaze swinging between him and Emma.

"Dad," Patrick said sharply. "I said we would talk about all of it later. This is my house, and I invited a friend to stay in my guest house. Discussion over."

"Okay then." Charlie backed out of the room, placing the game remote on the shelf. "I'll just go help my dad."

"I don't want to cause any problems," Emma's voice sounded small. "I can leave."

"Absolutely not," Stella answered before he could. "You're staying right there. Patrick is right, this is his home, and his friends are welcome. We don't mean to make you feel uncomfortable, Emma. I'm happy to meet you and get to know any friend of Patrick's. Actually, why don't all the men go shovel while us girl's chat."

Patrick debated staying where he was, but Stella made a shooing motion with her hand and gave him a look that said he would regret not doing as asked. It might be his home, but she was still in charge, apparently.

"You okay if I go," he asked Emma as he gestured toward the door.

"Yes, I'm fine."

"Just yell if these two get unbearable," he said with a smile.

As expected, Ben was standing just outside the kitchen door, yelling instructions to Jake and Charlie. He turned when Patrick stepped out onto the porch, frowning at him.

"Son, do you know this girl?"

"No, Dad. But I just finished telling Jake, she was here the whole time I was sick. If she wanted to kill me or rob me blind, she could have." He pulled a hat onto his head as he spoke. "And honestly, I'm almost thirty. Time to let me trust my instinct a little, okay?"

"It's just that—"

"I know," he interrupted. "I'm very aware of all the people who see me as a meal ticket, or a way to get ahead in life. I don't think she knows who I am."

Ben shot a glance at the door before he spoke. "I wasn't aware anyone in the world didn't know who you are."

"I mean, if the world wants to revolve around me, that's fine. But she honestly didn't seem to know. And if she's acting, she deserves to be in Hollywood, so I'll hook her up." Patrick sighed, glancing between his father and where his brother stood listening. "Let's just get this taken care of, okay? I still feel like crap and want to go back to bed."

"Why don't you go inside? We can take care of this," his father said with concern in his eyes.

"No, I want to see how it looks. Just give me a chance to figure out this Emma situation, without assuming the worst."

"I'm allowed to worry about you," Ben said. "That part doesn't go away, no matter how old you are or how much money you make."

"I know, Dad. I love you and appreciate it. But please, don't try to manage this." Patrick put an arm around his dad's shoulders and gave him a squeeze. "Besides, you've got enough on your plate with a new wife to handle."

"Boy, does she keep me on my toes," Ben laughed.

"We're ready over here," Charlie called out from the porch of the guest house.

Patrick waved for Ben to go down the narrow path first, then followed behind. Jake had opened the door using a key on his own key ring, which he then pulled off and handed to Patrick.

"You should have this. Just make a copy when you want me to start looking at some updates in here," Jake said.

"Got it." Patrick stuck the key in his pocket and looked around. The door opened to a small sitting room, with a couch pressed against the far wall and an aging recliner in the corner. A dusty television that was probably from the eighties and was likely a fire hazard sat on a stand next to the door. The rug underneath his feet was tan and needed a good cleaning.

Crossing the room to enter the kitchen, he saw the dated cabinets and appliances he was expecting. The refrigerator hummed and the air was slightly cool when he opened the door, but the light didn't turn on. The clock on the stove was out, and when he tried to click on a burner nothing happened.

"Jake," he turned and found his brother right behind him. "Oh, good. Can you get all these appliances swapped out right away? This looks like a fire waiting to happen."

"You're probably right. We unplugged everything but the fridge after the inspection to be safe, thinking you would want to wait until we could gut it before you replaced them." Jake jiggled a cabinet door that was barely hanging on. "I should secure these as well."

"I'm guessing it would take a long time to replace everything?"

Jake snorted out a laugh. "Yeah, that can't happen overnight."

"Charlie and I are going to shovel a path to the stable," Ben yelled from the living room just before the door slammed shut.

Patrick walked down a short hall to examine the bathroom, which looked serviceable once cleaned, and then the bedroom. The bed had seen better days, and the closet doors were hanging off their hinges. A bureau with missing drawers was on the wall across from the bed, and a nightstand that looked like it could collapse held a lamp, but the room was otherwise empty.

"Where can I get furniture delivered tomorrow?" Patrick asked Jake.

"There's a new store in Burlington, they've been quick to turn around. For you, I bet they'll be even faster."

"Do they have a website?" Patrick pulled his phone out and handed it to Jake to input the name of the store. "Looks like I can order on here, then maybe call and see if they can move the date."

"Before you do that," Jake said hesitantly. "Should we discuss the amount of money you're spending to make a stranger comfortable?"

"Money isn't an object," Patrick replied softly. "And I would need to furnish this anyway. I know it's less convenient for you if I do it now and then everything has to be moved, so I'll keep it simple."

"Not about that," Jake shook his head. "Just want to make sure you aren't being taken advantage of."

"She's been living in my stable. For weeks, it sounds like. Who would do that on the off chance that I would come home, furnish a house, and let them live there?"

Jake shrugged. "Stranger things have happened."

"I'd rather assume the best of someone than the worst," Patrick replied. "And I just see something in her that I haven't seen in a long time."

"You're surrounded by beautiful women every day you're on set," Jake argued.

"Not just that," Patrick shook his head. "Yes, she's beautiful, although it's natural and not like what I see in California. But she looks like she needs someone to give her a chance. Know what I mean? You're always rushing off to help fellow Veterans, and you know when someone just needs one person to show up for them."

"That's true," Jake said. "Just protect yourself, that's all I'm asking."

"I think I can handle it if she attacks me, she's all of five feet."

"I have a feeling we need to worry about more than your physical safety," Jake said as he disappeared into the bathroom.

Chapter 8

Emma glanced nervously at the women in the room, who were puttering in the kitchen making coffee and tea as if perfectly at home. She wasn't sure what to do with her hands, or if she should sit or try to help. Stella glanced over at her and smiled reassuringly, and Emma couldn't help but think that the older woman radiated kindness.

"Sit, honey," Stella urged. "You don't have to be uncomfortable around us. We're just regular old biddies. Well, I am, Shea isn't old at all."

"I feel like I am some days," Shea said. "It's so hard to get out of bed some mornings."

"You're making a baby," Stella reminded her. "That takes a lot out of you. Let Jake do more. And Charlie, that boy is a handful if he gets bored."

"Somehow, I don't think Charlie wants to grade papers for me. I'm a teacher," she directed at Emma. "I teach English here in Windsor Peak, which means Jake's son is in the same school."

"That's nice," Emma responded quietly.

"My son now," Shea said with a smile. "That takes some getting used to. I don't know if I'll ever formally adopt him, because he's already a teenager and I don't want to replace his mom, but I'm so lucky to get to be in his life. He's a great kid."

"This little bean is lucky to have him as a big brother," Stella said as she patted Shea's small bump. "Let's all sit on the couches, I'll bring this tray over so everything is ready when the boys come back in."

They all settled into spots with their hot drink of choice, before Stella turned her attention back to the stranger in the room. "What can you tell us about yourself, Emma?"

"I'm, uh," she stammered, feeling her cheeks blush. "I just got to town a few weeks ago. I am from New York originally. Up near Canada."

"Cold up there, so at least you're used to that," Stella smiled encouragingly. "Do you have family around here?"

"I think so."

"Oh?" Stella cocked an eyebrow as she set her cup of tea down.

"I have been searching for a while," she explained. "It's probably time I do something about it, I've been dragging my feet a little."

"Could we help," Shea asked.

"No," she shook her head. "Thank you. That's very nice, but no."

"And Patrick, how did you meet him?" Stella asked.

"It's kind of a complicated story," she hedged. She felt the instinct to squirm as both sets of eyes examined her and forced herself to sit still. It was a habit well learned over the years, to sit perfectly still while meeting the eyes of someone who didn't want to trust her.

"Patrick is—" Stella was cut off by the kitchen door opening, the men spilling inside.

"How's it going in here?" Patrick asked after kicking off his boots by the back door.

Emma couldn't believe the relief that flooded through her at the sight of his smiling face. She barely knew him, and yet she felt safe now that he was back in the room, a feeling she had to file away to study later.

"We just barely sat down to chat," Stella responded. "You boys were way too fast, you cut into our girl time. But your kitchen is a dream."

"You saying ours needs improvement?" Ben bellowed from where he was hanging up his coat.

"It's been a few years since it was updated," Stella responded, winking at Emma. "A little refresh couldn't hurt."

"Whatever you want, dear." He sat next to her, brushing a kiss across her forehead, and Emma was touched by the love between them.

Jake followed, plopping down on the sofa next to Shea and pulling her close. The two couples were so clearly enamored with each other, and they all shared such a loving bond, Emma felt the need to escape again. She was halfway to standing when Patrick sat on the other end of the couch, shooting her a look as he did that forced her to settle back down. Charlie disappeared through a doorway, and she resisted the urge to follow him. The teenager would likely be the easiest of the group on her, but Patrick's gaze kept her locked in her seat.

"The guest house needs some work," he said in a low voice. "Jake is going to make some calls and see how quick we can make it happen."

"I, uhm—"

"It's okay, they are all going to find out anyway. This is the nosiest group of people you've ever met, but they're people you can trust," Patrick reassured her.

"Want to fill us in?" Ben demanded of his son.

"Emma has fallen on some hard times," Patrick responded before she could. "She came to town because she thinks a family member might be living here, but she hasn't had a chance to do anything about that yet. I offered to let her stay in my guest house while she gets her feet under her."

"Where were you staying?" Stella asked softly.

"That's irrelevant," Patrick said. "She helped me when I got to town and was very sick, and I want to repay her the favor. Let's try to not overwhelm her with questions if that's at all possible."

"Maybe just a few," Jake said in a husky voice. "No offense, Emma."

"None taken," she whispered.

"We're all going to pretend I'm a grown man who can make my own decisions," Patrick warned them. "And focus on how you can help me get the guest house ready. Jake is going to work on getting appliances, I'll order some new furniture. Stella, do you have a cleaning crew that could come out first thing tomorrow?"

"Oh no," Emma said on a rushed breath. "I'll do that. Please."

"It would be faster if I hired a few people," Patrick said.

"No, you're already doing way too much. I'll be happy to clean it."

"We can help," Shea offered. "It's the weekend, so I'm free. Kendra might be busy at the restaurant, but I'm happy to pitch in."

"That's very nice, but I don't want to intrude on your time," Emma replied.

"If Jake is here, I'll probably be close by anyway."

"We can figure that out," Patrick cut in. "She can't move in there until the new furniture can come, that stuff has been there for way too long and who knows what's living in the bedding."

"I'm sure it would be fine—"

"It's not," Jake and Patrick said at the same time.

"I really don't want you to buy new furniture for my sake," Emma whispered.

"It's for my sake," Patrick insisted. "This all needs to be replaced, and I'll feel better when the furniture and whatever bugs they are probably holding gets out of here."

Emma shuddered at the idea of bugs. Living outdoors meant the bugs had frequently feasted on her, and she had yet to curb her fear of spiders. The idea of sleeping on a mattress possibly infested with spider eggs was enough to force her to stop objecting. She would find a way to make it up to Patrick somehow.

"If you men could haul it out now, we could start scrubbing," Stella suggested. "It's early and we have nothing else going on."

"We can do that," Jake nodded. "I can plow quickly, and Charlie can shovel a few more paths, so we can get everything over into the stable until we can get rid of it. Actually, let me make a call. Maybe I can get a dumpster delivered, then we can just toss it all. You don't plan to keep any of it, right?"

"No," Patrick shook his head. "Nothing worth keeping. Let's do that, it would be easier."

Jake stood and left the room, and Emma felt a slight relief when he did. Not that he didn't seem nice, but there was an air of authority to him that made her nervous. Of all the people in the room, he seemed the most unsure of her and the most likely to ask hard questions, so the less time she spent with him, the better.

***

As the sky began to darken, Emma felt exhaustion start to settle in. She had spent the last several hours scrubbing and hauling things out of the small house, shocked at how much crap had been left behind. Patrick had insisted on throwing away everything, from the furniture to the silverware, and the whole family had spent the hours traipsing to and from the newly delivered dumpster. The house was now empty, and she had scrubbed the kitchen from top to bottom. The other rooms she decided could wait until morning as she dumped a bucket of mop water over the porch railing.

Patrick came in the front door, having walked his family out to their cars to send them home. He held her small backpack in his large hands, and she flushed, suddenly ashamed of how little she had.

"I grabbed this from the stable for you," he explained, holding the bag up. "Thought you might want a hot shower and your own clothes. I was thinking of ordering some takeout, but I wasn't sure what you liked to eat."

"You don't have to do that," she said. "You're already doing so much for me."

"You need to eat," he pointed out. "And I'm starving. The lunch Stella made seems like a long time ago. But before I eat, I think I need something else."

She froze, sure the moment had come. He was going to demand she do something to repay all he was doing for her. She knew he was too nice, it was just a surprise that it had taken this long.

"Did I say something wrong?" he asked, looking concerned.

"No, I just," she sighed. "I kind of knew this would happen, but I guess after last night I thought maybe you were different."

"What?"

"This—" She waved a hand between them.

"I'm really confused, but maybe that's because I'm so tired." He rubbed a hand over his face. "I was just going to say that I need a soak in the hot tub, and ask if you wanted to join me or just go shower."

"A what?" She was blushing so hard she was sure her cheeks would catch fire. Did she really misinterpret the situation so much?

"Hot tub? Here, I'll show you." He walked over to a door off the kitchen, where Charlie had disappeared earlier. A flight of stairs was on the other side of the door, and he waved for her to go down.

At the bottom of the stairs, there was a whole world she couldn't have even imagined. To her right was what appeared to be a theater, with plush recliners and a huge screen. On the left, a bar was set up, along with a pool table, dart board, and a foosball table, a poker table and several bar height tables. Patrick crossed through that room and opened another door, which led to an enormous gym. Every piece of exercise equipment she had ever seen, plus some she had no idea what they were, lined the space. One wall was covered in mirrors, another had a ballet barre installed.

"Ballet?" She ran a finger along the bar, looking at him.

He shrugged, not looking concerned. "It's really great for flexibility."

"If you say so," she grinned.

"Come this way," he pointed to yet another door. The space was divided, with one portion almost looking like it was outside, there were so many windows. A huge hot tub sat in the center of a stone floor, and lush tropical plants sat in the corners. On the other side of the room was a large locker room type space, but fancier than any she had seen before. A massage table was in the middle, and a few nice wooden cabinets that held towels and supplies. She could see a shower though one opening, and what looked like a steam room on the other side.

"This is crazy," she marveled, looking around. "I can't believe this is all yours."

"Me neither," he laughed. "I'm going to change and hop into the hot tub, because I am sore all over. If you'd like to join me, I know there are a bunch of bathing suits and robes here." He opened a cabinet and showed her a range of bathing suits for men and women. "Easier to have a bunch here than to worry about someone wanting to go in and not having one."

She reached over and touched them, in awe that he had all this extra clothing here just in case someone needed it. "I've never gone into a hot tub, but I feel bad because I'm so dusty and dirty."

"So am I. I was going to rinse off first, but I don't have the energy. Luckily, I know there is enough chlorine in there to kill off whatever germs we probably just touched, and I can have it cleaned if needed. I'd like to order some food, then soak for a half hour, if that's alright with you."

"We don't need to order food, I can make us dinner."

"Really? I think the kitchen is fully stocked, but I didn't really look. I'm happy to get a pizza delivered," he offered.

"Oh, pizza." Her mouth salivated at the thought, she hadn't allowed herself the luxury of buying something so simple in a long time.

"That settles it. Pizza it is." He pulled his phone out and within a few minutes, looked back up to her. "I did one cheese and a pepperoni, and some other dishes. Plus, a salad, because I should at least try and not gain five pounds while I'm here."

"That would be tragic," she laughed, then sobered when she saw his face. "Really?"

"No, I'll be fine. I'll go change in the bathroom down the hall, you can use this one to change if you want to join."

He disappeared, and she pulled a one-piece black suit from the rack that looked like it would fit her. Grabbing a robe to pull on over it, she ducked into the bathroom with the shower and shed her dirty clothes before pulling it on. Thankfully she had used a razor in the shower that morning, because it had been months since she had last shaved. And she shouldn't be thinking like that, because he was not going to be looking at her legs or armpits.

When Patrick walked back into the room, she felt all the air rush out of her body. No man should look the way he did. He could be a sculpture with how his muscles were carved, every inch of his body rippled as he walked. She was busy trying to keep her tongue in her mouth and not fall over when he opened the door leading to the hot tub, and she could at least blame the swirl of heat for the redness in her cheeks. How was he just walking around looking like that? It explained all the gym equipment, but still.

She tripped over her own feet as she tried to walk toward the open door and met his bemused expression when she looked up. *Don't make a fool of yourself, he's human.* Taking a deep breath, she managed to make her way past him and into the room, where she shed the robe and climbed the stairs to the large tub. Poking a toe in, she jumped at how hot the water was.

"This might be too hot," she said to Patrick.

"That's the whole point. It won't burn you, I promise. Just make your way in slowly."

"Easier said than done," she whispered. Her whole life seemed to contradict the idea that a person could work their way into comfort, but if she didn't try this, it left her standing in a bathing suit in front of the fittest man alive. Taking a deep breath, she ignored the heat and plunged in, gasping as the hot water swirled around her. Patrick climbed the stairs and lowered himself into the opposite corner of her, and she was suddenly very aware of what a small space it was, and how intimate it was to be sharing it with him.

"No hot tubs, no cell phone," Patrick stated. "I'm starting to wonder if you were raised by wolves."

"Hot tubs are a common occurrence for other people?"

"Well, maybe not everyone. But the cell phone thing, that's unusual."

She shrugged, adjusting so a jet hit the small of her back where soreness had set in. "It seemed silly to spend money on. I didn't have anyone to call."

"What about for emergencies?" he looked shocked as he asked.

"I managed. I always find work, and there's a phone there that I can use. I've never needed to call the police for anything."

"But you were living out here all alone, that had to be nerve wracking."

"Maybe a little," she shrugged. "But it honestly wasn't so bad, it's not like this is a high crime area. And no one knew I was here."

"I don't suppose you want to tell me anything more about your life?" He asked with a gentle smile, and she had to clamp her lips shut to keep herself from spilling her life story.

"We're both too tired for that," she finally whispered. "Your family is really nice."

"That's one word for them," he laughed. "Nice, overprotective, invasive, and relentless would all do."

"You're lucky to have them."

He sobered, as though sensing the story behind her words. "I am. You're right, I shouldn't make light of it."

"It's okay," she smiled. "I think it's nice that you are all so close, and that everyone came to help."

"I can assure you, now that they have met you, if you need anything while you're in Windsor Peak, they would be happy to help you. That's how they are." He glanced out the window before checking the time on his cell phone. "I'm hoping you'll be sticking around for a while, take this time to get on your feet."

"I appreciate that," she said. Committing to anything before she knew if she was on the right track would be a mistake, although a free place to live and a nice town were very tempting. The last time she had a space that felt safe was so long ago, it would be hard to walk away from this place. And if she had to admit, hard to turn her back on Patrick, who had shown her such kindness without any expectations. Maybe the majority of the world was good, and she just kept falling into the bad parts.

Patrick checked the phone again for the time before groaning. "As much as I don't want to get out, I should dry off and get the pizza."

"Can I help pay for it?" She knew the amount in her wallet wouldn't cover the full dinner but felt badly not offering any money at all.

"No, already paid for." He stepped out of the hot tub and grabbed a towel from the rack. "I'll meet you in the kitchen."

She watched him disappear through the door that would bring him out by the stairs as he toweled his torso and was grateful his back was to her as she stared openly. Honestly, it wasn't fair that someone could just walk around looking like that. If she wasn't already tempted to stay in town, Patrick shirtless would have been enough to sway her decision.

But she couldn't let herself get distracted, or throw herself at her benefactor, it would only end with an embarrassing rejection. He clearly had no thoughts of her as a woman because he had no idea what she was talking about earlier when she had assumed he was coming on to her. Best that she put the idea of him and his perfectly chiseled body out of her mind, the last thing she needed was a crush that would end badly, forcing her to move on too quickly.

Chapter 9

"Dan, this better be an emergency." Patrick struggled to sit up in bed after being woken at dawn by the ringing of his cell phone.

"My baby brother comes home and doesn't even call me, of course it's an emergency," Dan replied. "Besides, I called you and texted at least a dozen times yesterday with no response. Kendra figured I did something to annoy you."

"No, I was just busy," he yawned. "Why are you awake so early?"

"I live with a six-year-old now. We are up for sunrise most days, it's great," Dan laughed. "I'm taking her skiing today, want to come?"

"No, I have a million things to do here."

"I heard you have a house guest." Dan stated it, but Patrick knew his brother was digging for information.

"Jake is the biggest gossip in town, and never tell me otherwise."

"Actually, Shea told Kendra," Dan argued.

"I take it back. Your wives are the biggest gossips in town."

Dan laughed. "That's probably accurate. But they love you and are concerned."

"Nothing to worry about," Patrick replied curtly.

"Don't get snippy," Dan said. "Are you alone right now?"

"Yes, I'm alone right now," Patrick sighed. "It's not like that."

"Tell me what it is like," Dan insisted.

"She needs help. I don't know her full story, but she was living in my stable. She has this one small backpack that has all her belongings in the world. And no one to turn to, no one to ask for help." The words gushed out as Patrick twisted the sheet between his fingers, sure his brother's disapproval would follow.

"Everyone knows how generous you are, Patty," Dan said gently. "There's not a person who has ever met you who didn't feel lucky they did. We just want to make sure this isn't some kind of scam or way to take advantage of you."

"I get that, I really do. But she doesn't know who I am. She asked me if I was a model last night, said that I looked kind of familiar," Patrick huffed out a sigh. "I have to trust my instinct about this. She took care of me when I was sick, and she could have just left me there. She's skittish and a little afraid, but at the same time, she has nowhere else to go."

"I can find a shelter. Or a room for her in town," Dan offered.

"She has a room. The guest house will be ready by tonight, and she can stay there as long as she needs to."

"Patty," Dan huffed out a breath. "Let's get some more information from her at least."

"So you can run a background check?" he snapped.

"That would help, yeah," Dan replied.

"I tried to ask her some questions last night, and I feel like she's warming up to tell me more of her story. Let me see if I can find out who she's here in town to meet, and we can go from there," Patrick suggested. "She's been on her own for a while now, and I know she bounced around a lot before that. All she's told me so far is that she was born in upstate New York, she's here because she thinks a relative might be in town and she slipped last night and said she had never met her father."

"You think she's here to find him?"

"Maybe, I don't know."

"I hope it's not our dad," Dan chuckled, then sobered quickly. "You don't think it is, do you?"

"No," Patrick shook his head even though his brother couldn't see him. "No way."

"Because you want to sleep with her, or is there another reason?"

"Both, jerk. I'm hanging up now, you're annoying and you woke me up."

"Say hi to Calle first before she implodes," Dan said before handing the phone to the six-year-old. Dan was in the process of adopting his new wife's daughter, who had been born after Kendra escaped an abusive relationship. Calle had never known her father until a few months prior, when he had kidnapped her, causing panic for the town. Eventually they had been tracked down in Boston, and her father had been killed by the police. Fortunately, the little girl showed no ill effects, and it had spurred Dan and Kendra to get married quickly and not waste more time.

Calle chattered in his ear as he climbed out of bed and brushed his teeth, amusing him with the thoughts of a first grader. As usual, she had a million questions for him, but fortunately Dan got her off the phone so they could head out to ski. Patrick jumped in the shower, deciding to use the early morning hours to get some cleaning done in the guest house before the appliances and furniture started arriving. Emma had refused to allow him to pay for a cleaning service, insisting she could do it on her own, but it was too big of a task for one person to complete before deliveries started. He might be spoiled now when it came to cleaning, but he had done his chores as ordered when he was younger and Stella had taught him well, so he could roll up his sleeves and get dirty with the best of them.

***

He had taped a note to the coffee maker and headed out to the cottage, figuring an early start would help. When she appeared in the doorway with two steaming mugs in hand, he grinned at her. "Just in time, I was about to go get a refill."

"You really don't have to do this," she said.

"I don't mind the cleaning. I'm not great at it, but I figured running a vacuum was within my abilities."

"I meant all of this," she gestured with her empty hand. "Letting me stay here, buying all the new stuff. Everything."

"I feel like we covered this already," he said with a smile. "It's an empty guest cottage. I was going to fix it up anyway and buy new furniture. This was always in the plan, I'm just making things a little harder for Jake because he can't remodel before the furniture comes. But he'll deal."

"Still, this seems like a lot. I'm a stranger," she insisted.

"So am I. And yet you took care of me and trusted me enough to stay under the same roof as me," he explained. "Maybe now we could be friends?"

He watched as the emotions crossed her face, as though the concept of a friend was beyond her imagination. While she studied her coffee, he placed his down on the now clean counter and glanced around the room in search of something to distract her from where her thoughts had taken her.

"Want to do the bathroom? I know that's gross but there's just no way I can tackle that," he admitted.

"Sure," she responded quietly. "I think I saw some gloves around—"

"Here." He opened the cabinet under the sink and pulled out a package of yellow industrial gloves. "These should protect you."

"Thanks," she said with a small smile. "For the gloves and all of this."

"Friends?" He dared to try again, glancing at her over his shoulder as she walked toward the bathroom.

Her soft laugh met his ears before she spoke. "Friends."

***

Hours later, Patrick flopped down onto the new couch and surveyed the room. The couch faced a new TV, sitting on a stand that could hold a few decorative trinkets eventually. A club chair and ottoman were on the opposite wall, along with a small table in the corner and a coffee table in front of the couch. The kitchen had been fitted with new appliances, all plugged in and ready to go, and a small high-top table was nestled by the window. A small closet between the kitchen and bathroom now held a new washer and dryer, replacing the ones that looked to be from the early sixties if he had to guess.

They had worked side by side all day, sharing small laughs and a comfortable companionship. He was amazed at how easy it was to be around her, and how drawn he was to her already. The attraction only grew the more time he spent with her, but if he made any indication that was the case, he was certain she would run the other way. The panic on her face when she had thought he was coming on to her earlier stuck in his brain, so he knew he needed to tread carefully.

Emma had been putting sheets on the new bed, which he had opted not to offer to help with, the image of her and a bed would be imprinted on his mind enough as it was. The bedroom set had been simple, small enough to fit into the tight space, but warm and comfortable looking. A shocking amount had been delivered from the local box store, containing bedding, towels, kitchenware, and every item Patrick could think of that she might need. She was well set up to move into the space immediately, which made him realize he would miss her in the main house.

"This is really too much." She came into the room and sat on the edge of the chair, pushing a strand of blond hair behind her ear in what he recognized as a nervous habit.

"It's perfect," he responded. "If you find anything missing, just let me know. Jake fixed the major issues we saw with the cabinets and closet, but if anything feels loose or dangerous, I'll have him come right over and take care of it."

"I'm sure it's all fine," she said softly.

"Just in case. And if you find you're missing anything, just say the word," he grinned at her. "Like when you go to open a can and realize we forgot a can opener, because the only time you ever think of it is when you urgently need it."

"I can always get a can opener," she objected.

"You know what I mean," he said as he waved a hand. "If you see something missing it will save me the trouble down the road. And speaking of down the road, I'm too tired to cook and I want a good meal. Want to go into town with me to grab dinner?"

She glanced down at her knees, and he could feel her thoughts churning from across the room. The kitchen, although well stocked with what she would need to cook, was lacking any food. She wouldn't want to continue poking around in his house now that she had her own space, and her funds were likely limited. And she had to eat.

"I could figure something out here," she finally said. "I don't want you to feel like you have to keep providing for me. This is already too much."

"What do I have to say to convince you that it's not too much?" His voice was sharper than he meant for it to be, so he softened it purposely. "That I would have furnished this house anyway, and it's not a problem?"

"I don't know," she whispered. "I just feel bad. Like I'm charity, which I am."

"I don't see you that way." He rubbed a hand over his chin, debating his next words. "A few months ago, I found out that a friend was struggling a little financially. Nothing huge, but she was making payments on a business to buy it from the original owners, and she couldn't afford to do that and also hire a manager so she could have some free time. I called the original owners and paid the loan off, and she has no idea."

"She still doesn't know?"

"No," he shook his head. "She assumed my brother Dan did it, because they got married a few weeks later. I would tell her, but it's more fun that she keeps poking Dan about it."

"Oh, it's your sister-in-law," she exclaimed. "I bet she would be so grateful if she knew."

"Yes, but she really doesn't need to ever know," he said. "I'm trusting you with this secret so you can see that it's not just you. If I see someone with a problem that I can fix, I do it. Money isn't an issue, and it makes me happy to help others. I've sponsored all of the town sports teams for years. I buy books for the library and the school when they are low on funds. I pay for so many kids to go to college, my accountant is ready to walk out on me if I don't set up a scholarship fund and at least get a tax break out of it. I've been very lucky in my life and passing that luck on to others is good for me."

She studied him silently for a long moment, until he thought she wouldn't respond. "You're a good man, Patrick. I hope you know that."

"I appreciate that," he said, feeling the words more than usual. Somehow her thinking that of him made him feel better about himself. "Now, can we shower and go for dinner? Please don't make me eat alone, I'll explain when we get there."

"Okay," she smiled briefly. "I already grabbed my stuff from the house, so I can take my first shower here."

"Perfect. I'll meet you in the driveway in a half hour." He stood to leave and stopped at the door. "Is that enough time for you?"

She laughed. "To shower and put my last pair of clean jeans on? Yes."

A half hour later, he chatted with her as he drove them the short distance into town, telling her about some of the neighbors who had lived there since he was a kid. As he drove slowly down Main Street, looking for a parking space, he asked if she had explored the town much.

"A little," she admitted. "Mainly the grocery store and the library. It's a small town, and everyone had a lot of questions about who I was and where I came from. But the library was warm and had plenty of books to read, so I couldn't resist that. And obviously I needed to get food."

He pulled into a parking spot, glad to distract himself from the thought of her spending all day alone in the library just to stay warm. The jacket she was wearing didn't look thick enough to withstand the Vermont winters, and he made a mental note to ask his sisters-in-law if they could find an old one to offer her. Even he was smart enough to realize that she wouldn't accept offers of new clothing from him.

Half a block away, the sounds of families dining and individuals yelling at sports events could be heard from the street. The Windsor Palace, owned by his sister-in-law Kendra, was the old Town Hall. A solid white building with pillars in front had been converted into a restaurant on the first floor and an apartment on the second. A long porch allowed space for diners to wait for tables outside, weather permitting, and an area in the back had been converted into outdoor dining and drinking in the summer.

Emma hesitated as he indicated the steps to the porch. "Oh, I didn't know we were coming here."

"What do you mean? This is the best place in town, especially since we had pizza last night. I suppose we could go there and get something different, but I'm dying for a steak."

"Okay." She bit her lip, and he couldn't help but notice her cheeks had gone paler.

"Is everything alright?"

"Yes, I'm sure it will be fine." She took a deep breath as though steeling herself against an unseen enemy and reached for the door.

He followed her inside, waving to Kendra behind the bar and seeing faces swing his way immediately. It was only a matter of time before even more people recognized him, even with it being slower and more filled with locals since it was a Tuesday night. He smiled at the few who called out to him and led Emma to the bar.

"Emma, this is my sister-in-law, Kendra. She's married to Dan, and the mom of my favorite niece, Calle."

"I don't know what you'll do if this is another girl." Kendra replied, patting her small bump. "Or if Shea has a girl. It's nice to meet you, Emma. I've heard a lot about you. And you look so familiar, have we met?"

"No, I don't think so." Emma still looked nervous but smiled at Kendra as she shook her hand.

"Not from around here?" Kendra continued studying Emma.

"No," Emma shook her head. "I've never been to Vermont before."

"Hmmm, I'll have to think on it. You remind me so much of someone." Kendra turned as the door to the kitchen started to open. "Oh, that's who it is—"

Patrick saw Zoe, Kendra's chef, step through the door and come to a stop suddenly, causing a busboy to drop a tray of dirty dishes just outside the kitchen door. Her eyes were locked on where he stood, though they had met several times, so he was surprised she would be starstruck by him. He raised a hand to wave, only to realize it wasn't him she was staring at.

"Emma?"

Chapter 10

"Emma?" Zoe's frantic whisper could be heard even across the room, after the dropped tray had silenced the room.

Patrick turned to look at her, a quizzical look on his face. "You know Zoe?"

She could only stare at her, tears brimming in her eyes and spilling onto her cheeks before she could stop them. Zoe crossed the room quickly, stopping a short distance away before rushing forward again and embracing her. Emma felt the sobs come even as Zoe whispered to her and rubbed her back and was finally able to get herself under control.

"I can't believe this." Zoe wiped tears from her own cheeks as she stepped back. "I never thought I would see you again."

"I've been looking for you for a long time," she admitted. "But then I got here, and I was afraid you wouldn't want to see me."

"Why would you think that?" Zoe looked horrified at the thought.

"I tried to call you years ago," Emma explained. "Your mother answered and told me you never wanted to see me again."

"That doesn't surprise me," Zoe admitted. "But why would you believe her? I always told you how she was."

"I don't know," Emma shrugged. "I was only twelve, and I was so lost. I knew she wouldn't help me, but I had hoped—"

"That was when your mom died," Zoe whispered. "How could she be so cruel? I tried to call you so many times, but the phone number was disconnected, and no one would tell me anything."

The room had come alive around them, families going about their meals and groups of people having fun at the bar. "Zoe, why don't you take a break and sit with them for a bit?" Kendra stepped between them and pointed to an empty table near the window, slightly hidden from the room by the half wall of the stage.

"I really can't take a break now." Zoe said, glancing around the full room. "But can I meet you for breakfast? Do you have a phone number?"

"No, sorry. I don't have a cell phone."

Patrick pulled his out and handed it to Zoe. "Put your number in here, and I'll text you. She's staying with me, so I can get a message to her."

"You're staying with Patrick? How did you two meet?" Zoe turned to him with a questioning look on her face. "How do you know my sister?"

"I'll explain it all when we get together," Emma promised. "I don't want to keep you."

"It's going to be hard to focus on work," Zoe said. Her short blond hair fell over her eyes as she entered her number into Patrick's phone. "Please, I need to see you tomorrow. Okay?"

"I'll be here. Or wherever," Emma laughed. "I am so glad I found you."

"Me too," Zoe said. She grabbed Emma in another quick hug, then turned to the kitchen. "Say bye before you leave."

Emma watched her disappear behind the swinging door before turning to see the questions in Patrick's eyes. "Why don't we sit, and then I can explain."

"Works for me." He led the way to the table Kendra had indicated, sitting with his back to the room. She could see many curious faces looking in their direction, some even whispering and pointing.

"I can't believe that made such a fuss," she said to Patrick.

"What do you mean?"

"Everyone is staring at me."

"Oh." He carefully pulled his silverware from the napkin and laid it on the table before meeting her eyes. "They might be staring at me."

"Don't get this wrong, you're handsome and all," she said. "But this is a lot."

He laughed, then leaned closer to her. "You think I'm handsome?"

"You already know you are." She rolled her eyes at him as she spoke.

"I appreciate that," he laughed. "But yes, most people are whispering about me being here, and I'm sure they're sending text messages, and within an hour the room will be full. Maybe not the locals, they're used to me, but the rest of them."

"Why would they do that?"

"You honestly have no idea?"

"None." She shook her head vehemently, feeling out of sorts. First, she was face to face with her sister for the first time in over fifteen years, and now she was apparently sitting with someone who was well known in the town. She knew he was wealthy and probably should have asked more questions when they were at the house, but she hadn't wanted to answer any, so it wasn't fair to ask.

"I'm an actor," he explained.

"Oh." She tented her fingers and propped her chin on them. "Around here? Or what does that mean?"

"Around—" He shook his head, taking a few seconds to stop his laughter. "No, I'm not a local theater actor. Not that I'm knocking it, but that wouldn't pay for that house, or my life. I started on a TV show, it got insanely popular, and when it ended, I went into movies."

She just stared at him, trying to process it. He was famous? Really, really famous? And he was at dinner with her, an unemployed, unexciting woman he just met?

"Don't get weird," he warned her.

"It's a little hard not to. All these people in here, they know you because you're famous, not because you're a townie?"

"A mix of both," he answered.

The waitress came to the table, clearly flustered to wait on him. Emma watched as he smiled at her and chatted, helping to ease her nerves. He ordered a couple of appetizers before turning to her.

"Is that good? Anything I missed that you want?"

"No, that sounds delicious." She had no idea what he had ordered but wasn't about to admit how distracted she was by him.

"Want to split a bottle of wine? Or would you rather something else?"

"Wine works."

He finished the order and smiled at the waitress before she walked off, glancing back at him over her shoulder.

"That must get weird," she said.

"It sure does," he laughed ruefully.

"I just can't believe I didn't know this. But I also haven't been to the movies in years, and I can't remember the last time I watched television."

"Enough about me, I'm already sick of myself. Could you tell me a little about yourself?" He held a hand up before she could instantly object. "Just what you feel comfortable with. Start with Zoe?"

She took a deep breath, steeling herself against her past. Revisiting it was usually reserved for nightmares, but she owed him some of her story. "Zoe is my older sister. Well, half-sister, we share a father. She was born in Canada, I was in upstate New York, so we didn't get to see each other much. Our mothers knew about each other, and both had watched my sperm donor run off as soon as the test turned positive, so they had that in common."

"You've never met him?"

"No," she replied. "For years, my mom told me he was working hard and would be back soon. She had pictures of him around the house. But he never came back. I think it's part of the reason she kept in touch with Zoe's mom and kept having Zoe come visit us. Just in case he went back to them, she would have a tie to him. My mom was a romantic at heart, and would have taken him back, I'm sure of it."

"She and Zoe's mom got along?"

"I wouldn't say that," she hedged. "Zoe's mom is not a nice woman, she can be very difficult. But my mom loved Zoe, and wanted for me to have a sister, so she put up with it. When her mom wanted to be rid of her for a time, she would send Zoe to stay with us, which was amazing. She would spend whole summers with us, so we were very close as kids."

"Then what happened? How did you lose touch?" He was leaning forward, looking drawn into her story as she talked.

"My mom died suddenly when I was twelve," she explained. "I gave the police Zoe's home phone number, hoping her mom would come and get me. She told them she didn't know who I was and to stop calling. They tried to find my father for a bit before they just gave up and stuck me in a foster home."

"I'm sorry about your mom," Patrick said softly. "I'd like to hear more about her one day, if you don't mind. But what kind of mother wouldn't feel sympathy for a kid going through that on her own? And not at least try to look out for her daughter's sister?" He looked outraged, and ready to throttle someone.

"That's who she was. Zoe told me the year before that she had accepted that she would never have a mother who loved her, or parents for that matter. Not everyone is kind, Patrick." She said it gently as she reached over and patted his hand. "I wish everyone in the world was like you, but sadly, that's not true."

The wine was brought to the table, and she watched as Patrick indicated the waitress should leave it and he would pour it. He lifted the bottle and filled her glass halfway before doing the same to his, and she took a sip of the wine and sighed. Red wine, or any wine for that matter, was a luxury she could never afford on her own.

"I don't know much about foster care, I have to admit," Patrick said. "My own mother died when she had me, but I obviously had my dad still, and my brothers and Stella. I never even thought about what would have happened if I didn't."

"You would have been okay," she smiled wryly. "You would have been an infant, and that's what everyone wants to adopt. No one wants a nasty twelve-year-old, then teenager, so you get bounced around a lot. Some of the homes are just in it for a paycheck, so they have multiple kids in a small bedroom and limited food. Then when they don't like you anymore, or you get in trouble, they send you to the next. I know there are many that are loving, clean, and stable, but I wasn't lucky enough to find one."

"That's horrible," Patrick responded.

"It is what it is. I was from an area that was poverty stricken, which makes it harder to find stable foster care."

"Couldn't they have moved you to another area?"

"I was moved a lot. I changed schools eleven times from seventh grade on. But overall, they try to keep you in the same state unless you have family elsewhere. As much as I would have loved to be whisked off to Manhattan and live an Annielike existence, that wasn't in the cards for me." She took a sip of wine, wanting to hide the pain she experienced when thinking about her past.

"I'm going to be singing that song in my head for the next week," Patrick groaned.

"Hey, you asked!" She laughed with him, happy that things had gotten lighter. "Let's talk about something else, if that's okay. This is kind of a heavy topic and I'm already exhausted."

"Just one last thing, which may put your mind at ease," Patrick said. "I've only known Zoe a few months, but Kendra trusts her. When Calle went missing just before Christmas, Zoe never left Kendra's side and helped every way she could. She seems like a good person. I know you haven't seen her in a long time and didn't know what to expect, but she's solid."

"Tell me about what happened with Calle," she asked. She leaned forward, feeling the draw towards him even as her brain objected. Patrick was so far out of her league, and this was not a date. It was two new friends having a meal together, and she needed to remember that. Someone with the world at their fingertips didn't date people who were down to their last three pairs of decent socks.

"Dan and Kendra were high school sweethearts," he explained. "They broke up when Dan went to college and acted like a buffoon. Kendra ended up married to a jerk named Brad, who she had Calle with. Brad took off before Calle was born, but after beating Kendra up several times."

"Oh no." She clasped a hand over her mouth and glanced over to where the woman was serving drinks and smiling.

"She didn't hear anything from him for years, other than apparently occasionally demanding money," Patrick continued. "When she finally stood up to him and stopped funds that were being siphoned out of her account to his, he apparently freaked. He was so used to her doing what he wanted, so he started calling her and showing up around town. Then one day he went into the elementary school, signed Calle out, and took off with her."

"How was he able to do that?" She was horrified at the thought and couldn't imagine the school allowing it to happen.

"He was her father," Patrick said. "Kendra had listed him on the paperwork, and they didn't have a custody arrangement. It didn't occur to her to list him as someone that couldn't pick Calle up, because he had never even met her. The woman working the front desk that day was new to town and the school, so it was the perfect storm. He was hours away with her before anyone even knew she was missing."

"That's horrible," Emma murmured. She had never met her own father, and the thought of him taking her at a young age away from her mother, where she felt safe, was horrifying.

"They found him in Boston, and Dan was able to bring her back safely."

"Is he in jail?"

"No," Patrick shook his head and seemed to hesitate. "He was killed. When they broke down the door to the hotel room, he fired off a shot at one of the FBI agents and they returned fire."

"Oh, wow. What a tragedy all around."

"Not so tragic that he's gone, if you ask me." Patrick sipped his wine. "Scumbag had been stealing from Kendra and had made her life miserable, and then scared all of us by taking Calle."

"But now she never has a chance to know her father."

"She has Dan," Patrick insisted. "He's a far better person than Brad."

"Still, there's something to be said for knowing where you come from." She held up a hand when she could see he was going to argue. "I'm sorry. You're right, he's a bad person and I'm just glad that it ended well for Calle."

The waitress returned, serving the appetizers Patrick had ordered. He asked for a few more minutes before they ordered entrees, glancing at her as she studied the menu. Everything in it cost more than what she had in her wallet, and that didn't count the appetizers and bottle of wine. She couldn't keep sponging off him like this.

"I'm not really hungry." She placed the menu down on the table and avoided his eyes.

"I have a thing about eating alone," he said quickly. "And this is my treat. Please reconsider."

"I can't keep taking handouts from you," she argued. "I need to start paying my way."

"Tomorrow we can deal with that. Tonight, I'm buying dinner and enjoying your company." He placed some food on the small plate in front of her. "Are you going to see about getting a job here in town? I can ask Kendra for you."

"No, thank you." She glanced over again at the busy bartender. "Working here with Zoe might be a little much. I will go around town tomorrow and see if I can find something else."

He started discussing the local businesses, suggesting places she could try, and she allowed herself the taste the food. It was delicious, and before she knew it, she had a dessert in front of her that looked incredible. She savored the warm cake and decided this would be a night that she would remember for a long time.

Chapter 11

Patrick wiped the sweat from his forehead with a towel he had slung around his neck before looking at his trainer, who was grinning at him like a sadist. "How come Jake and Dan are getting off easy today?"

"They don't have to go back to finish shooting a movie in tights," Mike responded. He walked over to adjust the weights on a bar before indicating Patrick should lie on the bench while he spotted him.

"It's spandex," Patrick grunted as he lifted the barbell. "And they've been lazy and eating for two, even though they aren't pregnant."

"Trust me, I'll make them work hard." Mike kept his hands just under the bar, making sure it wouldn't crash down on Patrick.

"Why are you whining? You're the one who hired him and had him start coming here rather than all of us going to the gym," Dan called over.

"I figured if I ordered all this equipment, we might as well use it," Patrick responded. "Plus, it's faster for all of us if I don't have to do the whole selfie thing every time. And I'm not whining, I'm pointing out the weight you've put on."

"I have not," Dan replied. "Have I?" He looked at Jake, who shrugged.

"Maybe, but I haven't. Shea has me so busy getting the house ready, I barely have time to eat," Jake said. "Certainly not enough time to be out to dinner in a cozy corner of Windsor Palace with a date."

Mike glanced over at Jake before looking back at Patrick. "You dating?"

"No, I'm not dating. You're all so annoying." Patrick sat up again, feeling the pull of muscles he had just worked hard.

"They're annoying," Mike pointed at the other two. "I'm not."

Patrick took in the sheer size of Mike, who hulked over him and his brothers, and grinned. "Even if you were, I wouldn't tell you. You get a pass."

"I have on good authority that you were nestled in a corner for a lengthy dinner last night," Dan said smugly.

"I had dinner with a friend," Patrick responded.

"A lady friend?" Mike asked with a raised eyebrow.

"A lady friend who happens to be living here," Jake inserted.

"What? You're living with someone?" Mike looked surprised and glanced toward the stairs.

"No," Patrick sighed. "She's living in the guest house. She fell on some hard times, so I offered to let her stay there while she gets her feet under her."

"Or she's a crazy stalker fan who is going to kidnap Patrick and keep him as her sex slave," Jake called over.

"She didn't even know who I was," Patrick growled. "I keep telling you guys that."

"Right, she said she didn't know," Dan replied. "But how could we possibly know if that's true or not?"

"Did you find out from your gossipy wife that she is Zoe's sister?" Patrick saw the surprise on Mike's face, but it was clear his brothers already knew.

"Zoe, the chef at the restaurant?" Mike asked.

"Yes," they all replied at once.

"Kendra did tell me that," Dan said. "But she didn't know much about the details behind it. What did she tell you?"

Patrick took a drink of his water, debating how much to share. His life in the spotlight had taught him to keep most of his cards close to the chest, but these were people he trusted. "They're going to breakfast this morning," he said. "All I know right now is that they share a father, but neither of them knew him. Emma lost her mom when she was twelve, and was in foster care after that, so she and Zoe lost touch."

"Ouch," Mike said. "That's rough."

"I know," Patrick agreed. "I don't know much about foster care, but I can't imagine it gave her a great start to life. She doesn't have much, and I have had to keep convincing her to let me help."

"Just looking out for you," Dan said. "None of us want you to get hurt or taken advantage of."

"Maybe get to know her a little," Patrick snapped. "Instead of being so closed off to the idea of her being a good person."

"He's right," Jake said. "We have been intent on proving her evil ways. Let's give her the benefit of the doubt."

"Thank you," Patrick said gruffly. He didn't know why it bothered him so much that his brothers were against Emma, but it did. If he was wrong about her, they would never let him live it down, but that was a risk he was willing to take.

"Does this mean that you and Natalie aren't a thing?" Mike asked. "Because if she's single and you want to fix me up, I'd be down with that."

"Trust me when I say you don't want that," Patrick warned. "But no, we have never been a thing. She just likes to make it seem like we are when we're in public, because it keeps people out of her dating life."

"Looked pretty cozy at the last movie premiere," Dan laughed. "I thought she was part of your suit."

"Yeah, that was a little much. I don't know what got into her, but she says it's better to have people thinking she's sleeping with me than Liam or Zane," he said. "And I'm not going to embarrass her by pushing her away in public."

"Again, I'm happy to take that bullet for you—"

"Mike, she would eat you alive," Patrick laughed. "Nat is a lot to handle, and I'm not dating her. Now I'm going to jump on the Peloton while you whip these two dad bods into shape."

"I bet I could handle her," Mike said under his breath.

"There must be some nice local girls for you," Jake said to Mike. "What about Ashley?"

"From the gym? No, she's like my sister. Plus, she's dating someone."

"We'll think of someone," Dan promised. "I'll ask Kendra if any of the girls at the restaurant are possibilities."

"I think I know everyone in this town, and the next three towns over," Mike sighed. "You guys got lucky when you found your wives."

"Sure did," Jake said, reaching up to high five Dan.

"Obnoxious," Mike and Patrick said in unison.

"Hey, if we can't gloat about how happy we are, what's the point of it?" Dan grinned.

"I'm going to make you pay for that," Mike promised.

"Go easy on me. I was widowed at a young age, don't forget," Jake said.

"You can't keep playing that card," Dan argued. "You're very happily married now."

"Maybe I deserve it a little more, because I was sad, and you were a jerk," Jake retorted.

Patrick tuned out as his brothers continued their good natured ribbing on each other as Mike pointed them toward the weights. He missed this when he was in Hollywood, or on location somewhere. Spending time with his brothers was one of his favorite things, even when they got on his nerves. He did envy the happiness they had found and wanted that for himself. His dinner last night with Emma was one of the few times he could remember being completely relaxed with someone other than his family, and it made him want to do it again.

He finished his ride, and jumped in the shower before his brothers finished their weights. Slinging a towel around his waist, he was combing his hair when his phone started to ring from the counter across the room. Grabbing it, he saw it was a facetime from Natalie, and grinned at the timing of it.

"Hey," he said as he answered. "Great timing, we were just talking about you."

"Who was?" She perked up, always enjoying being the center of attention. "Also, are you naked?"

"No, I have a towel on. I just showered after my workout."

"I'd like a full body scan, please."

"Nat."

She sighed. "You can't blame me for trying."

He laughed as he walked back into the gym, and flipped the phone so the other guys could see who was on the screen. "Nat, you know my idiot brothers. And this giant is Mike, my trainer."

"Well, hello, Mike," she purred.

He stood frozen, staring at the screen and not making a sound. Jake poked him in the side, and he didn't move.

"I think he's a little tired from his workout," Dan said. "Normally he's very charming."

"If he finds his tongue, let him know I could find a use for it," Natalie laughed.

"Nat," Patrick groaned. "Knock it off and be normal."

Her laughter rang through the gym. "I live to shock you, Patrick. Mike, I swear I'm harmless, don't believe a word he said about me."

Patrick realized Mike wasn't going to be able to function until he left the room, so he headed for the stairs to grab some clothes and give his friend a break. "What's up, Nat?"

"I'm just bored and lonely here," she complained. "It's so weird without all of you guys here."

"You have that whole storyline we aren't a part of, so it made the most sense to do it this way. Don't you have another shoot right after?"

"Yeah, but that one looks like it's falling apart. Trouble with the location, and my costar is being difficult suddenly."

"Maybe that's a good thing. You could use a break, take some time off."

"And do what? Go to parties and have my picture taken? I'd rather be busy." Her eyes widened as though just struck by an idea. "Or maybe I could come there? See what small town life is like."

"Did you see what you just did to Mike? Imagine a whole town like that. You'd have to tone it down if you came here."

"I can do that."

"You sure about that? There's not much to do here, you'd get bored pretty quick. Skiing is wrapping up soon, and then it's mud season. There's only a few restaurants and a few small stores. It's not Los Angeles."

"Don't tempt me with a good time," she teased. "I'm getting called back to set. I'll call you later."

He pulled on a pair of jeans, a t-shirt and an unbuttoned flannel quickly and jogged back down the stairs to where his brothers were still razzing Mike. Jake was yelling from the shower while Dan sat on the weight bench laughing, Mike looking flustered as he set the weights back.

"Sorry about that, Mike." He clapped a hand on the bigger man's shoulder. "I shouldn't have done that to you, especially in front of these guys."

"No worries," Mike shrugged. "I'll get to brag to everyone today that I talked to her, that will go a long way around the gym."

"But did you?" Jake's voice rang from the other room.

"I think we probably already reached the limit on teasing," Dan said as he stood up. "But I reserve the right to revisit this later."

"Thanks for putting up with us," Patrick said to Mike.

"No problem, it's one of the highlights of my day. I love when you're here, you make everyone work harder."

"Want to shower before you head out? Or use the hot tub or sauna?"

"No, thanks. I have an appointment at the gym in fifteen minutes, so I should run." Mike started for the stairs before looking back at Patrick. "And thanks for trying with Natalie, that was cool of you."

"Anytime, man." Patrick watched as he disappeared up the stairs before yelling in to his brothers. "I'll be in the kitchen."

He started a pot of coffee before glancing out the window at the guest cottage, where the lights were all off. Emma must still be at breakfast with Zoe, which meant it must be going well. He was happy for her, reconnecting with her sister would help her find her place in the world. He had offered to drive her that morning, but she had refused, saying the walk was good for her. It was odd that he missed her but having spent so much time with her over the last few days, he couldn't help but want more. His time was limited before he had to get back to California, he hoped he could spend more of it getting to know her. And that was a feeling he hadn't had in a long time.

Chapter 12

Emma had arrived at the small diner fifteen minutes early, after walking as slowly as she could manage. Seeing her sister last night for the first time in almost sixteen years had been surreal. She had barely slept last night, the emotions were so overwhelming. The grief over her mother, sorrow over the years missed with Zoe, and an intense hatred of Zoe's selfish mother had come in waves. She made sure to maintain a strong dislike of their father, constantly reminding herself that he was more at fault than a woman who was no relation to her. His absence in her life had been so absolute that he rarely entered her mind, unless she forced herself to focus on his role in her situation.

The bell over the door chimed as she stirred creamer into her coffee, and she was shocked to realize she felt relief when she saw Zoe's face. It hadn't occurred to her until that moment that part of her emotions had been fear her sister would turn her back on her, but she had shown up as promised this morning. She stood as Zoe approached the table, and they hugged before sitting back down.

"I still can't believe you're here," Zoe said. She pulled off her heavy winter coat and hat, placing them on the seat next to her. "I could barely sleep last night, I was so excited and happy. And I need to know everything."

"Me too," Emma admitted. "I want to know what your life has been like. Finding you was more difficult than I would have imagined, you have to be the only person on the planet with no social media presence at all."

"If I had known you were looking for me on there, I would be on all of them. I have an account for my work as a chef, but it's just Chef Zoe, so I can't imagine you would have found that."

"No, but I will now. One of my old foster sisters saw a post on Facebook about a new Chef at a small-town restaurant that everyone was raving about. When she saw your picture, she knew it had to be who I was looking for, so she tracked me down. I never would have found you otherwise." Emma smiled shyly at her sister. "I guess we look more alike than I realized."

"Just our hair length is different, I keep mine so short because I'm in the kitchen. I wish I had your long hair," Zoe laughed. "But the hairnets are a nightmare."

The waitress brought them menus and fresh coffee, pausing the conversation for a moment. Emma watched as her sister laughed with the waitress, and then waved across the room at someone else. She was clearly a part of this town, and people seemed to like her.

"Tell me everything," Zoe said after the waitress departed. "Where did you end up when your mom passed?"

"They put me into foster care, a temporary one at first while they spent time trying to track down our sperm donor. My mom didn't have any family left, and hadn't left any paperwork or anything to indicate what should happen to me. Who would have thought she would die so young?" Emma was surprised when tears sprung to her eyes and grabbed a napkin to dab them away.

"Not me, I was shocked when I found out. I was only fourteen, but I would have run away to find you if I had known what was happening." Zoe wiped tears away herself. "It was a car accident?"

"Yes," Emma nodded. "She worked late, which she had to do a lot. She had called me when I got home from school, she wanted to pick me up so I could come hang out while she worked. I did that a lot, I would sit in back and do my homework or read and have dinner. It let me spend time with her even when she was working. I was pouting over something so I said no, otherwise I would have been with her."

"She wouldn't have wanted that," Zoe chastened softly.

"No, but if I had gone without complaining, maybe she wouldn't have been in the right spot to be hit. I might have rushed her to leave earlier, or moved slowly and kept her longer. She was going through a green light, and a drunk driver ran the red and crushed her car." Emma took a deep breath, pushing the image of her mom's car out of her head. "She was killed instantly, which is a blessing I guess."

"You don't blame yourself?"

"A little," Emma nodded. "If I had been easier on her and just gone, or if I had asked her to come home early. Anything to keep her out of that intersection. I know it's unreasonable, but the last thing she asked me to do I said no, and I know that disappointed her. All I can think is that the whole night would have been different if I had gone."

"You can't think like that." Zoe covered her hand as she spoke. "There is no way your mom would want you to blame yourself. She loved you so much and was so amazing."

"Thank you for that," Emma whispered. She took a second to wipe more tears away and take a deep breath before continuing. "Her work friends tried to help me, but they weren't super close. And they all lived paycheck to paycheck, and most had kids of their own. I got sent to an older couple who were emergency housing, just to get me through the first few weeks until they exhausted all other options. The first foster house I went into was temporary, they were able to keep me in the same town so I could finish the school year, but they were also older and had been out of fostering for a bit. I was lucky, but I didn't know it at the time, that I was the only one in the house. After that, I moved almost every six months. New house, new foster family, new school."

"That must have been awful," Zoe's voice shook.

"It was," Emma nodded. "I won't sugarcoat it. There were some really horrible ones, and every once in a while, I would land somewhere that was almost nice. I would hope I could stay there, and I would try and be so good, but it never happened. I don't know why I was so easy to cast out, but no one chose to keep me."

"Oh, Em." Zoe was weeping now. "I'm so sorry."

She grasped her sister's hand tighter. "Please don't be. I survived it. And no one ever hurt me. I heard some horror stories from my foster siblings over the years, so I know I was lucky that way. I never had new clothes, and rarely had enough to eat, but at least I was safe."

"Even going to bed hungry is awful," Zoe protested.

"I learned over the years," Emma told her. "I would take food kids at school were throwing away and hide it. One of the lunch ladies saw me standing by the trash one day and told the principal, so they started to send me home with a bagged meal that I could have. That principal made sure it continued no matter what school I went to, so at least by high school I wasn't the trash picking kid anymore. But I still took my friends cast offs, which got easier when everyone was dieting for prom."

"You were able to make friends, even moving around so much?"

"I don't know if I would call them close friends, I never stayed in touch, but I found people to spend time with," Emma said. "I learned how to adapt very early on. Don't be a threat to the pretty girls, don't try to be the smartest, don't flirt with the cutest boy. I got involved in activities immediately and was usually able to find some friends easily. It helped that I would want to spend as much time in school or away from the foster home as possible, so I was always willing to volunteer for something. There were only a couple of schools that didn't want me there, but at least I knew that it would be short lived."

"What happened when you turned eighteen?"

"I was shown the door," Emma admitted. "I had a meeting with my social worker about six months before my birthday and talked about the options. I could go into a new home that would take me at eighteen and opt to stay in foster care until I was twenty-one. Or I could go to college, that would put a roof over my head and the state would pay for almost all of it. I was six months away from high school graduation when my birthday hit, so I had to find a way to stay in school and get to that point. The foster family I was with made it very clear that I would be shown the door on my birthday, since they wouldn't get money for having me any longer."

"What did you do?"

"I had been working at a local bakery, making bread and pastries before they opened. It was brutal to be up so early, but I was done before school, and I could go back after and work the counter. It was decent money, and the couple who owned the shop had a soft spot for me," she explained. "They had a tiny apartment over the bakery, it hadn't been used since they bought the building, so I asked if I could rent it from them. They agreed, and said I could just work an extra few hours a week in exchange for the apartment. Do things like accept deliveries, or be there if something needed to be picked up early on a weekend."

"Oh, that sounds like a great arrangement," Zoe gushed.

"It was," she smiled. "They were amazing, I was lucky. The apartment had been furnished by the previous owner, and they let me use everything. They never charged me for electricity or anything, and they were always handing me bags of groceries. Some nights I would finish work and find a full dinner waiting for me to bring upstairs, and they always invited me to spend holidays with their family. They taught me that kindness still existed, along with the teachers and school staff who always made sure to help me. Making sure I had jackets, or hygiene products, things you never think of until you're on your own."

"Did you stay with them after you graduated?"

"I did. I worked even more hours and took some classes at the Community College. I saved enough to buy a car, and they helped me get my driver's license. That was the first time I went looking for you," she said. "I had to study maps and print out directions at the library, but I was able to find your address. I rang the doorbell and a stranger answered."

"My mother sold that house when I graduated," Zoe said sadly. "I was in college, and she said she didn't need a big house anymore. In reality, she just wanted to make sure I didn't think I could come back to live with her when I finished school."

"Where did you go to college?"

Zoe glanced down at the table and her cheeks turned pink before she spoke again. "Le Cordon Bleu."

"What? That's amazing!"

"Thank you," she grinned. "I'm still surprised by it. I was chosen as the scholarship recipient, before that I had no intention of going to school. I had been in the technical studies program at my high school, so I figured I would go on to be a sous chef somewhere and learn on the job. My teacher encouraged me to apply for the scholarship, and next thing I knew, I was moving to Ottawa."

"What an amazing experience that must have been," Emma replied. "Did you stay there after you finished?"

"For a little while," she said. "Then I went to Paris to continue my training. Next thing you know, I found myself in this little town in Vermont and unable to leave for some reason. I think the universe knew I needed to be here so you could find me."

"Well, I'm glad for that," Emma smiled. "That explains why I couldn't find you for so many years. I never thought to check beyond Canada and the United States for you. And I don't speak a word of French, so finding you in France would be hard."

"Somehow I think you would have managed," Zoe blinked tears away. "I want you to know I've been looking for you for a long time. No one would tell me anything when I found out about your mom, and it had already been months when I finally heard. My mother has no shame and had no problem keeping that from me, apparently. It was only when I kept trying to call and suddenly a stranger answered, saying that I had the wrong number. They told me they had just gotten the number assigned to them, and I just knew something had happened. I knew your mom wouldn't move and not let me know."

"She would never have done that," Emma agreed.

"I started calling and writing to everyone I could think of, but I hadn't really paid that much attention to who your moms' friends were or when she worked. Your school told me nothing other than you weren't a student there. The librarian at my school helped me, but we couldn't find any trace of you. Even now, as an adult, I searched for you online every day."

"I guess one of us should have wised up and gone on social media," Emma admitted. "I don't know why I never did. Other than not having a smart phone, I guess. But I should have made a profile just in case you were looking. I just believed your mom, for some stupid reason."

"Not stupid," Zoe argued. "She was an adult, and you were a grieving child, of course you believed her."

The waitress returned, having been lingering behind the breakfast bar as if afraid to interrupt. "Do you girls want to order? I can give you more time if you need it."

"Sorry, Elaine." Zoe grabbed her menu and glanced at it quickly before placing it back down. "This is my little sister, Emma."

"I didn't know you had a sister," Elaine exclaimed. "How nice to meet you. Are you visiting?"

"Nice to meet you as well," Emma responded. "Yes, I am."

"How fun, I always love it when my sister comes to stay with me. We do facials and stay up way too late watching corny movies," she laughed. "Things our husbands would never watch. We send them off on hunting or golfing trips so we can enjoy the quiet."

"That sounds nice," Zoe smiled at the older woman. "Emma isn't staying with me, but maybe we can change that."

"Oh, are you at the Inn?"

"No—"

"She's staying with Patrick Burrows," Zoe interrupted.

"Oh, my." Elaine fanned herself with the notepad she held. "How do I make that happen for myself?"

"He's been very kind," Emma mumbled. She grabbed the menu again, hoping Zoe would get the hint, and was happy when her sister did the same.

"I think I'll have an omelet with tomatoes, cheese and bacon," Zoe declared.

"Sounds good. Toast and home fries?"

"Perfect." She wrote on her pad before turning to Emma. "For you, hun?"

"I think I'll try the macadamia nut pancakes," she answered. "And a side of bacon."

"Bacon makes everything taste better," Zoe grinned. "Thanks, Elaine."

"Sure thing. And if you have any details to share about that delicious Patrick, please include me." The waitress headed back behind the counter to put their order in, leaving the sisters alone again.

"What are the chances she won't spread that around town and make it sound salacious?" Emma bit her lip after she asked the question, already knowing the answer.

"She's been the waitress in this diner for about one hundred years. No one has more gossip to share than Elaine, and this will be in the top five things she shares. Us being sisters and you living with Patrick, and it will all be as blown out of proportion as she can make it." Zoe groaned and took a sip of her coffee. "I'm sorry, I should have just had you come to my place. Or kept my big mouth shut."

"It's okay," Emma said. "Enough people saw us last night to get the gossip whirling, now they'll just know who I am to link to him. I should probably get to work finding a job and a place to stay that is not with the hottest bachelor in town."

"You said you worked in a bakery, I know the owner of the one here in town and she's desperate for help," Zoe explained. "She does all the desserts for the restaurant, and does a solid business with her storefront."

"That would be perfect. I don't mind going in early to bake, but I don't have a car right now so it's a little tough."

"I'll text her." Zoe pulled her phone out and sent a text before placing it on the table. "I'm sure she'll get right back to me, she's asked me ten times this week if I have any waitresses looking for more hours."

"Are you sure it's okay if I stay in town for a while? I don't want to infringe on your life."

"Are you serious?" Zoe looked shocked. "This is amazing, and I never want you to leave. If you want, I can make space in my apartment for you? It's tiny but we can manage."

Emma considered the offer and then thought of all Patrick had done. "I don't want to leave Patrick and look ungrateful. You can't imagine the time and money he put into having the guest cottage ready for me in record time."

"He's amazing," Zoe gushed. "I haven't spent a lot of time with him, but when Calle was missing, he was so solid and ready to do anything for her."

"And he's famous?"

"Are you serious?" Zoe asked again. "Really?"

"I thought he maybe looked familiar, but it could have just been that he's so hot."

"He's incredibly famous. Like top ten actors right now," Zoe explained. "He was on the hottest show ever and went from a teenager in Vermont to being a huge super hero in movies. You need to google him."

"And he's—"

"What?"

"Single?"

"Oh yes. It's the source of much discussion among the Burrows women, they all want to find him the perfect woman." Zoe tapped the spoon on the edge of her coffee cup and grinned at her. "Maybe the perfect woman found him instead."

"He would never be interested in me," Emma said softly.

"You think he doesn't like beautiful, kind women?" Zoe sounded indignant on her behalf.

"If he's as famous and rich as everyone makes out, an orphan who barely made it through high school is not a good match."

"Let's see about that," Zoe said. "Oh, Piper from the bakery texted back, she said yes and to come see her as soon as possible. I'll tell her you'll be by in the next couple of hours."

Emma watched Zoe's fingers fly across the screen and let her mind drift to Patrick. In the perfect world, he would be everything her sister said, but she had learned long ago that the world was not perfect. Better to put the idea of romance with him out of her head before she got carried away. Focus on getting a job, connecting with her sister, and feeling safe for the first time in a while. A romance with someone so far out of her league was a distraction she didn't need.

Chapter 13

Two weeks in Vermont flew by faster than Patrick would have liked. Somehow the time spent in California dragged by, and his time spent in his hometown went by in a flash. He only had a few days left before he needed to head back to finish the shoot, and although he was happy to see his friends and work, he wasn't ready to leave. The days had been spent working out with his brothers, spending time with Charlie and Calle, and trying to catch Emma between her shifts at the bakery. If anyone ever tried to make a comment about their long hours on the film set, most spent lounging in a trailer, he would drag them here and make them work alongside her.

It was odd to miss someone you barely knew, especially when they lived mere feet away from you. But that's what it felt like, and he was determined to find a way to spend time with her before he left again. He had even taken to lingering in the bakery, eating treats he had to work off the next morning, but she was always too busy to sit and talk to him.

He was leaning on the side of the stable door when he heard the crunch of snow beneath a boot and turned to find her walking up the driveway. She smiled tiredly at him and waved. "What are you doing?"

"Hey," he smiled. "Jake just left; we were making sure the stable is structurally sound so I can think about bringing horses in."

"Oh, do you ride? I've always loved the look of them, but never been on one."

"I can take you," he offered. "We have a stable full at my dad's, plenty that are gentle enough for first timers."

"I might be a little too chicken," she laughed. "I kind of like having my feet on the ground."

"If Calle can manage, you can," he said. "Your next day off, let's try it."

"Okay," she agreed. "If you promise to keep me in one piece. Then I won't be so scared if I'm still here when you move horses in."

"You will be," he responded. "The stable is in good shape. I heard of a rescue that was having trouble finding space for some horses that were just surrendered. They need some fattening up, and some good care. I've donated to a rescue in California quite a bit, they save horses from being sent to Mexico. I love seeing the horses when they realize they've been saved and see the transformation. Tahlia who runs it even has a rescue Zebra, and a water buffalo."

"No way," Emma laughed, her eyes lighting up. "How did you hear about them?"

"Instagram, of course."

"If I get one of those, I'll have to find it."

"You should, it's a good reminder for me."

"Reminder of what?" She tilted her head to the side and waited for his answer.

"That kindness goes a long way," he said. "And that cruelty can be right in plain sight, and we can overlook it. Seeing those beautiful animals with their ribs sticking out or walking on a broken leg because an owner doesn't want to spend the money to put them down, that's wrong. Or working them to the bone only to stop feeding them or sell them to a trader when they can't work any longer."

"That's heartbreaking."

"It really is." He cleared his throat. "Anyway, I've done some fundraising events for this rescue in California, tried to help spread the word. I grew up with horses, and they are special animals who don't deserve this cruelty, so I try to help as much as I can through the rescue. They posted the other day that they had some horses in New England that needed a place to land until they could find them new homes. I told them if the stable was safe, they could come here, and it looks like they will be."

"You're amazing, Patrick." Her eyes were a little shiny as they met his, and he felt an urge to wrap her in his arms. She took a step back before he could move. "I should go shower, I smell like flour and sugar."

"Not a bad way to smell," he laughed. "Hey, I'm going to dinner over at my dad's tonight, the whole family will be there. Will you come? They would love to see you."

"I don't want to intrude," she said softly.

"No intrusion. It's always an open invitation at Stella's table, and there is nothing she loves more than feeding people."

"Okay, if you're sure."

"Very," he smiled. "I'll pick you up at six."

He jogged inside before she could change her mind, pulling out his phone to call the rescue and let them know he would be ready for the horses the next morning. While he was thinking of it, he also called the veterinarian his father used and scheduled him to visit the next morning, and the feed store for a delivery. With the horses set, he decided to kill some time in the gym to burn off what could only be described as nervous energy.

***

At six on the dot, Patrick opened the kitchen door to start the short walk to the guest house. Light was spilling out the windows, making the small space look more like a cozy home. He knocked and took a step back, waiting for her to answer.

"Hi," she said as she opened the door. "You could have just come in."

"That felt rude," he explained. "You need a few more minutes?"

"Just need my shoes," she responded. "Then I'm ready."

He watched her slip her feet into boots that looked like they had seen better days but bit his tongue. When she wrapped a scarf around her neck before pulling a thin coat from the closet, he lost his control. "You need a warmer coat than that."

"Working on that," she responded. "And please don't offer to buy me one."

"But—"

"Patrick." She leveled him with a steely gaze. "You have already done way too much for me. I cannot accept anything else."

"What if I have a warmer coat that you could wear?" He grinned at her and looked so charming, it was hard to resist.

"I think it might be a tiny bit too big," she said, gesturing between them. "You're well over six feet and I'm barely over five. I would look ridiculous. Besides, I am getting a paycheck tomorrow and a coat is top of the list. I'd also like to start paying you rent or paying you back for all you've done to this place."

"Absolutely not."

"We can discuss it later." She zipped up the thin coat and gestured to the door. "I don't want to be late."

He grumbled under his breath as they walked to the car, and her laughter ringing through the cold air warmed him more than any jacket ever could.

***

When Patrick parked the car, he turned to face Emma before opening his door. "My family can be a lot. They are loud, opinionated, and loving. Just ignore anything you don't want to answer, and hopefully have some fun."

"Maybe this was a bad idea," she responded.

"No," he shook his head. "You'll be fine. They will go far easier on you than they will me. Also, Stella already had a plan to invite you to dinner to thank you for taking care of me, and there is no one in the world who can say no to her. It's better if we do it tonight than you having to come alone. This way you can use me as a shield if you need to."

"Why would I have to come alone?"

"I have to go back to California," he explained. "Not for long, but long enough that they would have overwhelmed you."

"I didn't know you were leaving."

"Jake will be around at the house, and I hired people to come and care for the horses. They are highly recommended by the vet, and only live a few miles away, so they won't be staying on property." Patrick looked at her and couldn't figure out what her expression was. "Will you be okay there alone?"

"If I was okay living in your stable alone, I think I can manage from the guest house," she nodded. "I guess I just got used to seeing you around and knowing you were right there."

He leaned forward, feeling himself drawn to her. Her eyes met his, shining with something he couldn't quite recognize, but it wasn't repulsion. Just as he was about to reach for her face, a blaring horn came from behind them. They both jumped as he turned to see Dan's SUV pull in behind them.

"Guess we better get to it," he said, trying to hide his irritation at being interrupted. They both opened their doors, and instantly a tiny person in head-to-toe pink was next to him.

"Uncle Patrick! Did you get a girlfriend? Who's that? Who are you? I'm Calle. I'm here for dinner, are you? Can you help me carry in my stuff?" She bounced on her feet, clutching dolls and books to her chest. "Charlie promised to play princess with me."

"Did he now?" Patrick picked her up, holding her easily in one arm. "This is my friend Emma."

"I got a cookie from you yesterday," Calle announced. "Are you Patrick's girlfriend? Mimi Stella always says he needs one."

Emma laughed as she reached over to catch a falling book. "I'm his friend. And yes, I was working at the bakery when you came in. It's hard to forget all this pink."

"It's all she will wear," Kendra laughed. "Nice to see you, Emma. Calle, let's go inside."

They all piled into the foyer, removing boots and jackets and piling them on the hooks and racks next to the door. Loud voices came from the kitchen, indicating Jake and Shea were there, and something caused a wave of laughter that rode down the hall. Shea hesitated as she followed Kendra, causing Patrick to bump into her from behind. He placed his hands on her shoulders to catch himself and could feel the tension coming off her.

"Sorry," he said. "You okay?"

"I haven't," she hesitated before continuing. "Really been in this kind of situation before."

"I promise they won't bite," he whispered. He stepped around her and gazed into her eyes. "If you get uncomfortable, just tell me you're getting a headache and I'll bring you home."

She nodded, so he went into the kitchen first to absorb some of the attention and give her a moment to adjust. His whole family was piled into the one room, with the exception of the kids, who he could see in the living room.

"Emma," Stella's voice rang out. "I'm so pleased you could join us. Come, sit down and let me get you a drink."

"Well hello to you too, Stella," Patrick teased.

"Oh, you." She swatted him with the dishtowel she held. "You know I'm happy to see you, but I don't get to see Emma anytime I want."

Stella swept Emma to the table, where Kendra and Shea were sitting. His two brothers were pouring drinks at the counter, while their father sat at the island, the easiest place for him to talk to Stella as she cooked.

"Hey, Patty," Jake greeted him.

"Knock it off," Patrick warned.

"Oh, are we not supposed to embarrass you in front of your new girlfriend?" Dan asked in a low voice so the women wouldn't overhear.

"You guys are the worst," Patrick groaned. "And I didn't humiliate either of you when you first brought your wives around. Plus, she's not my girlfriend."

"Notice he denied that a little late," Dan said to Jake. "And the first time I brought Kendra around you were probably twelve, so I'm sure you did something."

"You know what I mean," Patrick replied. "She's a little nervous, so go easy, please."

"Nervous of us?" Jake's eyebrow raised. "Why?"

"In case you haven't noticed," Patrick replied drolly. "You are a lot."

"That's true for Dan, but I am certainly not."

Patrick poured two glasses of red wine before looking back at his brothers. "Just go easy, alright?"

"We'll be on our best behavior," Dan promised.

"That's almost a little scarier," Patrick admitted. "At least your wives are nice."

Chapter 14

Patrick placed a glass of wine in front of Emma before sitting next to her, his laughing brothers following him to the table. Jake pulled a chair to be even closer to Shea, leaning in to whisper in her ear as he sat. Dan sat and clung his arm around the back of Kendra's chair, smiling when she leaned into him.

"How are you both feeling?" Patrick asked, directing the question at the other two women at the table.

Shea smiled and placed a hand on her small belly. "I feel great. The first trimester was a little rough, but I guess I'm in the good spot now."

"Me too," Kendra nodded. "I'm still in the first trimester, but almost out of it, so hoping to have more energy in a few weeks."

"Does anyone else know?" Emma asked. "I had no idea you were pregnant, congratulations."

"Thanks," Kendra grinned. "Zoe knows, if that's what you're asking. I had to tell her it wasn't the food that was making me throw up every day. And Linda, the manager at the restaurant. She's been amazing, picking up the slack when I was exhausted or sick. And she'll obviously need to work more the closer to the end I get. We had planned to wait to get pregnant and give Calle the opportunity to settle in with a dad in her life suddenly. That plan went right out the window."

"I can't help it that you can't keep your hands off me," Dan laughed.

"Don't forget we're right here," Ben called from the island. "Keep it clean over there."

"Always," the three men chimed out in unison, making everyone laugh.

"We are excited that the cousins will be so close in age," Shea added. "Charlie and Calle get along great, but it will be nice that these babies will have a playmate the same age."

"Are you finding out what you're having?" Patrick asked.

"A baby," Jake deadpanned.

"You're an idiot," Patrick responded.

"We are going to wait," Shea replied. "What about you guys?"

Kendra nodded. "We're doing the same. We debated finding out, but we'll be happy either way, so it's more fun to have it a surprise."

"We should talk names one day," Shea said. "Make sure we don't have the same ones in mind."

"I know Jake, and if I say what names we like, he will steal it just because you'll deliver first," Dan said.

"I'm not stealing baby names, Danny," Jake said, rolling his eyes.

"You're the most competitive person I know, so I wouldn't put anything past you," Dan insisted.

"No one is stealing anything," Kendra soothed him. "We'll probably have two different genders anyway."

"I'm going to have a girl and name her Danni," Jake said.

"You two stop," Shea chided. "I feel like I'm at school."

Ben joined them at the table as Stella started placing platters full of food on the table. Once Charlie and Calle sat, the table was filled with even more noise as everyone seemed to be talking at once. Emma had no idea how anyone was able to follow along, with so many conversations and laughter all around. She accepted a platter of food from Kendra and placed a small portion on her plate before handing it to Patrick. He took the tongs and immediately placed another serving on her plate.

"If you don't take it the first time it comes around, you'll never be able to get seconds," he warned her. "This crew isn't known for leaving anything for second helpings."

"I don't know how she cooked all of this," she replied. "There is more food here than I think I've ever seen at once."

"She's amazing," Patrick smiled down at Stella. "She raised us, and she knows how much we like to eat."

"You're lucky," she replied quietly. She accepted another bowl of food from Kendra and took a scoop before passing it to him. "They're all amazing."

He nodded. "Every day of my life I'm grateful for this crew. I'm sorry you didn't have one like it to lean on."

"You can't miss what you didn't know existed," she replied. It was impossible for her to feel the sadness that wanted to creep into her heart when she was surrounded by such joy, so she pushed it aside. "But thank you, I appreciate that. And I'm so glad to have found Zoe, and to have met you."

She glanced over and got lost in his eyes for a moment, seeing the true concern in his. It was hard to keep reminding herself that she was likely something that he wanted to save, not a woman he was attracted to, when he looked at her as he was now.

"Patrick, I heard the veterinarian is coming by your house tomorrow," Ben's voice called down. "Did you get a pet I don't know about?"

"Kind of," he answered. "I'm fostering some horses for a rescue until they can find a new home for them."

"What kind of horses?" Calle asked, wide eyed.

"The kind that haven't had an easy life, or been treated well lately," he said. "They need somewhere to stay and get healthy, and then the rescue will either move them to a new farm or find people to adopt them."

"Daddy is adopting me," Calle announced. "Now I get to call him Daddy instead of Dan."

Everyone in the room grinned and sighed as Dan pulled her close to drop a kiss on her head. "You sure can," he said. "We don't need to wait for a day in court for me to be your dad."

"Maybe you can adopt the horses too," Calle suggested to Dan.

"We live in an apartment," Kendra replied. "It might get a little tight."

"We should talk about that," Stella replied. "Jake and Shea are close to moving next door, and Ben and I are settled into the cabin out back. You three should move in here."

"I could live with Charlie?" Calle looked overjoyed. "Can I share his room?"

"I'm actually going to move next door with Dad and Shea," Charlie replied. "But we can have sleepovers."

"You are?" Jake looked shocked.

"If you don't mind," the teen said quietly.

"Of course we don't mind," Jake sounded stunned. "I'm thrilled. I just didn't think you would want to move away from this house."

"It's just next door," Charlie shrugged. "And I kind of like hanging out with you."

"I kind of like it too." Jake pressed his napkin to his eyes surreptitiously before continuing. "We already had planned to make you a room, so now it won't be a surprise. But that's better, you can help me choose what you'd like. Let me show you the plans."

Charlie and Jake started looking at Jake's phone, Shea beaming happiness at the duo. Ben glanced down the table and Patrick tensed next to her, making her look and see the man's gaze locked on her.

"Emma," he stated. "How is life in the guest cabin at Patrick's house?"

"It's very nice, thank you," she replied quietly.

"And when Patrick goes back to California, what will you do?" Ben asked in a brisk voice.

"She'll stay right where she is," Patrick replied. "Because I'm a big boy and it's my house, which means I can decide who is welcome there."

Ben ignored him. "I heard through the grapevine that Zoe is your sister?"

"Yes, sir," she nodded. "We haven't seen each other in years. We have different mothers and didn't grow up together."

"Where is your father?"

She shrugged. "Your guess is as good as mine."

"And you got a job at the bakery?"

"Yes, Piper has been amazing to work for."

"That means you plan to stick around?"

She hesitated, glancing over at Patrick before replying. "I do, I like it here. And Zoe is here, so I'd like to spend more time with her. I can move—"

"Absolutely not," Patrick stopped her. "You are welcome to stay as long as you like. The cabin would be sitting empty."

"I can at least pay you rent," she insisted.

"We can talk about this later," he said. "Dad, did you have more questions, or can we go back to enjoying our evening?"

"When are you leaving for Los Angeles?" His father fired back. "And for how long?"

"Day after tomorrow. Zane and Liam are back now, but they needed a few days to detox and get camera ready before we start up. We should only be a couple weeks from wrapping."

The family chatter started back up again, everyone saying either that they would miss Patrick or his brothers teasing they were glad to be rid of him. Emma took a sip of her wine and tried to hide her feelings on the matter. Despite avoiding him as much as possible the last few weeks, she was going to miss him when he left. Sitting next to him now, sharing in the warmth that his family created, the idea of him being so far away had her already feeling lonely.

He was an unusual man, unlike anyone she had ever met before. Even if he wasn't as shockingly handsome as he was, she would be drawn to the kindness he seemed to show everyone. It was hard not to get drawn into fantasies about what it would be like to be the woman that he loved, or to feel what it would be like to kiss him. Earlier in the car she had a moment where she felt like he was about to do so, and she wouldn't have been able to resist. She was torn about whether the interruption was a good thing, because as much as she wanted to feel his lips on hers, the heartbreak that was sure to follow if she let herself fall would be too much to bear.

***

The sounds of trucks approaching woke her early the next morning, and a peek out the window revealed two large trucks pulling up to the stable. Patrick stood at the door, looking perfect in jeans and a heavy jacket, ski cap pulled down over his ears. He had looked confused, and maybe even disappointed, last night when she declined going into the main house to have a drink with him, instead almost running to the cottage. If she had gone into the house, she was afraid she would throw herself at him, and that level of embarrassment would be too much.

Pulling on jeans and the warmest tops she owned, followed by her flimsy jacket and a hat, she grabbed the two mugs of coffee she had prepared and headed to the stable. He smiled when he saw her coming, filling her with relief that she hadn't insulted him the night before.

"Morning," she called. "I brought you some coffee."

"You're a mind reader," he smiled. "Thank you. I was up way too early knowing these guys were on the way."

"What are they delivering?"

"Everything the horses will need. Hay, feed, shavings, some calorie boosters, buckets, floor mats for the stalls, blankets, cleaning supplies, heaters, salt licks, grooming supplies," he ticked off on his fingers before grinning at her. "If you can think it, I probably ordered it."

"I don't know much about horses," she replied. "I guess I'll learn fast."

"If you'd rather stay inside, that's fine. Dan, Jake and Charlie will be here later to help me get set up." He glanced at his watch. "The horses should be here early afternoon, so we have to be quick."

"The more hands the better," she responded. "What I don't know I'll make up for in the willingness to work."

"Appreciate that," he murmured. "Let me go show these guys where to unload."

She watched as boxes, large tubs and barrels were rolled off the truck and into the stable. It looked like way too much to be put away in the short amount of time they had, but she had no idea where to begin, which left her waiting for Patrick's direction. Two more trucks pulled into the driveway, and soon Jake, Dan, Charlie and Ben were part of the chaos.

"Dad, I told you it was alright if you wanted to stay home," Patrick griped when he saw his father. "Don't hurt your back."

"Son, I can give orders with the best of them. You need someone to oversee and call in reinforcements, because there is no way this is getting done in time." Ben stepped away as his three sons shook their heads at him, pulling his phone out of his pocket.

"Do we want to know who he's calling?" Dan asked.

"Nope," the other two responded.

"Let's start with the stable mats," Jake suggested. "Once we get a couple down, someone can start putting shavings in as we keep going through the rest."

"How many horses are coming today?" Jake asked.

"Eight," Patrick responded. "We can do it."

"Charlie," Ben called from where he was sitting on the back of his pickup. "Come here."

"Okay, down one. He can start doing shavings when he gets back," Jake said. "Dan and I will each take a stall on our own, why don't you show Emma how to do it."

The two men grabbed stacks of the black mats and disappeared, and Emma watched as Patrick grabbed some and led her into the stall next to where she had slept. She knew it was intentional and appreciated the small kindness but kept it to herself.

"These link together," he explained. "It's like a puzzle. They should fit without having to be trimmed, you just want to make sure it's all the way flat."

They worked side by side, clicking pieces together and handing each other a piece without needing words. When the stall was done, they moved into the next, and she ignored the part of her that suggested she could do one on her own. Being side by side with Patrick was too good to turn down, so she let herself believe it was easier to complete the task together.

Chapter 15

"We've got help on the way," Charlie called out from the doorway. "My team is coming, and Grandpa called some other people."

"Great," Patrick responded. "Start doing the shavings, okay?"

"On it," the teen responded.

Emma was on the floor, pushing a piece of floor mat into the corner of the stall they had just started. She hadn't complained, and although he wanted to insist that she go inside and relax on her day off, he was enjoying her presence. When the rest of the volunteers showed up, maybe he could force himself to send her inside, but not at that moment.

"Can you grab a few more pieces?" she asked, blowing a piece of blond hair out of her face. "I don't think I got enough."

He grabbed a stack and joined her on the floor, clicking the rubber mats into place at a slower pace than he would have done if he were alone. They reached for the same seam, brushing hands, and she jumped back from him so fast he startled and almost fell backwards. He saw the blush on her cheeks and decided to ignore it, but it was something he would have to revisit in the near future.

The sound of more vehicles pulling in snapped him out of his thoughts, and soon the stable was filled with noise. Charlie's entire hockey team had come, grabbing shovels and bags of shavings to work on stalls. Another group of them started opening boxes, pulling blankets and heaters out and placing them near each stall. Other adults started filing in, some holding tool bags, including his trainer Mike and friend JJ, who was a local police officer.

"Ben told us to start installing heaters," JJ called out, pointing at the boxes on the ground.

Before he knew what happened, the stable was filled with people all working in harmony to get the space ready for the rescue horses. He was touched that his neighbors, many of whom he didn't know well, would have dropped everything to spend their Saturday morning helping him. It was a far cry from Hollywood, where he doubted if anyone would cross the street to help him.

Within hours, all the tasks were done. The stalls were ready for horses, with supplies, blankets, heaters, and feed in each. Now all he needed was the trailers to arrive and the vet to inspect each horse, but for now he could take a much-needed lunch break.

"Stella and the girls are in the kitchen," Ben advised the group. "Zoe and Stella whipped up some food for everyone."

The whole crowd cheered and headed for his kitchen, the teens leading the pack. He glanced over at where Emma was washing her hands, cheeks pink from exertion and looking pleased at the idea that her sister was there.

"Hungry?" he asked, joining her at the sink.

"Starved," she grinned at him. "I might out-eat those boys."

"You should hurry," he said. "I've seen them in action, and I'll be surprised if we can find any scraps when we get in there."

She laughed and looked around. "This is really amazing, Patrick. You should be proud of yourself."

"I'm prouder of this town," he replied. "And you. I'm just amazed that anyone who wasn't related to me and forced to do this was willing to help."

"I'd do anything for you," she replied softly. "You've been so good to me, I can never replay you."

"Please stop looking at it like that," he responded sharply before softening his voice. "I don't want you to feel like you owe me anything."

"But I do," she replied. "I can't believe how generous you have been with me, not just in giving me a roof over my head. Although I really appreciate that, don't get me wrong. But you've also welcomed me into your life, and shared your family, and it means a lot."

"I told you before, it's who I am. I'm not expecting anything in return, other than your friendship. But if you decide you can't stand me, that's okay too."

She stared up at him, their eyes locked together, a long beat strumming between them before she responded. "I don't think that will ever happen."

"I'm glad, because I—"

"Let's go, you two," Jake called from the porch. "The kids are eating everything in sight."

They both dried their hands and headed out of the stable, and he was once again left feeling like an important moment had passed and he had screwed it up again.

***

He filled a plate with food, then managed to squeeze into a spot at the island next to Emma. She was trying to talk to Zoe over the chaos teenage boys and abundant food caused, laughing when her sister added another portion to an overflowing plate.

"These boys can eat," Emma marveled. "I think that kid had more food on his plate than I ate last year."

"Don't say that, it makes me feel awful," Zoe groaned before waving to the man next to her. "This is JJ. He should probably be on duty with the sheriff's office but seems to have chosen a path of danger by being in my way in the kitchen."

"I can't help it that I want to hang out with my best friend," JJ grinned. "Nice to meet you, Emma."

"You too," Emma said, observing her sister and her clearly besotted friend. JJ was tall, with sandy hair and bright eyes, handsome and looked strong enough to handle her sister. "Best friend, huh?"

"He says that all the time," Zoe waved her hand. "He clearly has a sad life if his best friend is the person who feeds him."

"Hey, my dog considers me his best friend and I am his provider," argued JJ. "Only makes sense I see you the same way."

"Am I the dog in this scenario?" Zoe stopped moving for a minute, leveling the man in her gaze.

"I think I am?" JJ tried with an endearing grin. "Someday we will go out to dinner, and I'll explain all of this in great detail."

"We aren't dating," Zoe warned him. "I keep telling you that."

"We will one day," he said confidently, winking at Emma. "I'm going to talk to the boys while you two chat. Come on, Patrick, kitchens getting too hot for us men."

He followed his friend, casting a glance at Emma where she was huddled with her sister. Zoe looked up and met his eyes, smiling at him as if she could see right into his thoughts. Maybe getting her on his side would help him break through Emma's walls.

***

The sound of approaching trucks brought the party inside to a standstill.

"Are the horses here?" One of the teenagers called out excitedly.

"Looks like it," Ben said from the front window. "We shouldn't all go out right now. Let Patrick get them safely into the stables and pasture, we don't want to spook them."

Patrick nodded, knowing his father was right. When his brothers stood to accompany him, he shook his head quickly and turned to Emma. "Want to come with me?"

She looked uncertain but nodded, pulling on her coat and hat as she walked in front of him. He wanted her to be a part of this moment and was glad she had agreed.

Two men were at the back of the trailers, having a short discussion as he and Emma exited the house. The taller of the two approached Patrick with his hand outstretched. "Nice to meet you, Patrick. I'm a big fan. I'm Hank, that's Sam back there."

"Nice to meet you," Patrick responded. "This is my friend Emma."

Hank nodded at her, then went back to Patrick. "We'll get these guys unloaded for you, looks like you have plenty of space. They are a little shy, I'll warn you. And they need a lot of love and care."

"I've got the vet already on the way," Patrick responded. "And more than enough people who want to love on them."

Hank looked over his shoulder and laughed. "Sure looks like it."

Patrick looked and saw all the windows facing the stable filled with faces, hoping to catch a glimpse of the new horses. "They all helped get the stable ready and will be more than willing to spend some time helping. Plus, I hired a trainer and a manager to be here, so they'll fill in whatever I don't already know about horses."

"Alright, let's get them unloaded." Hank headed back to Sam and unlatched the closest trailer, reaching in to encourage a frightened horse out.

Patrick held his breath, seeing the frail, too-skinny horse come down the ramp hesitantly. The animal was clearly afraid, despite the two men being gentle and using flags to help direct her toward the stable.

"Should we put them in the pasture first?" Patrick called over.

"Best to get them in their stalls so your vet can see them," Sam responded. "Plus, it will give them a chance to adjust and not be so scared."

Patrick moved closer, feeling Emma right at his side. The horse sidestepped away from them, so he stopped moving and waited while the two men guided her into the furthest stall. They repeated the process until all eight horses were in their stalls, most eating or drinking as if afraid the supplies would be removed before they had a chance. One was pacing the small space, seemingly unable to settle down.

"She's the most nervous," Hank advised them. "The rescue was able to grab her at the last possible second, but she's been through the wringer. Tossed from stable to stable, each one treating her worse than the one before. Keep your distance, she could be dangerous if she gets scared. She likes the colt we put in the next stall, we don't think it's a mom and baby, but she seems most content when he's nearby."

"They all need new shoes," Patrick guessed. "And obviously to be well fed. Any injuries you've noticed?"

"No," Hank shook his head. "We kept the injured and sick ones at the main ranch. These guys seem like they just need to remember how to be horses, and then should be either adopted or make great pasture horses at our main location. We just need to find homes for a few to make room for them, we got overwhelmed."

"What happens to them if you don't rescue them?" Emma's voice asked, sounding small.

"Well," Hank pushed his hat back on his head. "Most end up being transported to Texas, where they either find another rescue or a farm, or they end up in a kill pen headed to Mexico. It's a brutal business. We just do what we can."

"That's horrible," Emma said, her gaze going to the horse pacing in her stall.

"That's why we appreciate your help," the man said, nodding at Patrick. "We should get on the road, long drive ahead of us."

Patrick shook both men's hands, posed for pictures with them and autographed a few items that Sam's kids had sent along. He saw Emma looking over with interest as he signed, but by the time he was done she had wandered further into the stable. When he waved the two trucks off, he noticed she stood outside the anxious mare's stall.

"Be careful with her, okay?"

"I will," she replied. "She just looks so scared. And it's a little ironic that she's in the same spot that I used to sleep."

He moved closer, putting his hands on her shoulders as he stood behind her. "I'm glad you aren't in there anymore."

"Me too," she said softly before turning to look at him.

There was no chance he could have prevented himself from kissing her in that moment. The vulnerability in her eyes, the emotion he could feel coming off her as she identified with this horse, drew him in. He desperately wanted to soothe away her every worry, at the same time knowing he needed to be sure he was getting involved with her for the right reasons. He kept telling her that didn't view her as something to be saved, he honestly felt a connection with her that he hadn't felt with anyone before.

The second his lips touched hers, he felt a connection he had never had before. Not since his first kiss had he experienced this feeling of wonder, the discovery of something that was magical. He drew her closer, relieved that she responded equally, molding herself to him and wrapping her arms around his waist. His mind went blank as he could only focus on the feeling of her in his arms, the taste of her, and the overwhelming urge to make her his.

Chapter 16

In the week that Patrick had been back in California, Emma had done little but think of the kiss they had exchanged in the stable. They had been interrupted by the surge of people rushing from the house to see the horses, and Emma had used the opportunity to sneak away with Zoe when Patrick had been distracted with his family. She knew it was cowardly, but the moment had rocked her to the core, and she needed the time to process it. By the time she got home from work the following day, he had been gone.

Of course, being who he was, a new iPhone had been left outside her door with a note attached. *Wanted you to have this since you'll be out here alone while I'm gone. I programmed my number and my brothers into it for you. I hope you'll use mine.* He had planted the ball right in her court, and she had no idea what to do with it.

After a long day at work, she stopped by the Windsor Palace to see Zoe before the dinner rush started. Her sister was a whirlwind in the kitchen, overseeing the other staff and seemingly cooking ten things at once. JJ was settled against a wall, calmly eating a sandwich and watching Zoe.

"Hey, Emma," he called over, waving for her to join him. "How's things at the bakery?"

"Great, thanks. How's crime?"

He laughed. "Lucky for me, not much happening. Means I have more time to sit here and try to charm your sister."

"Are you serious about wanting to date her?"

"As a heart attack," he said, popping the last bite of food into his mouth. "I've never met anyone like her."

"It's not just about the food?" She pushed, wanting to know how he really felt about Zoe.

"That's how it started," he admitted. "The woman can cook. But then I started hanging out here more, and seeing how she treats the staff. And seeing how she steps up to help in the community any chance she gets, even though she pretends she's keeping a healthy distance from everyone."

"I get that," she murmured. "She's really special."

"She is," he agreed. "Maybe you could put in a word for me?"

"I'll see what I can do," she smiled at him. "But she's pretty stubborn."

"I know. I just have to find a way to force her hand a little. Not in a bad way," he added quickly. "But just make her take a chance on me." He stood as he spoke, neatly stacking the plate, cup and napkins together and placing them near the sink. "Thanks for the food, Zoe. I'll swing by later and walk you home."

"No need," she called after him, laughing when the door closed behind him. "He does that every night, even though I tell him I'm fine. Of all people, he should know there is no danger to me in this town."

"It's sweet," Emma offered. "He's got it bad for you."

Zoe glared as the entire kitchen staff called out their agreement, then laughed. "He just likes the food, that's all. What's happening with you?"

"Not much, just finished work and thought I would visit with you before I go home."

"Want some food?"

"Sure, if you have something I can take home with me. I'm desperate for a shower," Emma admitted.

"Something must be on your mind if you came by first," Zoe pushed. Her sister crossed the kitchen and dropped into the chair JJ had vacated. "Spill."

"Patrick left me a cell phone," she said in a rush of air. "And I don't know what to do."

"Use it? Here, let me put my number in," Zoe said, waggling her fingers for the phone.

She passed it to her sister and waited while she entered her details and passed it back. "He put his number in too. And his brothers, in case I had any problems."

"And that's a bad thing because…"

"He kind of left it up to me to get in touch with him," she confessed.

"I don't see why that would be weird," Zoe said, face scrunched up as she thought. "Unless – did something happen between you guys?"

"Kind of."

"What? Tell me everything this instant," Zoe demanded. "I can't believe you didn't come to me immediately."

"I actually did, but I didn't tell you why," Emma laughed at the shock on Zoe's face. "It was the day the horses arrived."

"And?" Zoe waved her hand in a circle, indicating she wanted more details.

"We kissed in the stable," she admitted.

"Was it amazing? He's so gorgeous. It must have been amazing."

"It was," she paused, searching for the words. "It was like the best thing that's happened to me in my life. And also, maybe the worst?"

"Why would it be the worst?" Her sister looked shocked.

"He sees me as a charity," she said. "Something to be saved. Like the horses, or someone who had a tree crash through their roof. Did you know he even paid off the loan for this place?"

"He what?" Kendra's voice broke through, and Emma felt herself shrinking, horrified she had revealed Patrick's secret.

"Nothing," she said quickly.

"No, tell me." Kendra was standing in front of her now, shock on her face. "Was he the one that paid it off?"

"Please don't tell him I told you," she begged. "I feel awful. He told me that in confidence, trying to make me feel more comfortable accepting help from him."

"I can't believe I never thought of him," Kendra sagged against the counter next to her. "I should have immediately. I just still think of him as Dan's little brother, not a hugely successful movie star."

"You're going to tell him you know, aren't you?"

"No, I'll figure out a way to get him to tell me," Kendra said confidently. "I promise I won't rat you out."

"I always figured it was Dan," Zoe admitted.

"Me too," Kendra laughed. "And he accepted the fact that I credited him, even though he insisted it wasn't him. Patrick is really something."

"He is," Emma said softly. "He's been so nice to me."

"Should I give you my protective older sister lecture?" Kendra asked with a smile. "I see how you two are together, I am rooting for you."

"Oh, we have a long way to go before anything like that," Emma cautioned her.

"Did you see the craziness that happened when the pictures from the rescue went up on social media?" Zoe asked.

"I'm not on social media. What craziness?"

"You were in one of the pictures the rescue posted." Zoe pulled her phone out and clicked a few things before passing it to her. Pictures of Patrick, Hank and Sam filled the screen, as well as the one that they had insisted she join them for. "People are going nuts trying to find out who you are, and if he has a secret girlfriend. Someone in the comments said your name, that they knew you in elementary school. Even said the town you were from, but that they hadn't seen you in years. A few other people have chimed in that they've worked with you, or went to school with you."

Emma started reading through the comments, horrified to think this many people were invested in who she was. "Why do people care about who I am?"

"Obsession with Patrick, most likely. Anyone that he is seen with is the subject of interest," Kendra suggested with a shrug. "He's normally so careful about who he's seen with and keeps his private life out of the press, so now the speculation is running wild that he has a secret girlfriend hidden in Vermont."

Emma groaned and dropped her head into her hands. The thought of this perfect bubble she had been living in for a few weeks bursting made her want to cry. It was ridiculous, because who really cared whether someone who knew her as a foster kid knew she was living here now? But somehow, the life she was creating slowly here seemed so different than her past, she didn't want anything other than Zoe to carry over. And knowing that it would bother Patrick added to her worry, she didn't want him to pull away because of the speculation.

She gathered the food that her sister had packed for her, which was too much for one person, but she didn't bother to fight it. She knew there would also be a large slice of something delicious for dessert, and it would be a struggle to choose the healthy meal over the sugary treat. But after a shower and the walk home, her hunger would probably win over her sweet tooth. She said goodbye to everyone, making Kendra promise one last time to not mention her spilling Patrick's secret, and headed home.

***

After a quick shower and a change of clothes, she gathered her food, a book and the new cell phone and snuck over to the stable. The manager and trainer were there all day, and once things settled down at night, they both left for their nearby homes. The first few days one or both of them had slept in the stable, not wanting to leave the horses alone, but now everything seemed settled.

She walked slowly down the rows of horses, greeting each with a pat and a treat, before arriving outside the last stall. The mare was still restless, pacing and barely eating, and Emma found it hard to be away from her. Even though the horse wouldn't accept a pat or a treat, she felt like her presence somehow comforted the beast. She placed a blanket on the ground right outside the stall door and set everything down, before talking to the horse in a quiet voice.

"Hey, Whiskey," she called over. "I'm going to have my dinner here, and then read to you for a bit. I hope you'll eat something at the same time."

She settled down, eating her dinner in record time, not realizing until the first bite how ravenous she was. Once the main course was done, she pulled her book out and held it up for Whiskey to see. "I think we'll like this one," she told the horse. "But I'm sure you'll let me know if not."

Over the last few nights, she had spent hours exactly like this, sitting outside the stall and reading to the horse. The first night she had tried just talking to her, and it seemed to help calm her. However, she had grown tired of coming up with topics to discuss with a horse, while also avoiding her complicated childhood and her feelings for Patrick. The second day she had gone into the library and chosen a popular mystery book, which Whiskey did not enjoy. She had snorted and pawed at the ground when the crime had taken place, so they had put that one aside. The next night, she had tried science fiction, with more of the same reaction. She moved on to romance, and Whiskey so far approved of her selection. She even seemed to move closer to where Emma sat, bumping the stall door softly with her head.

After she had yawned for the third time, she knew it was time to pack up and go to bed for the night. Her shift was early the next day, and it was a long walk into town. She made a mental note to be on the lookout for used bikes for sale, which would shorten her commute significantly, before turning to say goodnight to Whiskey. With a smile she realized the horse had been eating as she read, and she snorted at Emma after taking a drink of water.

"Good girl, Whiskey. I'll see you tomorrow, and we can find out what happens next," she whispered to the giant horse as she tucked the book away.

Walking slowly down through the stable again, she called out a goodnight to the horses as she went. The horses made quiet sounds as she passed, a few poking their heads out for one last pat before she left. She made sure everything was secure before heading to her cottage and recoiled when she saw a figure sitting on the porch of Patrick's house. Backing slowly into the stable before he noticed her, she felt the cold fear work its way though her. He was sitting in one of the chairs on the porch, a hat pulled low over his face so she couldn't make out any features. The light outside the kitchen door cast a shadow on him, or she would have missed him entirely.

She pulled her phone out and tried to unlock it with trembling fingers, dropping it once before finally able to see the screen. Who should she call? Jake was the closest, but also the one she was least comfortable with. However, Patrick had mentioned Jake's military background several times, and he was the most logical choice. Hitting call before she could chicken out, she waited while the phone rang.

"Hello," his voice came through the phone.

"Jake, this is Emma. Patrick gave me your number in case of emergencies," she whispered.

"I can barely hear you. Emma?"

"Yes," she said a little louder. "I'm here at the house and there is a strange man on Patrick's porch."

"I'll be right there. Did you call the police?"

"No, I called you first."

"I'll call JJ on the way over. Do you want to be on the phone with me until one of us arrives?" She heard him say something to someone near him, asking for another phone. "I'm calling him on Shea's phone and coming right now. Stay on the phone with me."

"Thank you," she whispered. She tiptoed over to glance out the window that faced the porch, and realized the man wasn't there anymore. "Jake, I don't know where he went."

"Where are you? Can you lock your doors?" She heard the truck start as he spoke.

"I'm in the stable," she responded.

"Lock yourself in the bathroom," he ordered. Realizing he was right, and she never would have thought of it on her own, she dropped her belongings and rushed into the small room. Too afraid to turn the light on, she locked the door and then sat on the floor, feet pressed to the bottom with her back against the wall to further prevent it from opening.

"I'm in the bathroom," she told Jake quietly. "Thank you, I wouldn't have thought of that."

"I'm two minutes away," Jake told her. "JJ is coming as well."

It seemed like a lifetime before she heard the truck screech to a halt in the driveway, and heard Jake call her name. Emerging slowly from the stable, she found Jake with the man sitting on the steps of the house, hands in the air. The sheriff's car pulled up behind Jake's, lights on.

"Are you alright?" Jake called over to her.

"Yes," she nodded. "Thank you."

JJ ran from the car to where the two men were, casting a glance over to her before turning to the man. "Sir, can you please identify yourself and explain why you're on private property?"

The man tilted his head up, and Emma started to feel uneasy. There was something familiar about him, but she couldn't place it. It wasn't until he looked right at her and spoke that everything became clear.

"I'm her father."

Chapter 17

"Wait, what?" Patrick pressed the phone closer to his ear, trying to hear what Jake said over Zane and Liam's voices ricocheting off the walls of his trailer. "Guys, shut up for a minute."

"Yeah, we were all shook. Emma especially."

"Tell me again what happened," Patrick demanded.

Jake recited again about getting a frantic call from Emma, racing over to the property, only to have the man reveal himself as her father. "He said he saw her picture and name on Instagram and knew it had to be his daughter. They look alike, it's crazy."

"How was Emma?"

"She was really scared when she called me, and she still looked unsettled. JJ made him leave, told him to go see her during the day at work like a normal person. I asked her to come over and stay with us, and she refused," Jake explained.

"You should have made her," Patrick groaned.

"You sound like my wife," Jake said. "Who packed me a bag and sent me right back to sleep at your house."

"Thank her for me."

"Will do," Jake said. "I'm currently sitting in your hot tub, so I'll thank her myself."

"Where is Emma?"

"She's at work, of course. I insisted on driving her this morning, which she wasn't too happy about. But what if this guy isn't her dad?"

"That's what I'm worried about. I have a few more days left out here, then I'll be home for a while."

"Don't rush on our account," Jake told him. "Dan and I can take turns staying here. Calle was more than excited about the chance to stay at the 'really big house' as she calls it."

"Thanks for that. I wish I could do more," Patrick said. "Why was she in the stable? Did you ask her?"

"I did," Jake laughed. "You won't believe this. Seven of your new horses are adapting well, eating and working with the trainers, and just doing great. None have been saddled yet, or anything along those lines, but they seem happy. One, Whiskey, has been reluctant to eat, still rarely settles down and just paces around her stall. When they're all out in pasture she only stays near the one colt, won't let any other horse near them."

"Okay?" Patrick rubbed a hand over his face, trying to focus on what his brother was saying through his exhaustion.

"Emma dropped all her stuff when I told her to lock herself in the bathroom. I went back and picked it up," his brother reported. "She had a takeout bag from Windsor Palace, a blanket, a big bottle of water and a couple of books."

"No crime there," Patrick guessed.

"Obviously," Jake scoffed. "I asked her what she had been doing, and she looked embarrassed. Finally told me that she likes to sit in the stable and eat dinner with the horses, give them some company."

"That's really nice," Jake said.

"I was telling Travis about last night," Jake said, referencing the new stable manager. "He said he had come out the night before last because he forgot something and saw her."

"Doing what?"

"Sitting outside Whiskey's stall," Jake said. "Reading to her."

"Reading to the horse?"

"Right? That was my reaction too. But Trav said that she was on the blanket right outside Whiskey's stall, just reading out loud. And get this," Jake said excitedly. "Travis watched for a bit, and Whiskey was calm. Even ate some of her food, drank some water, which Travis said was hard to get her to do. The poor horse doesn't trust anyone, and somehow when Emma is there, she's calm."

"I hope she knows to stay outside the stall," Patrick said worriedly. "That horse could kill her in a second."

"She still seems a little skittish around them. Travis said in the mornings when the horses are in pasture, some of them will go over to see her when she's nearby. He said she will pet them, but it's still from a healthy distance," Jake said. "She's definitely not comfortable around them. I even asked if she wanted to go riding one day when I was taking Charlie and Calle out, and she said no. Said it would be humiliating to go out and have a six-year-old know more than her."

"Be careful," Patrick said. "It sounds like you're starting to warm up to her."

"Shea has good instincts, and she trusts Emma," Jake said. "She's even been visiting her in the bakery, asking her to join the girls for a night out soon."

"That's great," Patrick responded. "I'm glad she's being included and making friends. Any idea how things are with her and Zoe?"

"Seems to be good, she's in the restaurant most nights according to Dan. And Zoe spends her mornings sitting at the bakery. They both work so hard, it's probably hard for them to get time away to spend together."

"Maybe I should—"

"Neither of them is going to accept a handout from you," Jake cut him off. "So don't think like that. Just let them figure it out on their own."

"Fine," Patrick huffed. "I was just thinking maybe I could arrange a day for them to spend together, but I'll mind my business. You'll keep an eye on this father situation? And Emma in general?"

"Already on it," Jake agreed. "Get your butt back here soon so I can get back to my normal life, will you?"

"Few more days, hopefully. I'll let you know once I have a date." Patrick hung up and then drummed his fingers on the table in front of him, wishing he were in Vermont.

"What's up at home?" Zane asked, eyes focused on the TV screen and the video game he was playing against Liam.

"I told you guys about Emma," he said slowly, debating how much to share. "Her dad showed up at my house last night. Or someone claiming to be her dad."

"I'll bet you a thousand he has no relation to her at all," Liam said. "Someone trying to make a quick buck off you."

"I think the same," Patrick replied. "But it's hard to be all the way out here and have no idea. I have to trust my brothers to keep an eye on the situation."

"Think she's safe there alone? Maybe you need to hire some security," Liam suggested. "Or at least put cameras in."

"I have cameras and a security system already," he protested. "It's so private and quiet, and if a stranger shows up in town everyone knows in five minutes."

"Unless they are the dad to your new niece, or the dad of the woman mysteriously living in your stable," Zane deadpanned. "Honestly, more is happening out there than in Los Angeles, and you think it's some sleepy small town."

"It normally is," Patrick sighed. "But you're right, it's been a weird year."

"Maybe we should come back with you," Liam said. "See what it's all about."

"No, thanks. I've had enough of listening to you two, I need a break."

"Rude," they both replied.

"You missed a great time in Hawaii, and now you're going to race back to the mountains right when we're about to have some free time here. You should stay for a week. Fly this Emma out if you're so concerned about her, although Zane would absolutely try to sleep with her," Liam joked.

"I probably wouldn't have to try hard," Zane grinned at him. "But I guess I can leave this one woman alone if you'll stay and hang out for a while."

"No, I need to get home. I have the horses there too, don't forget."

"Oh, right. You need us to jump on that fundraiser live thing with you?" Liam glanced at his watch. "That's coming up soon."

"Sure, if you guys want to stay. That will drive up the number of people watching," Patrick responded just as a knock sounded on the door.

Natalie opened the door and sauntered in, her smile widening when she saw it was all three of them. "What's up, boys?"

"Thought you had to be in Atlanta for some secret shoot," Zane grumbled. "Threw off our whole schedule, and now you're back?"

"Wow, how to make a lady feel welcome." She held a hand to her heart, drooping her lips into her trademark pout.

"He's teasing," Liam soothed her. "You class up the joint. Want to get dinner with me later?"

"Is dinner code for something else?"

"Always," he responded. "But we can have dinner and then you can turn me down again."

"If I'm still here when you finish, sure." Her eyes turned to Patrick. "What are you doing?"

"I'm doing an Instagram live fundraiser soon for a horse rescue," he explained. "And I have at least one more scene to shoot with Zane before we can call it a night."

"Sorry I messed things up and then my new dates got moved," she said. "Let's all go to dinner when you finish, I'll treat and make up with you all."

Patrick glanced at his watch again. "I have to go live in a few minutes, do you guys want to do it with me or not? I'll log in on the laptop if you do."

"Yeah, we'll do it. Tell her to tag us," Zane responded.

"I'll stick around too," Natalie offered.

Patrick pulled the laptop out and spent five minutes trying to remember his password to Instagram before resetting it and logging in successfully. Once he was logged on, he texted his contact at the rescue that he was ready, and that his friends would be with him to help them gain exposure. He gave all their names and handles so she could tag them and waited for the live to begin.

"It's going to start now," he called to the room.

Zane and Liam tossed down the Xbox controllers and moved closer to take the seats on either side of the couch, facing the laptop that Patrick had placed on a table in front of them.

"Be right there," Natalie called from the bathroom.

Patrick clicked to join the livestream, and smiled back Tahlia, who ran the rescue, as her face came on the screen. He could see the numbers rocketing up as notifications went out that they were all on the live with the rescue and could tell by her face that she was thrilled. After a few minutes of chatting, she began to explain what the rescue was and what they were raising funds for. In the middle of her explanation, Natalie came out of the bathroom and Zane nudged Patrick.

Somehow, she had lost half her clothes, the chunky sweater was tossed aside to reveal a skin tight tank top that left little to the imagination. Her leather pants were already like a second skin, so she now looked every bit the woman men around the world were obsessed with. She seemed to be considering her options as to how to join them in front of the screen before shrugging and sliding onto Patrick's lap.

"Sorry, this was the only empty seat," she winked to the screen. "I apologize for interrupting."

The screen erupted in hearts and instant comments, asking over and over again if they were a couple. Zane and Liam hid their laughter and Patrick tried to stem the fury that he was feeling. This was the image that would be strewn across gossip magazines, and another round of speculation about their love life was about to start. Why couldn't she just go along with pretending to be in love with Liam? At least he was already half in love with her and wouldn't have to act.

He went along with the live, declining to answer any questions about his love life. They watched as the rescue showed some of the horses they had saved, and talked about an auction they were planning to attend that weekend. Patrick was surprised to see Nat wipe a tear away and hated that he had to wonder if it was authentic.

"If I could interject for one second," Nat said, smiling at the woman on the screen. "I'd like to match what you raise in fundraising from this video. And I'll challenge these three to do the same. Save as many horses as you can, and please let me know if I can help in the future."

The people at the rescue all started cheering, growing louder when all three men agreed to do the same. They signed off from the livestream and Patrick dumped Natalie on the couch unceremoniously. "Why do you always have to do that?"

"What?" She batted her eyes at him, the picture of innocence.

"You know what. Now that's all people will talk about, and that image of you sitting on my lap will haunt me for months."

"I really don't get you," she said as she stood slowly. "Sometimes we're friends and can have some fun, but as soon as I touch you, you can't stand me and are embarrassed to be seen with me. You should probably figure that out. Boys, I'll meet you at the Marmont for dinner. I hope the stick in the mud will come too, but he probably has to go home and pout."

"I'm sorry, Nat. I didn't mean to hurt your feelings—" The trailer door slammed shut on his words, and he sat back, pushing his hands into his hair. "Why do I always manage to screw up?"

"Well," Zane drew out the word. "You've got the world's hottest woman trying to get in your pants, and you push her away constantly. And you've got some lost mystery woman in Vermont who appeared out of nowhere, seemingly in need of your help, and now has a crisis on her hands that you want to solve. I can see how this is confusing. Definitely don't pick the hottest woman who you know well, and who is our friend. That would be foolish."

"She doesn't really want me," Patrick sighed. "It's an act. But I'm still a mess."

"Agreed," Zane stated. "And we are getting called to set, so get it together. I don't want to have to keep resetting because you are distracted."

Patrick stood to follow his friend back to set, where he would pretend to fight some guys who were going to appear as aliens on the movie screen. It couldn't be any crazier than his own life lately.

Chapter 18

Emma sat at the bar at the restaurant, where Zoe had told her to wait for her. Her sister was taking time out of the busy kitchen to catch up and discuss the appearance of a man who claimed to be their father. Although she had teased Zoe about finally discovering what it was that would force her to take a break, Emma was feeling rattled and desperately needed her sister to help her make sense of everything. She had barely slept the night before, rocked from seeing her own eyes stare out at her from the man's face.

She had known the instant he looked up at her what he was going to say, but it still hadn't made it any easier. Thankfully, Jake and JJ had been there to bolster her up and take care of it. JJ had shuffled the man off to the waiting police car, explaining that he was just giving him a ride back to town, but if he came back, he would be arrested for trespassing. Jake had waited until they were gone, and then shocked her further by putting a hand on her arm and asking if she was alright.

The last word she would have used to describe herself in the moment was alright, but she had nodded at him and said she was fine. She knew he would call Patrick and he would worry, so it was easier to laugh it off with Jake and speculate that the man was lying. Jake had wished her a good night, and then a half hour later, sent her a text warning her that he was on his way back to stay in Patrick's house to make sure nothing else weird happened. She was both grateful and nervous that he expected trouble, which hadn't helped her to relax.

"Hey." Zoe slid onto the stool next to her in one fluid motion.

"Hi," she replied. "Thanks for taking the time to sit and talk about this. It's crazy, right?"

"Beyond. I could barely sleep last night, I couldn't stop thinking about it," Zoe said with a sigh. "Tell me again what happened."

Emma reiterated the whole story that she had already shared with her sister last night on the phone and again this morning in the bakery. Zoe's cheeks turned pink, and her eyes flashed angry as she spoke.

"How nice of him to turn up when you're staying at a rich movie star's house," she sniped. "Clearly that's what he's here for."

"We don't know that," Emma argued. "Maybe he's been looking for us this whole time."

"Did he ask about me?"

"No," Emma admitted. "But I didn't talk to him for long. Just a minute before JJ had him in the back of the car and was driving off. And I really was too shocked to even speak."

"JJ wasn't," her sister reported. "He grilled him all the way to town, and dear old dad wasn't giving anything up. But he specifically asked if he had any other children, and the dirtbag said no."

"Is there any chance he doesn't know about you?"

"I called my mother first thing," Zoe went on. "She was shocked. She and your mother compared pictures and stories, and there is no doubt that we have the same dad. And she assured me that she told him about me. She's ready to get in a car and drive down here, but that's way more than I can handle right now."

Emma winced at the possibility of Zoe's mother showing up over the next few days. "Same. I definitely can't handle a run in with her."

"What are we going to do about him? A DNA test?"

"Maybe we should talk to him first, see what he says."

"How is it possible that I'm more of a cynic than you are, after all you've been through," Zoe wondered out loud.

"I just think we need to hear him out," insisted Emma. "If he knows about my mom, and yours, then he has to be telling the truth."

"Not necessarily," insisted Zoe. "Anyone could look you up and find your mom's obituary."

"I hate this," Emma sighed. "Why can't I be lucky and have a loving parent show up?"

"If he was a loving parent, where has he been all these years," Zoe asked gently. "You know how hard they tried to find him before putting you in foster care. You can't tell me he didn't know about that and choose to stay away."

"Oh my god," one of the women next to them at the bar exclaimed loudly. "Look at this Instagram live!" She held her phone out in front of her so her friend could see.

"Is that Patrick Burrows?" The friend squinted at the screen.

"And Zane Ramsey, Liam Dorsey and Natalie Cloud."

"Natalie and Patrick are so cute together," the friend said. "Look at how she's draped all over him."

Zoe pulled her own phone out and pulled up the video, turning down the sound but holding it so Emma could see. Emma felt her jaw drop as she saw Patrick, two more ridiculously gorgeous men, and a woman so beautiful it almost hurt to look at her. A woman who happened to be draped all over Patrick, one hand playing with his hair as she smiled at the camera and offered to match donations. Not only stunning, but generous as well.

"I thought he was single," she whispered to Zoe.

"So did I," her sister confessed. "I've seen pictures of them together, but everyone always says it's fake."

She leaned closer, examining the duo on the screen. Nat was beaming up at him, and he appeared relaxed and happy. "That looks pretty real."

"Kendra," Zoe waved her boss over. "What's this all about?"

Kendra grabbed the phone and watched for a minute before handing it back. She leaned across the bar so they were the only two who would be able to hear her. "No idea," she said. "He insists they are just friends, and that she likes to keep people thinking they're a couple, so they leave her alone."

"It looks like they are hot for each other," Zoe responded. "JJ and I are just friends, and I don't sit on his lap and play with his hair."

"He'd like it if you did," Kendra said with a pointed look. "All I know is what Patrick says, and he's been pretty adamant. After the pictures came out last month from the movie premiere,

Jake and Dan were all over him about it. Not to mention Charlie, who was crushed thinking his uncle was secretly sleeping with the woman of his dreams."

"She's a little old for Charlie," Zoe laughed.

"Don't tell him that," Kendra replied. She waved at someone at the other end of the bar before straightening up. "I have to go grab that order, things are about to get busy."

"That's my cue to leave," Emma stood from the stool. "I'll let you get to work."

"Hang on, I packed a dinner for you."

Emma waited until her sister reappeared from the kitchen with a bag of food. "You have to stop doing this, or at least let me pay. Kendra must be getting upset at all the free food you're giving me."

"She's fine with it, I talked to her."

"Are you paying for this?"

Zoe gave her a quick hug. "I have to take care of my little sister. Listen, we didn't get to talk enough about dear old dad. If you see him again, tell him to meet both of us in the morning, you pick the day. Otherwise, I'll have JJ track him down and set something up."

Emma nodded. "That might be easier, I think he's going to be scared off from approaching me for a while. But if I see him, I'll let you know."

She walked home quickly, anxious and unable to identify why. She wasn't afraid of her father, although she supposed it was nerve-wracking to think about getting to know him. It wasn't until she was set up in front of Whiskey's stall, downloading Instagram on the phone Patrick had left her, before she realized what her stomach was in knots over. The idea of him with another woman, especially one as beautiful and rich as Natalie, was sending her into a tailspin. Even if that woman would be better suited for him, she let herself wish for one moment that she was the woman he could fall for.

***

Early the next morning, a light knock on the locked bakery door startled her. Peering between the blinds, she saw JJ's smile and let out a sigh of relief. Quickly unlocking the door, she waved him inside before closing it again.

"Morning," he said with a smile. "Thought maybe I could steal a minute of your time, and maybe a cup of coffee."

"Of course," she said as she went behind the counter. "I just brewed a pot. Would you like a pastry as well?"

"I admire your restraint in asking if I'd like a donut."

She laughed, seeing the amusement in his eyes. "It was hard to resist."

"As are donuts," he admitted. "I'd love a glazed."

She popped one into a bag and put a lid on the coffee cup before handing both to him. "What did you want to talk about?"

"Hoyt Ridge," JJ said. "That's the man who claims he is your father. I saw him last night, sitting out in front of the Inn, so I stopped and talked to him. He asked me if there was a way he could communicate with you without the drama, so I suggested he come here around ten this morning. I know you have a big rush early, but it looks slower mid-morning. I also told him that if you didn't agree, I would ask him to leave town."

"Did you tell Zoe?"

"I did, and she's not happy, but I'm sure I don't have to tell you that. She'd prefer he leave, but she said you were interested in hearing him out. I asked her to let me talk to you, so I can be sure you're comfortable with this."

She nodded slowly, considering her options. Having the man – Hoyt – come into her work seemed odd somehow. Like this was a safe space for her, and she didn't want her family issues to raise questions with her new boss. "Could you ask him to meet us at the Inn instead? In the lobby, I guess. I've never been there, but wherever we could have a private conversation. I'll talk to Piper and tell her I need to take a break around that time, I don't think she'll mind."

"No problem," he said as he stood to go. "You'll let Zoe know?"

"I will. Hey, JJ," she called as he opened the door. "You ever going to ask her out?"

"I've asked her out so many times I got sick of myself. Now I ask her to marry me five times a week," he smiled. "One of these times she'll say yes."

"Starting with dinner might help," she laughed.

"Too easy, that would bore her," he said as he shut the door.

She laughed and pulled her phone out, asking her sister to come by at just before ten so they could walk over together. To meet their father. She shivered, the gravity of the situation hitting her. This was a make-or-break moment in her life, she could either have a parent or have her heart crushed, there was no middle ground.

***

The two sisters entered the library off the lobby of the Inn, where they had been directed by a helpful front desk attendant. The room was small and cozy, and only one other person was there, seated in a large armchair in front of a fire. He stood as they entered and gestured toward the couch across from him.

"Thanks for meeting with me," he said quietly as they all sat down. "I'm sure this is unsettling."

"To say the least," Zoe muttered under her breath.

Emma nudged her with an elbow as she smiled at him. "I'm Emma, and this is Zoe."

"I'm Hoyt Ridge, but you probably already know that." He smiled again, a reserved one that didn't quite reach his eyes. The young, blonde man with the twinkly eyes that she had seen pictures of had aged, but she could see hints of what her mother had been attracted to. His eyes were soft brown, his hair tinged with some grey now and his face creased in a way that suggested he had spent a lot of time out in the elements. It was easy to see how handsome he was as a young man, and even how he would still be considered ruggedly good looking in his early fifties.

"It is a little strange to be meeting you like this. How did you find us?" Emma pressed on, trying to keep the peace.

"I saw a picture of you, Emma, and it led me here. Just a lucky coincidence that I found both of you at the same place."

"Although I'm not staying on a famous actors property, so you decided to skip right past me?" Zoe practically snarled, and Emma had to put a hand on her arm to try and settle her down.

"I didn't know you were here," he responded. "Once I saw Emma I just came, and then the nice police officer told me that you were here as well. I wouldn't have had any way of knowing, or I would have come."

"You knew about both of us," Zoe challenged. "I asked my mother again, and she insisted that you knew she was pregnant and that she told you when I was born."

"Yes, I did. And I'm deeply regretful of my behavior, I have no excuse. But after that, Marise told me to leave you both alone, that she never wanted to see me again. I didn't dare cross her."

"And my mother?" Emma asked softly.

"Gwen also told me that she was pregnant," he admitted. "And I once again acted like a coward. I only knew your first name because she told my mother when you were born. She wasn't able to reach me, so she sent her a letter."

Emma met Zoe's eyes and saw the rage burning, so pushed on with the conversation. "Maybe you could tell us a little more about that time in your life."

"Sure," he sighed, leaning forward and putting his elbows on his knees. "I was young. When I got Marise pregnant, we were both barely twenty. We had been friendly in high school, but never dated. I stayed in town and worked, she went off to college, and one night we ran into each other. She was never the nicest person, I'm sorry if that's untrue now or rude."

"It's fine," Zoe allowed.

"She was icy, I think that's the best way to describe her. Anyway, this one night, we were at a mutual friends house. And, uh, one thing led to another."

"I'm familiar with how babies are conceived," Zoe said drolly.

"It was a one-night thing. I don't know how much she told you, but it seemed a little out of character for her. I tried to see her again, tried to talk to her, but I didn't get a response until she called to tell me she was pregnant." He leaned a little further forward, as if trying to catch Zoe's eye. "I offered to marry her. She said no."

Zoe's head snapped up, studying his face before shrugging. "Then you disappeared."

"She told me she wanted me to, that she would raise you and wanted to do it alone. And I admit, I was happy about that. I took the freedom and ran, became a little wilder than I should have. I started running with tougher groups, traveling with work crews and drinking more than anything else. I can't say I'm proud of any of that, but it's what happened." He looked over and met Emma's eyes. "Then I met the sweetest girl, who was working at a diner. I don't know why she even looked at me, but she did. We started dating, and the next thing I knew, she was pregnant. It was like Deja-vu. I had been drinking to forget I had a little girl out there that I had never seen, and to try and make myself feel less worthless. How could I raise a baby with Gwen after walking away from Marise?"

"You could have gone back to my mother, insisted you wanted to be a part of my life," Zoe insisted.

"You're right," he nodded. "I should have. I should have done a lot of things differently, but I was a weak man. I just kept making bad decisions and trying to forget that you both existed."

"Until Emma showed up on a millionaires property," Zoe said. "You can't claim to have been looking for us, because my mother is still around, and she hadn't heard from you. And when Gwen died, they looked for you. Did you know that Emma grew up in foster homes, because you were nowhere when her only parent died?"

He hung his head and shook it slowly. "I'm so sorry."

"Good for you," Zoe spat as she stood up. "We grew up without you, and we are doing just fine. You can go back to whatever it was that was more important than your two daughters, because we don't need you. Let's go, Emma."

"Zoe—"

"No," her sister pointed at her. "We are sticking together. It's time to go, and we can talk about all of this. If he wants to stick around in case one of us decides to talk to him, he can. But we are done here."

Chapter 19

Patrick placed his luggage near the front door, relieved to be back in Vermont after weeks away. He had hitched a ride with his friends on a private jet to New York, then chartered a small plane to make the rest of the trip quickly. After his last trip from Los Angeles, taking the fastest and easiest route home had won out. Dropping his keys in the bowl by the door, he crossed to the kitchen without turning on any lights. Jake had been texting for days, saying that Emma's dinners with the horse had continued, and he hoped he had made it home in time to witness it himself.

Seeing the soft lights coming from the stable, he switched from his sneakers to boots and went out the kitchen door, closing it softly behind him. Crossing the ground quickly, he spied Emma sitting on a blanket with her back against Whiskey's stall, the horse's head over the side as if reading over her shoulder. She was reading out loud, reaching out once in a while to stroke the horses nose when it nudged her shoulder.

All the reports from the veterinarian were that all the horses were healthy, but the mare named Whiskey wasn't trusting of anyone. She was quieter these days, especially when the young colt in the next stall was nearby and no one approached her. As soon as the trainer or vet tried to get close, she would snarl and kick, making it difficult to determine if she could be trained to ride. All of which made the image in front of him even harder to believe, as the horse looked completely content to be as close to Emma as possible.

He hadn't decided how to make his presence known, but Whiskey solved the problem by letting out a snort and what sounded like a growl as he got closer. Emma looked up sharply, but then her gaze softened when she saw who it was. He dared to even hope that she looked happy to see him, although she was always so guarded it was hard to tell.

"Hey," he called out. "Thought I might find you here."

"Who ratted me out?"

"Jake," he admitted. "He said you come out here every night and sit with Whiskey. And the trainer told me that you are the only person this horse allows to get near her."

"She has good taste in books, and I think she enjoys them as much as I do," Emma said, smiling at the horse. The horse snorted again and bobbed her head, while pawing at the ground.

"I don't think she likes me being close to you," Patrick remarked.

Emma stood slowly, giving the horse an apple as she did. "She seemed so scared when she first came here, she couldn't seem to get calm. When she's out in the pasture she sticks with the colt, and even then, she doesn't want anyone else near them. I can relate to that fear, and I think she knows that. Plus, I think she knows that I was terrified the first few nights I came out here alone, I was sure she would knock the door down and trample me."

"It was brave of you," Patrick said softly. "To extend your kindness to her over your fear. I already thought you were the bravest person I knew, after all you went through as a kid."

She shrugged, avoiding his eyes. "It's not like I had a choice. My mother was an only child, and she didn't choose to leave me."

"She must have been a good mom," he said softly, fighting the urge to take her in his arms.

"The best," Emma smiled sadly. "I just wish I had gotten to spend some of my adulthood with her, ask the questions that I never asked. You know?"

"Kind of, but not really. My mom died giving birth to me, so she's always just been a person in pictures or that my dad tells stories about."

"I'm sorry, that was insensitive of me to say. That's much worse," Emma said.

"No, it's fine. And I don't think it is worse, when you think about it." He thought about it as he leaned against the stall across from her, petting the horse who came to say hello. "It's one of those things that there is no good answer to. I'd love to have a memory of her, some little thing to hold on to. But I also can't mourn her like you do your mom, because I never had her. You got to make the memories, but it made the goodbye harder."

"So true."

"And I got Stella, where you got put into foster care. I'd say you win the sad award," he smiled gently, hoping she would get the humor he was trying to infuse into the comment.

"Oh, I didn't know there was one. Do I get a prize?" She smiled at him as she asked, pulling her hair over her shoulder to keep Whiskey from chewing on it.

"Dinner with me." The words came out before he could even think about it, but he was happy they did.

She froze, staring at him for so long he started to wonder if something was wrong. Then a shy smile came across her face and she nodded slowly. "I'd like that a lot."

"Tomorrow?"

"Sure," she said. "One thing though, if I can ask."

"Go ahead."

"Your costar, Natalie?"

"Is that a question," he teased her, needing to hear that she was at least a little anxious about another woman near him. That meant that she was interested, and he wasn't misreading the situation.

"You know what I'm asking. Are you two a thing?"

"Never have been, never will be. She just makes it look like we are so people leave her alone. A single woman in Hollywood brings a lot of speculation and rumors, so this is easier for her. Not so much for me, but I respect her and go along with it. Eventually she'll find someone, and I'll be off the hook." He helped her pick up the blanket from the ground, folding it before handing it back. "I have to admit, I'm a little happy that you're jealous."

"Oh, I just wanted the inside gossip," she laughed. "Besides, it's not like this can be anything between us."

"Why is that?"

"Patrick," she rolled her eyes at him. "Look at you. Look at your life. Then look at me. We don't fit."

"That's bull, and you know it." He stepped forward, purposely invading her personal space so she backed up against the stall. When she looked up at him, he could see the attraction there, in her eye and the way she licked her lips. "You felt something when we kissed."

She swallowed and looked everywhere but at him before her eyes came back to his. Then to his lips.

"I wonder," he said slowly, dipping his head so his lips were just a breath from hers. "Whether you can convince yourself we aren't a good match or if you'll be the one kissing me next time." He stayed where he was for a beat, then slowly moved over to kiss her on the cheek, allowing his lips to linger just a second too long.

She let out a shaky sigh as he took a step back, then shook her head. "Maybe dinner isn't a good idea after all."

"I'll pick you up at six," he called over his shoulder as he started jogging toward the house. She ran after their first kiss, he could make a break for it this time before she had a chance to change her mind.

***

He knocked on the door promptly at six, flowers he had run out for clenched in one hand. Thankfully neither of his brothers were around to see that he had changed his clothes twice and debated calling Maria, his favorite designer, for advice before settling on his outfit. Nervousness usually evaded him, but it had him in its firm grips this evening, and he took that as a good sign.

When Emma opened the door, her hair bouncing around her shoulders and a soft pink sheen to her lips, he felt the butterflies amp up even more. She was in a dress, simple and black, and the heels she wore showcased her legs, which seemed much longer than her height would allow. Words left his brain as he stared at her, before he thrust the flowers forward.

"For you," he said quickly. "You look stunning."

"Zoe helped me," she said shyly. "These are all her clothes. Luckily, we are still the same size, and she has a whole closet full of date-worthy clothes. Which is sad, because all she does is work, so it's only fair I take them out."

"It looks like it was made for you," he smiled. "Do you have a warm enough jacket?"

"I do, Zoe let me borrow her nice one." She paused, then waved him inside. "Let me put these in some water and grab my jacket."

He watched as she puttered in the kitchen, pulling a mason jar out of a cabinet to place the flowers in. She lowered her head quickly to sniff them, a smile tracing her lips as she did, before realizing he was watching. Quickly placing them down on the small kitchen table, she crossed to the small closet and grabbed a coat and purse off a hook.

"Ready." She stilled as he took the jacket and helped her into it, turning her so he could do the buttons on the front. The long wool coat was warmer than what he usually saw her in, although more formal than she would probably be comfortable in for walking to work.

She hesitated again as he held open the door to his Range Rover, before sliding into the passenger seat. As he started driving down to the main road, she glanced over at him.

"Would it be rude to ask where we are going? I'm new to this dating thing."

"There's a small restaurant in Stowe, it's a short drive. I probably should have asked you if there was anything you don't want to eat," he questioned her.

"I'm not picky," she answered. "There's almost nothing I would say no to."

"Oh good, because this place is fully Vegan." She stared at him, mouth agape but not saying anything. "It's a new thing I'm trying."

"That might be interesting," she said slowly.

"Good, because I'm only kidding," he laughed. "They have normal food. I might be able to give up a lot of things, but cheese is not one of them."

"Oh, thank you. I was already trying to figure out how to secretly find out what time the latest pizza delivery is in town."

He filled the time during the drive by telling her stories about growing up in Vermont, feeling her relax more as they drove. She laughed as he told her the trouble he and his brothers had caused and shared some gossip she had picked up from the bakery. Although he wanted to know what had happened with her father, he waited, not wanting to spoil the mood.

When they pulled into the parking lot of the restaurant, she glanced around with a questioning look on her face. "Where are all the cars?"

"Oh, did I not mention," he asked as he unclipped his seat belt, waiting until he had walked around and opened her door before continuing. "They're closed tonight."

"What do you mean?"

"It's hard for me to have a private dinner, or to not be interrupted. I wanted tonight to be special and be able to focus on you," he explained. "I called and the chef was happy to agree to come in for us. I met him a few years ago, he was on a reality show or something, came to a movie premiere. Nice guy."

"Wait," she stopped walking and stared at him. "Did you close it down for the night, or ask them to open?"

"I asked them to open," he said softly. "I wouldn't force them to cancel a bunch of reservations, or ruin other people's nights. This is a small favor he's doing for me, and I'll repay him by posting about the restaurant a few times."

"This is weird."

"I think we can agree that my life is weird and move on from there. I would rather you think of me as just the guy next door, for tonight at least," he suggested.

"The guy next door who bought out a restaurant for dinner?"

"For our first date," he responded, satisfied by the stunned expression on her face. He opened the door to the restaurant and was happy to see soft candlelight and hear quiet music playing. A table was set for two by the front window, a fire roaring on the opposite wall.

"This is amazing," she whispered.

"Patrick." The voice boomed from the darkness where the kitchen doors must be hidden before the chef came into sight. He was short and stocky, with a buzzed haircut and the look of an ex-Marine. "I'm so glad you called. You must be Emma; I'm Wyatt."

"It's nice to meet you, and it's so nice of you to do this for us." The two shook hands and Patrick wasn't surprised to see Wyatt's normally stern expression soften.

"It's no problem at all," he insisted. "I'm thrilled to cook for you both, I hope you don't mind that I planned the menu."

Patrick rubbed his stomach and grinned. "I can't wait to see what you come up with."

"Sit, I'll get you some wine. I do have a waitress here, but if you want me to send her home I can."

"It's not a problem," Patrick said quickly. He helped Emma with her jacket and placed both on an empty table before pulling out her chair. Settling in across from her, he was surprised when she reached across and touched his hand before settling hers in his palm.

"This is the best first date I've ever been on," she said shyly. "Just in case I forget to tell you later."

Chapter 20

Emma felt slightly dazed, as if she was in a dream, as she and Patrick talked among the plates of amazing food and wine. This was unlike anything she had ever experienced before, and the man across the table only added to the lightheaded feeling. He was so gorgeous, so kind, she couldn't believe that he had chosen her to take on this date.

Even thinking of it as a date made her stomach feel funny, although Patrick had used the word frequently as if knowing she needed to be assured of his intention. The last few weeks since their kiss she had savored the idea of a romantic connection with him, before pushing it from her head as a fantasy. Although they had texted regularly after her father's first appearance, it had remained fairly casual. Stories of his days on set, pictures of the horses grazing in the pasture, jokes they found funny. It had made her feel closer to him, but this was a new level.

"Would it ruin the mood if I asked how things went with Hoyt," Patrick questioned as he poured her more wine.

She sighed, wrestling with the emotional rollercoaster she had been on since the man had appeared. "It was tough," she admitted. "Zoe was angry and has now decided that she doesn't believe anything he said. He painted himself as an immature boy when Zoe's mom got pregnant, but also kind of made her out to be the villain. Claims he proposed but she refused, and almost suggested she had used him."

"How?"

"It was weird. Zoe's mom is a difficult person, doesn't have a lot of close relationships. He said she was the same growing up, but then one night suddenly came on to him. Zoe was debating talking to her mother about it, but ultimately, we decided it's so far in the past, there's no point in upsetting her." Emma sipped her wine before continuing. "When my mom got pregnant, he says he freaked out because he already had one baby out there that he had nothing to do with, and now a second coming."

"He could have tried to do better the second time," Patrick responded. "Or even repaired what had happened with Zoe, she couldn't have been more than three at the time."

"Yes, exactly. And that's part of her argument, that he continued to choose to be an absent father. He claims he just started drinking and lost himself in the bottle, but that he's sober now," Emma paused, a thoughtful look on her face. "I honestly don't know what to think."

"How did you and Zoe know about each other?"

"Good question," she smiled at him. "My mother lived not far from them when she met Hoyt. When he took off, she was working at a diner that had a good amount of traffic from truck drivers who went over the border. One of them happened to be Zoe's grandfather, who had seen Hoyt hanging around my mom."

"I can't imagine what my father would have done," Patrick laughed.

"Probably the same as him," she replied. "He waited for him in the parking lot, tried to talk some sense into him about the daughter he had no contact with. Hoyt ignored him, and the next time Zoe's grandfather went through, he had taken off. He asked the waitress he had seen him talking to, and my mom burst into tears. Ended up telling him the whole story, and he told her about Marise and Zoe."

"Wow, that's crazy. Your mom must have been stunned," Patrick said.

"I'm sure she was, but she also thought that maybe they could get to know each other," she explained. "After all, they were raising sisters, and she wanted us to be close. She wrote to Marise and tried to call her. As I said, Marise is difficult and didn't want to be friends with the next woman Hoyt impregnated. I was four when my mom packed me in the car and drove to their house, determined for me to meet my sister."

"No kidding? Good for her." Patrick looked impressed, and it warmed her heart that he felt that way about her mother.

"After that, Marise agreed to send Zoe to visit us over school vacations, but she never allowed me to go there. Zoe loved coming to our house, my mom was everything hers wasn't."

"What was she like?" He asked the question gently, inviting her to share her memories with him.

"Soft and warm, she always smelled like something sweet, and she loved to cuddle up and read with me," she reminisced. It warmed her from the inside out, talking about the mom she had hidden away in her heart so many years ago. Foster siblings all had their own sad pasts, and no one wanted to talk about her mother with her. Over the years, she had become accustomed to no one asking, and to keeping her memories to herself. "She loved to bake, and her favorite holiday was Christmas. She would go all out every year, even though money was always tight. We made decorations together, watched every holiday movie, and sang carols all day long. Most importantly, she was a safe place to land, always knowing the right kind of comfort or discipline to dole out."

"She sounds amazing," he said as he reached for her hand.

"She was."

"What happened to her?"

"A drunk driver hit her one night when she was on her way home from work." Emma braced herself to tell the story again, knowing it would break her heart all over again. "It was just before my birthday, she had worked late, probably to buy me a present. I was always complaining about the things the girls at school had, when I had secondhand clothes and donations for school supplies. I was right at that age when things like that mattered, and girls were starting to not want to be my friend because I was a poor kid."

"Those middle school years are rough," he sympathized.

"Oh, please," she laughed. "There is no chance anyone bullied you or didn't want to be your friend."

He laughed, the sound forcing her to smile despite the topic of conversation. "You're right, other than my brothers, no one really gave me a hard time. But I have heard stories."

"Well, I'm a survivor of them. And it only got worse when I went into foster care, changing schools constantly. The only consistent and true friends I had were the ones in books, and fortunately, they never let me down," she said. "I had acquaintances at school, people who would let me sit with them at lunch. I knew how to play the games, to try and not be the target of bullies. But I wasn't always successful, and at the foster homes it was always impossible."

"I've never known anyone who was in foster care," he admitted.

"It's not a picnic, and I made it even worse because I was a teenage girl with a bad attitude. I wanted my mother back, and nothing else would suffice."

"Can't blame you for that," he said softly. "Losing her at that age and having your world flipped upside down would cause anyone to act out."

"I also felt guilty." She heard the words leave her mouth and couldn't believe she had said them. She had never admitted that to anyone before, in all the years since her mother had died, and now suddenly she had told Zoe and Patrick. "She had asked me to come to work with her, and I refused. Plus, the only reason she was working extra hours was for me, she should have been home watching Bravo instead of on the road."

"I get that," he said as he gripped her hand tighter. "But it's not your fault."

"She should have been home with me," she argued tearfully.

"Maybe she would have run out to get milk, or gone to meet a friend, and been heading home at the same time. Or the next day, driving to work, the same thing could have happened. You can't change the past with guilt." He waited until she met her eyes before continuing. "I've felt the same way as you. I'm the direct reason why my mother died. But I had to let that guilt go, because what did it get me? A miserable life, a bad relationship with my dad and brothers because I felt like I stole something from them."

"But that clearly wasn't your fault," she said, leaning forward to be closer to him. "You didn't choose to be born or do anything that would have caused her death."

He met her eyes with a sad smile before replying. "And neither did you. Your mom made her own choices, and nothing you did or didn't do would have changed that. Same with my mom; my dad says she wanted even more kids after me, so if it wasn't with me, it could have been a year later. We can't change that. We just have to live our lives to honor their memory."

She wiped a tear with her napkin, shocked at the sudden relief she felt. Had she been carrying that much guilt with her all these years? Maybe she had been doing her mother a disservice by being so isolated and miserable for so long. It was the opposite of what her mom had been, and she knew it would have driven her crazy. Her mom would have encouraged her to be open to people and new experiences, even the bad ones, so she could learn from them.

"It's really not right," she half laughed, half cried. "That you could be gorgeous, nice, and smart. You should have some faults because it's simply not fair to be so perfect."

"I encourage you to spend a few hours with my brothers, and they will be quick to point out my many flaws," he laughed.

"Name some."

"I get hangry, and that can be ugly," he said, holding up one finger to count. "I get spoiled on set, and I let people do things for me that I could do myself, even when it makes me uncomfortable. I don't like to lose, and act like a toddler when I do. I am a little slobby, and a shockingly bad cook."

"All seem pale in comparison to the good things," she said softly. "What is your dating life like normally?"

"What *is* normal in my life? I honestly don't date much, especially not in the public eye. In a lot of ways, Nat's behavior has helped me too, so I'm a little guilty for allowing it for selfish reasons. Less speculation about my dating life, my sexual preferences, and whether I've been romantically involved with someone I brushed elbows with on a red carpet." He sipped his wine and met her eyes. "I haven't really connected with someone in a long time, if ever."

"But you must have had some contact with females over the years," she challenged.

"Of course," he smiled. "I'm not a saint. I dated an agent for a few years, but when she tried to sign me, I had to break it off. I have tried dating actresses, but that never ends well. The ones that are more famous were tough, because our schedules made things hard, and the ones who were just starting out usually wanted to be seen with me for their own face to get out there."

"I bet everyone hooks up when you're on location."

"Some people do. We're stuck together in a strange city for weeks or months, and only have each other for entertainment," he explained. "When you do a project with people you know, there's some comfort there. You know how long the relationship will last; you know what to expect. The movie franchise that I'm in is a lot of recurring characters, and mainly men. Which is why Nat would rather people think we have something going on, she's outnumbered on set. And even though she could have her pick of them, she knows we all spend too much time together for her to leave a string of broken hearts behind."

"And you've never—"

He shook his head, stopping the question. "Don't ask questions you don't want the answers to. What happened in the past is in the past. I am here with you, and that's the only focus I have. I'm not a cheater, I would never be here with you if I were involved with Nat. Can that be answer enough?"

She chewed on the inside of her cheek, mentally comparing herself to the voluptuous and stunning movie star. Then she looked at the man across from her, daring herself to give him a chance she hadn't given anyone since her mom died. "Yes," she whispered. "That's enough."

"Should I ask about your dating history now?" He smiled as he sipped his water, waiting for her answer.

"I don't have much," she admitted. "A few high school boys that I dated, a very few short relationships as an adult. It's been hard, just trying to keep a roof over my head is the focus most of the time. I didn't want or need a man to come in and solve all my problems, although I guess I let you do that."

"I'm not solving your problems," he protested. "You're working hard for yourself, I'm just providing a little help. Where had you been living?"

"Primarily upstate New York, although I moved to Montreal for a few months to look for Zoe. She wasn't there, and I was trying to save money to travel and find her. But then I got lucky, and a coworker of mine heard that she had moved to this little town in Vermont," she explained. "Zoe was a big deal in the culinary world in that part of Canada, so her up and moving to a little town caused a lot of buzz. I packed up my meager belongings and started to make my way here."

"Why not just try to call her, or reach out some other way?"

"I wish I could answer that," she responded. "It's been half my life since I last saw her, and I wasn't sure how she would react. My last interaction with her mother left me questioning whether Zoe would want to see me. Not to mention, being alone for so long has made me question even the simplest things. I find it hard to trust that things will go well for me."

The chef interrupted, asking about their meal and thrilled to receive praise from Patrick. They posed for pictures, Emma taking one of the Chef and Patrick that could be posted for promotion of the restaurant, before finally saying their goodbyes. The ride home was quieter, they chatted about the town and shared laughs, but Emma couldn't stop herself from thinking ahead to what would happen when the car stopped. The tension she was feeling could be entirely one-sided, but it was hard to take a breath, the anticipation was so tight in her stomach.

When he parked and came around to open her door, she found herself shaking slightly as she stepped out of the car. Seemingly unaware, he took her hand and walked with her towards the small cottage she lived in, stopping on the tiny front porch.

"Thank you for an amazing date," he said, pushing a hair back from her cheek with his free hand.

Remembering what he had said after their last kiss about leaving it to her to make the first move, she took a breath of courage and then stood on her tiptoes and pulled him closer so she could press her lips to his. She felt herself sink into him, soaking up his strength and warmth, until the soft sounds from the stable reminded her where they were.

"Come inside," she urged, pulling on his hand.

"I want to," he assured her, meeting her eyes. "But this was our first date, and I'm going to make damn sure you're ready when I do."

"I'm ready now." She couldn't believe the words that came out and had to stop herself from clamping a hand over her mouth.

He bent down and kissed her softly before releasing her hand. "I'll see you tomorrow."

She was unlocking her door, unsure if she should be embarrassed or pleased that he was unlike any other man she had ever encountered, when she heard him call her name. Turning, she saw that he had stopped on the first step to his back door, smiling at her.

"I want to be the thing that you trust will go well," he called to her.

She closed her eyes, feeling the words hit her in the heart, and when she opened them again, he was out of sight. Closing the door softly behind her, she felt the first glimmers that her life could be on the right path for the first time in a long time.

Chapter 21

Patrick was awake early the next morning, immediately needing to resist the urge to cross his backyard to finish what he had started the night before. He had already gotten so far as to open the door before closing it, determined to stay the course. She needed to trust him, and he needed to prove that he saw her as more than a problem to solve. A little time, that's all it would take.

"Morning," Dan's voice called from the front door, walking in with Jake. "You really should lock this."

"No one knows I'm here," he responded, placing his coffee mug in the sink. "Other than family, and you all come and go as you please regardless of whether it's locked. Not to mention, I knew you guys were coming to work out, so it's easier to leave it open when I'm awake."

"Everyone knows you're here now," Jake laughed. "Have you not gone on social media?"

"No, why?"

Jake handed him his phone, open to a popular celebrity magazine's Instagram page. A picture of him with the chef from the night before was the lead story, with a second picture of him and Emma that had been taken from further away.

"That mother—" Patrick stopped himself as he stormed to grab his cell phone. "He promised he would only use the picture of him and I." He swiped angrily at his phone, seeing texts from his agent asking him to call, along with a series of apology messages from the chef, claiming he hadn't taken the picture.

"Everyone wants to know who Emma is," Dan commented. "I also wouldn't mind knowing more about the woman who you are apparently dating now."

"Shut up, Dan," he growled. "Wyatt claims he didn't take the picture, he thinks the waitress did. He already fired her, so now I feel terrible about that."

"Don't," Dan replied. "Not your fault, she was likely told this was a private dinner, and she violated his trust."

"Still, I should have known better." Patrick sighed and threw his phone down, not wanting to respond to any of the messages yet.

"Patty, at some point, you have to be able to just live your life. Take a pretty girl on dates, make some mistakes, settle down like us two. You can't be so careful all the time," Jake offered.

"Do you know how many times I've asked them to kill my character off?"

His brothers looked stunned, staring at each other before turning back to him. "What?"

"Yeah. The last three movies I asked them to kill him so I could be done. Just come back here and live a quiet life," he sighed. "But they won't do it."

"You have no obligation to do more," Dan said. "After the next two, I mean. Those you are contractually obligated to do."

"But think about the people I'd be letting down," he argued. "If they killed him off, it would be easy to carry on. But if I just refuse to film, it impacts everyone else at the same time. I can't do that."

"Where is this coming from?" Jake asked, pulling out a barstool to sit at the island. "I thought you loved your career."

"I do," he explained. "It's just a lot. I've never not been famous, you know? I went from being a sixteen-year-old working the ski lift to on the cover of a teen magazine, just about overnight."

"And that's bad because..."

"Because I can't just take a pretty girl on a date," he erupted. "It has to be a circus. People wanting pictures, now they'll dive into her life and rip her apart. I'm trying to get her to trust me, and now she will have all this criticism and a spotlight on her."

"And a father who appears suddenly," Jake offered.

"Exactly. Her life will be flipped upside down, because I took her on one date."

"The risk might be worth it in the end," Dan suggested. "If you really like her, screw everyone else."

"I have to warn her, though. Tell her about this."

"You can," Jake said. "Or give it a minute and see if it dies down. Let your publicist make a statement that she's a friend and have them stir up some other nonsense. There's more than enough speculation about you and Nat, maybe she can do something to take the attention away from Emma."

"Nat," he dropped his head into his hands. "She is going to freak out."

"But you aren't dating, right?" Dan asked.

"No," he shook his head. "I wouldn't have asked Emma out if we were."

"But you clearly have a history," Dan observed.

"I don't talk about that," he responded.

"Don't talk about it all you want," Jake laughed. "But it happened. And whether Nat wants more or not, you have to deal with it. Maybe she won't care, and she'll be happy to deflect."

"Mike is going to be crushed if he finds out about you and Nat," Dan said.

"It was years ago," he replied. "We were on location for the first movie, it really isn't a big deal."

"Make sure she's not embarrassed by this," Dan suggested. "Have your publicist deal with it, and then let's work out. I need to get to the office."

"You guys go start," he said as the doorbell rang. "Let me send some messages."

He heard them greet Mike at the door, and the three of them headed to the basement gym before he fired off some messages. His agent and publicist promised to do their best to take the focus off the picture, and to try and pull some strings to get it taken down but wouldn't make any promises. Debating what to say to Nat, he finally shot off a quick text asking her to call when she was free.

The facetime ring came through instantly, startling him. Answering, he saw her smiling at him from a couch in a room he didn't recognize. "Hey, love," she smiled at him. "I'm in Japan doing a commercial so you caught me awake. What's going on?"

"Hey, Nat. Wanted to warn you that a picture came out of me on a date last night."

"Should I throw a jealous hissy fit?"

"I would rather you didn't," he said. "Since we aren't dating."

She pouted briefly before continuing. "You calling me about this means you must like this date. Before it gets any further, can I ask one question?"

"Go ahead."

"Is there really no chance for us? I thought we were having fun, and a good match. I had feelings for you," she said softly.

"Nat," he responded back quietly. "We did have fun. And now we have an amazing friendship. I think you romanticized it all these years, because when the shoot ended, you took off and I didn't hear from you for months. When they signed us all for the sequel, you remembered I was alive."

"That's not true," she argued.

"It is true. And it's all we can ever be," he said. "I want to be your friend, your best friend even. But I can't be more than that."

"Why?"

"I don't know," he said. "We were so young, and even then, when the shoot ended, I wanted to come home to a little town, and you wanted to do the Hollywood scene. We just want different things in life."

"I guess you're right," she sighed. "What do you need me to do now?"

"Go on a date?"

"With who," she laughed. "I'm in Japan."

"I don't know, see if your agent has anyone over there that can take you out. Just be seen somewhere very public and with a man, please. That will stop people from speculating that I'm cheating on you, or that you're heartbroken."

"Maybe I am," she teased.

"Please."

"It's already almost nine here," she said. "I'll see what they can do. Maybe there's a hot concierge who wants to go out."

"You say nine as if you were going to go to bed for the night," Patrick laughed.

"I'll find someone," she promised. He heard a soft vulnerability in her voice that wasn't normally there. "I'm sure my agent has someone that she wants some exposure for."

"Thanks, Nat." He paused before hanging up. "Are you okay? You sound a little down."

"Just jetlagged," she said, not sounding believable.

"Nat," he cajoled. "Be honest with me."

"Sometimes this whole life seems silly, doesn't it? Racing around the country, spending hours worried about what I look like, what I say, who I socialize with," she said quietly. "Maybe it would be easier if you would fall in love with me, and I could be a housewife in east bum Vermont."

"In another life, that would probably have happened," he offered.

"I hope she's worth it," Nat said.

"She is," he promised. "I can't wait for you to meet her. And I know you'll find someone who makes you feel like this one day. Go and have fun, call me when you get home."

***

Two hours later, Patrick was drying off from the shower when a text came through from Nat, with a screenshot from the same magazine. Nat was cozy next to a B list actor in a booth at a popular restaurant in Japan in the picture, his arm around her pulling her close to him. Satisfied that it would take some of the pressure off him, and grateful for her help, he arranged to send a bottle of champagne to her room before getting dressed.

Walking into the bakery a short while later, he frowned when he saw the man sitting at a table by the window. Emma was hard at work behind the counter, frosting a cake while also trying to make conversation with her father, and she looked relieved when he walked in.

The other man jumped to his feet and rushed to Patrick, hand outstretched. "What a thrill to meet you," he gushed. "Emma was just telling me how great you've been."

"Thanks," he said. "You must be Hoyt."

"I am, I am. Come, sit down."

"No, I just stopped in for a minute to talk to Emma," he explained.

"I'd love to buy you lunch, get to know you," the man persisted.

"Thanks," he said politely. "Another day, maybe. Emma, can I steal you for one second? Hey, Piper."

Piper nodded from where she was working, not looking up from what looked like a wedding cake. "Head into the kitchen," she offered. "I can hold down the fort for a minute."

Emma wiped her hands on her apron and nodded her head for him to follow her through the swinging door.

"I'm sorry about him," she said immediately. "I didn't know he was going to be here, or that you would stop by."

"First of all," he said. "You don't need to be sorry about anything. Second, good morning."

She smiled and let out a sigh of relief. "Good morning."

"And now," he kissed her softly. "It really is. That's all I really came by for, and to ask if you were free tonight?"

"I am," she said.

"Will you come to karaoke with me at The Palace? A group of us try to go every week, it's a lot of fun."

"I can't sing," she said, looking terrified at the prospect.

"You can be my groupie," he laughed. "Most people can't sing, it's just a lot of fun."

"I'm in," she smiled at him.

"I'll get you at six, we can eat there first?"

"I'll be ready," she smiled at him. "I'm done here at two, so I'll have some time to spend with Whiskey first."

"You're amazing," he said softly. "I hope you know that."

She grinned, pushing him softly towards the door. "Get out of here, I have work to do. I'll see you at six."

Just before he left, he dropped his keys on the counter. "Here, take the Jeep home. It's parked right out front."

"I don't want—"

He put a finger over her lips. "It's the Jeep that I use when I want to be less visible in town, it's not anything fancy. Jake or Dan can bring me home, or JJ will drive me. I'd rather you be able to get home quick and see Whiskey before our date."

He pushed his way through the door, not giving her a chance to object. Waving to Hoyt before rushing out the door, he escaped without a further interaction with her father. Something about him was off, and he needed to find out what it was, so he headed for the person who could help.

***

JJ was busy when Patrick arrived at the Sherrif's office, so he sat in the small waiting room trying to ignore the desk clerk's stares. He was relieved when his friend yelled from the back for him to come through, nodding at the woman as he passed.

"Hey," JJ said as he stretched. "What can I do for you?"

"I can't just pop by to say hi?"

"You'll see me tonight, so no."

"True," Patrick laughed. "I hope you plan to do that Bon Jovi song again."

"That didn't work, so I'm moving to Celine tonight."

"I can't imagine why Zoe isn't falling at your feet," Patrick said.

"Me neither," JJ grinned. "All this and a singing voice that can break glass? What more could she want? Now, for real, what's up?"

"Their father."

"I figured," JJ grabbed some papers from his top drawer. "I've been digging and not finding much. Trust me, this bothers me as much as you."

"Guy just comes from nowhere and wants to be Emma's best friend apparently. He's sitting over at the bakery now watching her work."

"He tried to go to the restaurant yesterday, Zoe had him thrown out. She said she hasn't spoken to him since they all met, but that was the only time he had tried."

"He's focused on Emma?" Patrick questioned, seeing the knowing look on his friend's face. "Shit. This is about me, isn't it?"

"Looks that way, bud. I'm sorry."

"She was excited, even hopeful, when she talked about him."

"We could be wrong," JJ warned. "But I have a good sense about people. He's living beyond his means right now, running up a huge tab at the Inn. Told the manager there he was your girlfriends dad, and the bill would be covered."

"No." The word burst out as he jumped to his feet, furious at the thought of this stranger trying to take advantage of him. "Do I need to call over there and set them straight? They should kick him out."

"I assured the manager that was not the case, but the man is a smooth talker. I even heard he was doing some dating of his own, mainly wealthy widows from the Stowe area, even a few up in Burlington." JJ showed him some notes and social media profiles of older women. "Seems to have a regular schedule of women, but this one gets the most time. Her husband retired from Wall Street and dropped dead on a golf course a month later, leaving her loads. She doesn't have any kids and doesn't know a lot of people in the area. We're keeping an eye on it; he spent the last few nights at her place."

"As much as I would like to worry about her, I honestly don't care what he does in his free time," Patrick responded. He sank back into the chair at JJ's hand wave, stopping him from pacing the small room any longer. "I don't want Emma to get hurt in this."

"Neither does Zoe," JJ said. "She shares the same concerns and wants him gone. I'll see what I can do."

"I'll talk to Dan, see if he has any ideas," he suggested. "There are always people trying to get something from me, and they usually have a price. Maybe Dan can find it and get him to leave quietly."

"No bribes," JJ warned. "I don't want to arrest either one of you."

Patrick laughed. "Think of the fame. My mugshot would probably be worth a pretty penny."

"I don't need that kind of trouble, or the press that would swarm on this town. I'll keep you posted," JJ said. "Let me know if anything changes."

Walking the short distance to his brother's small law office, Patrick convinced him to take a break for lunch and then drive him home. Spelling out the problem with Hoyt to Dan helped, and he felt better knowing that JJ and Dan would come up with an answer. For now, he wanted to focus more on winning Emma's heart, and less on it being broken by another man.

Chapter 22

Emma had driven Patrick's Jeep home earlier, careful as she steered through the roads she had grown accustomed to walking. The extra time had meant she arrived home when the trainer was still working with the horses in the paddock, where Whiskey had been refusing to participate. She had, however, walked right to where Emma stood and put her head over the fence, accepting some of the treats offered and asking for pats. The trainer had shaken his head, saying he would take advantage next time and try to put a saddle on the horse while Emma read.

Emma had simply stroked the horse's face, reassuring her that nothing bad would happen to her. The other horses were happy to run and play, didn't mind having a saddle put on, and were settled into their new lives. Whiskey would get there when she was good and ready, and if Emma could help, she would. Granted, the idea of climbing onto the back of a horse still terrified her, but if she wanted Whiskey to be brave, she had to be as well.

Preparing for a night at the local bar was easier than preparing for the first date, Emma decided. Jeans and a cozy sweater swiped from Zoe's closet were simple and yet flattering, and she was ready before Patrick knocked softly. She enjoyed a second with the butterflies in her stomach before opening the door. Dressed in worn jeans, a button-down flannel and a baseball hat, he could blend in with anyone in town. Unless they took a careful look at his chiseled cheekbones and shockingly blue eyes, or the muscles that he was trying to hide under the loose-fitting shirt.

She took a few minutes to explore the muscles with her hands as they greeted each other with a kiss before he took a calculated step backwards and took a deep breath. "We have to get out of here, or we aren't going to make it to the bar."

His frazzled expression brought a smile to her face, pleased that he was as affected by her as she was him. "I'm ready," she replied. "Oh, here are the keys to the Jeep."

He waved his hand at them. "No," he insisted. "You keep them, please. I'd rather you drive to and from work, especially with your early start in the morning."

"Patrick," she rolled her eyes. "You can't give me a house, and a car, and everything else. This is crazy."

"I have three cars here," he pointed out. "And four in Los Angeles. I think I can lend one to a friend. Trust me when I say my friends in California would have no issues taking one of my cars."

"They can afford to replace them if something happens."

"It's insured," he said, dropping the keys on the counter. "And it's the cheapest car I own, I bought it for fun. Please, drive it."

"Fine," she huffed. The extra half hour of sleep it would provide her was a welcome thought, especially since the nights seemed to be filling with activities that would keep her up way past her normal early bedtime. But she still had to find a way to survive without him taking care of everything for her.

He filled her in on the horses' progress as they drove, mentioning an upcoming fundraiser the charity had planned. "It's in a few months, maybe you'll want to come with me."

"Where is it?"

"Las Vegas," he responded.

"You want me to go to Vegas with you?"

"Well, not right now," he laughed. "In a few months. I think it's in June, if I'm remembering correctly."

"Why are they doing it there? Is that where they are based?"

"No," he shook his head. "They have stables in Texas and California, but my studio is doing a big event there, which means I have to go. I mentioned to the charity that if they could get something planned, I'd have a lot of friends looking for something to do. Not to mention, it will get them major attention to have all these actors at their event. They reached out to some contacts and were able to get it scheduled. All my co-stars agreed to go, and a bunch of other people who have work with the same studio."

"That's amazing," she said. "That will be huge for their fundraising."

"You could say that," he laughed. "I told them to aim high for the ticket prices, worst case I'll buy a bunch and fly people in. But I think people will pay up to be in the same room as some of these celebrities."

"Like you," she teased.

"Hopefully I'll have you by my side to protect me," he laughed. "You look like you'd be a fierce bodyguard."

"Hey, I could hold my own. Especially if it's your body I'm protecting," she objected. "One day I'll use that punching bag of yours and show you."

He laughed as he parked and helped her from the SUV, holding her hand as they entered the restaurant. A table near the stage already held his brothers and their wives, along with Zoe and JJ, and a couple she hadn't met. Patrick steered her into the seat next to Zoe, then slid into the empty seat next to her. The man on the other side of Patrick reached over with his hand to greet her.

"Hey, I'm Ryan. I'm Patrick's personal security, and my wife is Christine," he indicated the perky redhead across the table from him. "She's incredibly pregnant and may go into labor at any second."

Christine rolled her eyes. "He's very dramatic," she said. "I'm only five months, but he is constantly asking if I'm having contractions or if my water broke."

He shrugged, a grin on his face. "I want to be prepared."

"I know you were considering being my bodyguard, but Ryan is good at staving off fans," Patrick explained.

"It helps that I'm his biggest fan, and I want all his attention," Ryan interjected. "But I think JJ is the biggest deterrent to anyone."

JJ frowned intensely before grinning at her. "I have a resting arrest face. Stops most people in their tracks."

Zoe sighed. "You have to stop saying that."

"But it's true," he argued.

"You have the look of a golden retriever," she responded. "No one is scared of you."

"I'm choosing to take that as a compliment, my love." JJ winked at her.

They all ordered food, and Emma found herself feeling comfortable and enjoying the company at the table. She and Zoe were able to catch up quickly before joining the banter around the table, which they all made sure to include her in. By the time the singing started, she felt as though she was enjoying a night out with old friends, and she joined in the cheers as JJ tried to serenade her sister in the first song.

"You should give him a chance," she whispered to Zoe.

"He's not being serious," Zoe rolled her eyes. "This is all just fun for him."

"I think he is," Emma argued. "Patrick thinks so too."

"Trust me, he just wants the food." Zoe crossed her arms, a signal that the conversation was over.

They turned their attention to the stage, where Patrick was getting ready to sing. He had mentioned to her once that he had been on Broadway, so she had assumed he had a decent voice, but she was shocked at how good he was. He was singing a fun pop song from a boy band and had the crowd up and dancing along with him. Jake joined him next, the two of them equally talented as they sang a Hall and Oats song she remembered from her childhood. Although most of the crowd got up to sing, everyone chanted for Patrick and Jake most of the night, so they performed song after song before collapsing at the table.

"I'm exhausted," Patrick said in her ear. "Want to get out of here?"

She nodded and hugged Zoe goodbye, waving to the others at the table. As they walked hand in hand toward the door, she felt all eyes on them. A giant of a man stood to block a small group of women from interceding them, and Patrick fist bumped him as they went by.

"That was fun," she said as she buckled her seat belt. "I can't believe how amazing your voice is."

"Thanks," he smiled at her. "I enjoy it. Open mic night is on Thursdays, Jake and I try to go as often as we can. Sometimes the crowd would be more than Kendra can handle, so I try to do it when people don't know I'm in town."

"Word has definitely gotten out from that Instagram post," she reflected. "That was a big crowd tonight. And those women would have swarmed you if that guy hadn't gotten in the way."

"That was my trainer, Mike," he explained, laughing. "He's a big dude."

"Stopped them right in their tracks," she said. "That must be weird for you."

"A little," he shrugged. "I went from being a nobody in a small town to being a face everyone knew. There was no in between or time to get used to it. I think it helped that I was young, and my dad and Dan were there to level me out, so my ego didn't get too big."

"How old were you?"

"Sixteen," he answered. "I was working at the ski lift when an agent came through. She took one look at me, took her skis off, and asked me a million questions as I was loading people on. Finally, she asked me to call my dad and have him come meet with her, and the next thing I knew I was in Hollywood. She had been tasked with casting this new teen drama and knew right away I was the missing piece. They did a screen test and signed me right away, and the show was a huge hit. One day I was here in high school, the next I was a poster on the wall of my former classmates."

"Really?"

He laughed. "Maybe not my literal classmates, they weren't terribly impressed. But my peers across the world, yes."

"I can't imagine that."

"And now I can't imagine what my life would be like if it hadn't happened," he said. "I probably would have tried to go into music, or who knows. I was still thinking that I would try Junior's hockey, maybe try to play in college."

"Did you go to college?"

"No," he shook his head. "I tried, but it was too crazy. And my schedule didn't allow it. I was barely able to finish high school with private tutors while on set."

"In some ways you're really lucky," she said. "And then I feel sad for you, that you didn't get a chance to do what is considered normal for a teenager."

The car filled with silence, and she was afraid she had upset him before he finally responded. "I think you're the first and only person to ever really get that about me. But compared to what you went through—"

"It's not a contest," she interrupted. "We can be even in our dysfunction."

He laughed softly and reached for her hand. "I'm glad you found my stable."

***

The alarm woke her, and although it seemed as though she had only been asleep for minutes, she rolled over with a smile on her face. The night before had been perfect, even with Patrick retreating to his own house at the conclusion of the night. He had laughed at her frustration, telling her that their second date was complete and that he couldn't wait for the third.

As she showered and dressed for work, an idea brewed for their third date. Shooting a text to Zoe before she left, she reluctantly grabbed the keys for the Jeep to drive to work. Even when he wasn't right in front of her, Patrick was doing things to make her life easy. Planning a night for him would be fun, and she was smiling as she flipped on the lights at the bakery.

An hour later, her happiness had moved to the backburner as Hoyt – her father, she supposed – had been sitting at the table moping for most of the time they had been open. Piper pulled her into the kitchen between customers, gesturing to him as she spoke.

"You have to get him out of here," she said. "He's killing our vibe."

"I know, but what can I do?"

"Take him to the diner and have breakfast," Piper suggested. She pulled cash out of her back pocket and stuffed it into Emma's hand. "On me, I insist. Then maybe he'll find something else to do with his day."

"I don't want to take your money," Emma objected.

"It's worth it if you can convince him to spend his day elsewhere," Piper sighed. "I'm sorry, I know he's your dad, but something about him just rubs me the wrong way."

"It's okay," Emma looked down at the money in her fist. "I really don't know him."

"Maybe that's for the best," Piper suggested. "I heard a little of your story, and I know who you are, Emma. That man out there, he doesn't deserve you. He had every opportunity to step up as your father, and he didn't. What would your mom say about this?"

"I wish I knew."

"My parents are divorced, and they made my childhood difficult," Piper said. "Always fighting, constantly demeaning the other one in front of me. It wasn't pretty, and as an adult, I now wish they had put me first and gotten over the anger. But they didn't, and yet they both still showed up for me when I needed them. That guy? He only showed up when something good happened for you. Remember that."

"I will," Emma promised. "I'll be quick."

"Take your time. Just make sure he goes somewhere else when you leave the diner," Piper laughed. "Maybe Zoe could help?"

"No, she wants nothing to do with him. I'll deal with it." She took off her apron and grabbed her jacket off the hook, shrugging it on as she walked toward Hoyt. "Want to go grab breakfast?"

He looked up, surprise written on his face. "Don't you have breakfast things here?"

"I need a change of scenery," she lied. "Let's walk over to the diner."

They walked in silence, and slid into an empty booth toward the back, where they would have some privacy. Several people greeted her as she passed, and she couldn't help but notice that all ignored Hoyt.

"What's going on," she asked him, pouring cream into her coffee. "You're moping around the bakery."

"I'm not moping," he argued. "I just had a bad night."

"What happened?"

"The lady I was seeing broke it off. I don't know why. I guess her friends got in her ear. I knew they didn't like me."

"Not the end of the world," Emma argued. "It's only been a couple of weeks."

"There's not a lot of women to pick from around here," he said.

"That's not true at all, I've met a ton of single woman around your age, just here in town."

"Maybe I liked this one," he said, sounding so childish it made her wince.

They ordered breakfast, then sat silently for a moment as she tried to decide what to do about him. They hadn't spent a lot of time together, and she felt like he was primarily a stranger sitting across from her. It was odd, because she hadn't spent a lot of time with the people she had been with the night before yet had felt instantly comfortable. This was the opposite.

"I was thinking," he said, leaning across the table. "Maybe I could come stay with you for a while? Plenty of room up there at that huge house."

"It's not my huge house, it's Patrick's," she said, stunned at what he was saying. "I live in a tiny one-bedroom guest cottage."

"I'm sure he wouldn't mind having your dad stay with him," Hoyt said confidently, leaning back in the booth.

"I wouldn't know because I'll never ask him. He's already done so much for me."

"That's a little selfish, don't you think?" He leaned back, and she could see a calculated look in his eyes. "You get a little luck and don't think you can spare some for your old man?"

"Selfish?" The word came out so sharp, she was surprised her water glass didn't burst. "You deserted me before I was even born, and never looked back. Don't talk to me about being selfish."

"Your mother—"

"No." The word burst from her mouth, far louder than she would have preferred, but she couldn't help it. "Don't you dare speak about her. She was everything a parent should be, and you were not. I grieve for her every second of every day, and you were never even a passing thought until you showed up here. Do you know what my life has been like? Orphaned before I was even a teenager. In and out of foster homes, changing schools more often than I got new sneakers. And all this time, you were out there, not willing to find me until something went right for me. I think you need to leave; this is not working out."

She stood, almost bumping into the waitress who was bringing their food. "Sorry, Lacey." She handed the waitress the money that Piper had given her. "This is for the food, please keep the change."

Racing out of the diner, she ignored the feeble attempt Hoyt made at calling her back. She ran straight for Zoe's house, banging on the back door, startled when a shirtless JJ answered the door.

"Are you okay?" He pulled her inside, holding her by the shoulders as he looked at her. She hadn't been aware of the tears streaming from her eyes until he did so, and she swiped at them angrily.

"What are you doing here? Where is Zoe?"

"I'm here," Zoe rushed into the room. "What happened?"

"I just had an argument with Hoyt, and the only place I could think of to come was here" she said, fighting off tears. "But I'm interrupting, so I should go."

"No, stay. JJ was just leaving."

He sighed, then turned and went down the hall towards Zoe's bedroom before reappearing fully dressed. "We'll talk later," he directed at Zoe. "If I can do anything to help, Emma, you know where to find me."

"I have to get back to work, so I don't have time to figure out what that was," Emma said. "I just needed to vent before I go back as a mess."

"I'll walk with you," Zoe offered. "Let me grab my shoes."

Walking and talking to her sister helped her calm down, and by the time she reentered the bakery, she was calm. Her sister had seconded her thoughts about Hoyt, and the desire to have him leave town. Zoe asked her to call for backup next time, they could chase him out of town together if he wasn't already gone. The thought of having her sister in her corner had made her feel better, and she realized how lucky she was to have found her again.

Her sister reminded her of the text message she had sent this morning, distracting her from her worries about Hoyt. Before she disappeared into the bakery again, Zoe had helped her plan out the surprise for Patrick. The thought of the night ahead was enough to push the unpleasant thought of Hoyt from her mind, and she was determined to leave him as a thing of her past. She had Zoe, and Patrick, and a new life she was building here in Windsor Peak. That was more than enough, and she wasn't letting anyone ruin that for her.

Zoe gave her a quick hug at the bakery door and turned to go. "Hey, Zo," she called out before her sister walked far. "What was happening with JJ this morning? In all this chaos, I almost forgot to ask."

"Nothing," Zoe rolled her eyes.

"Looked like something," she teased. "Are you giving him a chance?"

"We'll talk about it later," Zoe promised. "I had a moment of weakness, that's all it was."

"He's a good man, you should really consider giving him a chance."

"We've got bigger problems right now," Zoe said. "Let's focus on you and Patrick, and getting to the bottom of this situation with our so-called father. Then I'll deal with my love life." She trotted down the steps, waving before she crossed the street towards the restaurant.

Chapter 23

Patrick carried his golf clubs into the new building at the local golf course, where a simulated system had been set up to get the locals through the long winter. Dan had texted him to meet there at four, and although his brother wasn't there yet, JJ was waiting by their lane, four beers on the table in front of him.

"Hey," JJ called out. "Glad at least one of you can be punctual."

"I'm surprised I beat Jake, he's usually five minutes early to everything." He set his clubs down and grabbed a beer, swigging a sip. "How did you manage to get off work?"

"I'm pulling more weekend shifts, so I have a little time off during the week. We need to hire someone fast, or I'm going to lose my mind." JJ glanced around before speaking again. "Any other trouble with Hoyt?"

"Not that I know of," Patrick replied.

"I heard he got kicked to the curb by the woman in Stowe," JJ shared. "He had been spending a lot of time there, now he's back to the Inn and lurking around town. You might need to check on Emma, I heard from Lacey at the diner that they had some kind of altercation this morning."

"Who did? Lacey and Emma?"

"No," JJ shook his head. "Emma and Hoyt."

"I haven't seen her today," Patrick said. "Maybe I should go check on her."

"I went by later, grabbed some cookies, and she seemed okay. I hope the guy hits the road, leave them alone." JJ sipped his beer and looked around the room. "I don't know what it is, but he just rubs me the wrong way. He hasn't been arrested, but he also doesn't stay in one place for too long. That's never a good sign."

"I try to avoid him because I feel the same way. Something's just not right," Patrick said. "And one hard lesson I had to learn was to be able to spot the people who are only after me for what I can do for them, and he's got that written all over him."

Jake and Dan entered the building, filling the space with their laughter as Jake announced that Dan had made him late. Patrick struggled to push the thoughts of Emma and Hoyt out of his mind, wanting to enjoy the afternoon. He watched as Jake set up to tee off, laughing when the ball went into the woods on the screen.

"Hey, I'm still recovering," Jake protested.

"You finished physical therapy months ago," Dan teased. "Maybe the shoulder injury will save you money, no point in throwing it away on golf."

"I'll still beat you," Jake said. "I just need to get warmed up."

"Kendra is convinced you and Zoe went home together last night," Dan announced to JJ, causing the other man to choke on the beer he had just swallowed.

"Why's that?" JJ asked.

"Said you two looked cozy," Dan replied. "She has a feeling about you. It was all she would talk about last night."

"You might want her to get that checked out," JJ said. "After all, she married you."

"Luckiest day of her life," Dan retorted. "And you're not answering the question."

"It's no secret that I've been chasing her since she moved to town," JJ said slowly. "Maybe I made a little progress last night."

"Not that I like to gossip," Jake joined them at the table. "But I drove Charlie to school today and saw a very familiar truck outside Zoe's house."

JJ stared at Jake before laughing and shaking his head. "You guys are brutal. Maybe I parked there and walked to the bar with her, and then decided that I shouldn't drive home."

"Your house is too far to walk," Patrick pointed out. "That makes me think you didn't go home last night." At JJ's guilty look, they all burst out laughing.

"You spent the night with her," Dan laughed. "Good for you. Finally wore her down."

"Let's talk about something else," JJ tried. "Patrick and Emma seem pretty tight."

"Nope," Jake laughed. "Not getting off that easy. We'll come back to that in a minute."

"Guys," JJ stood and grabbed a driver. "I'm going to marry her. She just needs to get on board with the idea."

"Good luck with that," Dan said. "She doesn't seem to want to date you, so marrying you might be a stretch."

"Maybe you should try and get her to agree to a date first," Jake agreed.

"Her words and her actions are two different things," JJ said mysteriously. He lined up and drove the ball straight down the fairway before turning to point the club at Patrick. "Now let's do him."

"What's going on with you," Jake asked.

"You saw me last night," Patrick said. "And you talk to me every day, so you already know."

"You really interested in her?" Jake pushed.

"Yeah, I am. And before you both get all protective and claim she's after me for the wrong reasons, I'm the one chasing her. Not the other way around."

"Playing hard to get can be a smart strategy," Dan said.

"That's not what this is. Trust me, I've been around enough people who want me for the wrong reasons to know when someone is being sincere. We enjoy each other's company, and we understand each other. Let me have this chance," he said, looking at each of his brothers as he did.

"All we want is for you to be happy," Dan said gruffly.

"And fat," Jake said. "If you could get fat and ugly, we wouldn't mind that."

***

When he pulled in the driveway two hours later, he saw a soft light coming from the stables. Knowing that's where he would find Emma, he left his stuff in the car and crossed the grass to open the door, stunned to find a small table set for two in the space in front of Whiskey's stall. Exactly where he knew she usually sat on her blanket, reading to the horse. Emma was standing, stroking the horse's face, and turned as he entered, a shy smile on her face.

"Hi," she said. "I wanted to surprise you with dinner."

"Wow," he grinned. "You definitely surprised me. This must have taken a lot of work."

She laughed. "You forget you have a bunch of guys here all day, so it was pretty easy to get one of them to carry this table out."

He walked closer, noticing it was the small table from her kitchen. A tablecloth had been draped over it, and two chairs sat close together, facing Whiskey. Candlelight flickered, and a bottle of wine sat on the table.

"The candles are fake," she said in a rush. "I would never light actual candles out here, I know that's a risk."

"Thanks," he smiled at her, moving closer until he could wrap his arms around her. Dropping his head to kiss her softly, he laughed when the horse pushed him away. "I'm making Whiskey jealous."

"She doesn't want me to have other friends," Emma said. "But she's doing so much better, she walks on the lead now and socializes with the other horses more. The trainer said she's working well with him, finally."

"He said the same to me," Patrick said, reaching over to stroke the horse's head. "He thinks she's finally feeling comfortable here."

"Let me grab the dinner," Emma said. "I had to keep it away from the horses. Why don't you open the wine? That is, if you're okay with having dinner with me?"

She looked so vulnerable, standing there twisting her hands and not meeting his eyes, that it flustered him. "Of course. I was going to ask you if you wanted to order food when I got home, so you saved me some time."

"I'll be right back," she promised, a relieved smile on her face. She darted out of the stables, and he went to work on the corkscrew then filled their glasses as she came back in. "I had Zoe make this, I hope you don't mind. I'm not much of a cook, and she's so good. And I didn't want to risk hot food, because I didn't know what time you would be back." She took out two plates, both with a large salad topped with chicken, and then pulled a loaf of fresh bread out from under her arm.

"This is perfect," he assured her. "Especially since my brothers just told me they hope I'll get fat."

"They did not," she laughed.

"Oh, trust me, they did. But they are ridiculous, so forget about them," he said. "More importantly, how was your day?"

He saw the color change on her face as her eyes averted his. She spread something on a piece of the bread and passed it to him, before doing the same and putting it on her plate. "Did you talk to JJ?"

"Yes, I just golfed with him."

"In this weather?" Emma looked shocked, glancing out at the mounds of snow outside.

"No, it's an indoor simulator," he explained. "You hit the ball into a screen, but it looks like a course. Kind of like a video game but you're actually hitting the ball the way you would on the course."

"That sounds fun, although I don't golf," she grinned at him. "Something else I'll maybe learn one day."

"I'll take you there, see how you like it. In the spring you could take some lessons at the golf course," he offered. She smiled at him in return, and he found himself relieved at the thought of her still being here in a few months' time.

"JJ must have told you I was upset this morning," she guessed. "Hoyt was sitting in the bakery all morning, moping. Piper finally asked me to get him out of there, and we ended up having words at the diner. He called me selfish, and I snapped."

"He called you selfish? What basis could he possibly have for that?"

"He wanted me to do something for him, and I said no. It's not important. What is important is that I told him to leave me alone, and then I was a mess, and I ran to Zoe's house crying."

"I'm sorry," he said softly, taking her hand. "Are you okay now?"

"Yes," she nodded. "Zoe and I talked, and then Piper was a good friend, listening to me all day. At the end of it, I just decided with Whiskey that I need to stick to it and tell him to get lost. He never looked for me before, and he hasn't done one thing since he came to town that would be considered fatherly. I so badly wanted to believe what he said, but Zoe is probably right, he's manipulating the past to make himself look innocent. And now it's all about what I can do for him, not how he can make up for all these years. When I look at your dad, and how quick he is to help you, and how happy he is to see you all, I know that's what a real father is."

"Should I ask what it is he wants you to do for him," Patrick ventured. "Or is that something you don't want to talk about."

She fiddled with her fork before sighing and turning to face him. "I don't want to, but I also do, because I want you to know that I would never do anything like this. Today he wanted me to ask you to let him stay here."

He stared at her, taking in the words and seeing how upset she was getting. He had assumed it had something to do with him, but asking to move into his home wasn't even in his head. He had figured it would be a money grab or wanting to get famous somehow.

"I told him no," she said quickly. "That it's not a possibility at all. And I want you to know that this is not me asking. I just want to be honest with you, so it won't reflect on me later. I asked him to leave town, and to leave us all alone. There is nothing that I would ever ask for you to do for him, I hope you believe that."

"I believe you," he said slowly. "Yes, it makes me uncomfortable, but I don't hold you responsible."

"Thank you," she reached over and squeezed his hand as she spoke. "I was so worried. I had already planned this dinner, and then I thought I should do it a different night or just leave you alone entirely."

"That's the opposite of what I want," he laughed.

"I'm glad." She smiled at him, and he wasn't able to resist kissing her until the horse let out a snort in their direction, making them both laugh.

"I was just with JJ and my brothers," he said. "There's a rumor going around that JJ spent the night with Zoe last night."

"Oh, yes," she smiled. "When I showed up banging on the door at eight this morning, he answered it without a shirt. I need to get back to Zoe to find out what is happening."

"According to JJ, he finally made some progress with her. But he wouldn't tell us anything else," he told her. "Jake saw his truck outside her house, that's how he was busted for spending the night there."

"Small town, can't get away with anything."

"Unless you live halfway up the mountain," he winked at her.

"Trust me, everyone in town is fully invested in your life," she laughed. "The number of customers that come in just to get a look at me is shocking. But Piper is all for it, said it's increased her sales over fifty percent since I started working there."

"It's a blessing and a curse, I guess." He pushed the plate away slightly, pouring them each a little more wine. "That was delicious, thank you."

"I have dessert too," she said, her cheeks turning pink. "I put it in your refrigerator."

"Oh, did you," he drawled out, twirling a piece of her hair with his fingers. "Why don't we clean this up and go check that out."

He made record time of stacking the plates, grabbing them and the bottle of wine before asking her to grab their glasses. "We can move the table later," he said as he ushered her toward the door.

Her laughter filled the air as they half raced across the lawn, shooting into his kitchen, where he unceremoniously dumped the load of dishes in his sink. She winced at the sound as he placed the wine on the counter, then took the two glasses from her hands and put them next to the bottle.

"Stop me if I'm misunderstanding," he said, kissing her softly. "I'm hoping that dessert can wait for a bit."

She wrapped her arms around him, urging him closer until he scooped her up and deepened the kiss. When she slid down from his arms and took his hand, he followed her up the stairs. "Date three," he said as he chased her. "My favorite so far."

Chapter 24

Days turned into weeks, and then months, as Emma fell into a life in Windsor Peak. The bitter cold of winter let way to what the locals referred to as mud season, as the snow melted, and any unpaved area was suddenly a hazard. Suddenly ice on the sidewalks seemed safer than stepping onto a grassy area, and she learned quickly why locals continued to wear boots long after the snow was gone.

Easter came and went, the day filled with joy at the Burrows home. Emma had been slowly getting to know Shea and Kendra, as well as Stella, and enjoyed being folded into the family for the holiday. They had insisted Zoe come as well, who had dragged JJ along with her. When Stella sent them out on an adult egg hunt, she and Patrick had chosen to hide in the hayloft. Just the thought of it had her smiling as she drove home from work the next day.

As she drove, a weather advisory came on the radio that had her laughing. Only in Vermont would a few feet of snow arrive in April, and few would bat an eye to it. She ran into her cottage to shower and change into leggings and a sweater, knowing she and Patrick would be staying in with the weather forecast. Grabbing the box of treats she had brought home with her, she darted across the lawn to his house, shocked at how cold it was already.

"Hi," she called as she let herself into the kitchen. "It's just me."

"Hey," his voice called from the front of the house. "Be right there."

She set the bakery box next to the open bottle of wine on the counter and heard his low voice coming closer. As he stepped into sight, he pointed to the cell phone to his ear and rolled his eyes. He was freshly showered and dressed casually, so they had similar thoughts about the plans for the night. He said goodbye to the person on the phone before tossing it on the counter and pulling her close to him.

"Hi," he said before kissing her. He kept his arms around her as he looked down into her eyes. "How was work?"

"It was good," she said. "Busy. I brought us some dessert to have later."

"Oh, did you," he said, a gleam in his eye. "Tell me more."

She laughed and pushed back against his chest. "How do you make everything sound dirty?"

"Sexy, not dirty."

"You're brutal," she laughed. "Who were you talking to?"

"That was Nat," he sighed. "She's on a spiral."

"About what," she asked as she opened the refrigerator and pulled out a block of cheese. Grabbing a plate and a box of crackers, she set them on the island in front of them.

"There's nothing she won't freak out about," he said.

"Is that code for mind my own business?"

"No," he sighed. "I just don't want you to feel bad or think the wrong thing."

"This doesn't sound good." She poured them each a glass of wine and pushed his towards him before sipping her own. "Lay it on me."

"The magazines are running wild with speculation over our supposed breakup, and about my hidden girlfriend," he explained. "Nat is beside herself because next they'll start speculating about her love life. She's playing it off now with some fake dates, but she doesn't want to be seen as single for long."

"First, why is that an issue? She's a gorgeous movie star who could date anyone she wants."

"True," he nodded. "But she got burned a few years ago and hasn't dated publicly since. Having me as a buffer means she isn't getting questions about the ex, or about any potential love interests she happens to cross paths with. When I do interviews, it's rare they ask about my love life or insinuate I'm a slut. For her, it's constant."

"That's horrible."

"It is, and she hates it. Most of the reporters have been on their best behavior because they all wanted the big scoop, to get the two of us together. Which clearly isn't going to happen because it was all fake to begin with." He popped a piece of cheese on a cracker and chewed it before continuing. "Not the friendship, that's real. I look at her like a sister, or a close friend. But I can't pretend to date her forever."

"Now, about that new girlfriend of yours," Emma said with a smile. "Anyone I know?"

"You bet you do," he said, pulling her close again. "Short little blond, likes to hide out in stables. You probably met her once or twice."

"Really, though," she pulled back to look up at him. "Is that where we are?"

"I thought so," he said. "I'm not seeing anyone else, and I don't want to. I hope you feel the same."

"I do," she said shyly. "This is just all new territory for me."

"Being in a relationship?"

"Yes," she nodded. "Not to mention, the fact that my boyfriend has been named Sexiest Man of the Year and is one of the biggest stars out there."

He leaned against the counter, looking as though he was trying to hide a smile. "You googled me, didn't you?"

"I didn't need to. Zoe, Shea and Kendra filled me in, and Christine was more than happy to help."

"Did you tell them I was taken?"

She shoved him lightly. "I don't think your sisters-in-law are trying to steal you away from me."

He laughed, pretending to fall from her light shove. "I've always suspected they had a crush on me."

"Oh, of course. Zoe too," she laughed.

"Speaking of Zoe, I did grab dinner from her earlier," he said, pulling open the door to the refrigerator. "I figured it would be easier to stay in with the weather turning, if that's alright with you."

She gestured at her clothes, laughing. "Great minds think alike. A night in front of the fire is perfect."

She helped him follow Zoe's detailed instructions for heating the meal before they took their wine and cheese tray to the sofa. Leaning back on the couch, she sighed, then laughed. "It seems like a lifetime ago that I slept on this couch, sure you would wake up and have me arrested."

"Is that what you thought?" He looked surprised, then nodded. "I guess that makes sense. You did break and enter, after all."

"I did not," she said, pushing him lightly. "You had the key. I just helped you get the door open."

"The police will completely go for that," he laughed. "But I really am glad that happened, even though I never want to be that sick again. If it hadn't, what would you have done? If I had been dropped off and was perfectly healthy."

"I would have freaked out," she admitted. "Ran to the stable to grab my stuff and disappear as quickly as possible."

"Where would you have gone?"

"I guess I would have had to approach Zoe earlier," she said. "I was so nervous that what her mom said was true, that she wanted nothing to do with me. I don't know why I felt like watching and waiting would tell me if it was true or not. But if I had nowhere else to go, especially on a night that was as cold and snowy as that, it would be go to her or possibly freeze to death."

"I'm glad that didn't happen," he smiled at her. "Will you tell me more about your life after your mom died?"

Feeling the pit in her stomach, she stalled by stacking some cheese on a cracker and then chewing slowly. "You had such a nice life," she said. "I worry that it will change your image of me."

"How do you figure?" He looked stunned. "You were a kid. And you survived it, that tells me so much about who you are."

"Barely survived, it feels like," she said softly, before taking a deep breath to continue. "The night she died, I was sent to a foster home that was used for emergencies. They never kept kids long, it was an older couple, they just kept kids for a few nights to get them through. They didn't talk to me much, and I was picked up by a social worker to go to my mom's funeral. If you could even call it that."

"What do you mean?"

"We didn't have any money. We lived in a rented apartment, my mom lived paycheck to paycheck, probably behind a lot. There was no money for a big funeral, so she was going to be buried by the state. My school principal started a fundraiser and was able to get enough collected to give her a nicer send off, but it was still very quick and small." She thought back to standing at the gravesite, her mom's circle of coworkers and a couple of friends nearby. The only people to offer her any comfort had been from her school, and she had never seen them again after that day. "Once she was buried, they moved me into what should have been a longer-term foster home. This one had eight kids, two of their own and six like me."

"Must have been crowded," he said.

"To say the least. They had one room for girls, one for boys, and then their own kids had their own rooms. Four of us were crammed into this tiny room with two sets of bunk beds. Since I was the newest, I got treated horribly by the kids who had already been there," she admitted. "I didn't know any better, and I was so full of grief I didn't really notice for a while. But the family had two meals, one for them and one for all of us, and I barely got any food. The others just took it away from me, and I didn't care. I wanted to go to heaven with my mom."

"Oh, Emma," he pulled her close, and she realized she was crying.

"They moved me after one of the boys broke my arm. I was trying to stop him from taking a piece of jewelry that I had from my mom," she told him. "I didn't get to keep much of her stuff, so I tried to just keep small things I could always carry with me, like the jewelry and some pictures."

"Did he steal it?"

"No, I fought back. Even after my arm was broken. Then they moved me the same night, to a new house."

"Was that one any better?"

"No," she shook her head. "This one was almost like a religious cult. They were so strict, and we were barely allowed to speak. I cried all the time, and when they couldn't make me stop, they made me leave."

"How many different foster homes did you live in?"

"Seven," she told him, seeing the shock on his face. "The longest was a year, I think."

"It's amazing you came through it and are still so positive," he said. "Is it weird that I'm proud of you?"

"Thank you." She laughed, leaning into his shoulder. "Now tell me more crazy stories about growing up here."

Patrick shared lighthearted stories, seeming to know when she needed the distraction away from her darker thoughts. Soon she was relaxing, the wine and company putting her past exactly where it belonged, in the rear-view mirror. Time to focus on the positives that were happening right now, starting with the man in front of her. Who she just so happened to be falling in love with faster than she could get her prayers up that this one good thing in her life could last. The only thing scarier than falling for him was losing him, and she saw the questioning look in his eye as she gripped his hand tighter than she planned.

"You okay?" he asked softly, squeezing her hand far more gently than she had his.

"Yes, sorry," she said. "I just was thinking about how much fun I have with you, and how good things seem to happen when I'm around you."

"Ditto," he responded, leaning in to kiss her. "I have to tell you, I haven't felt this way in a long time. I hope that doesn't scare you off."

"How do you feel?" She held her breath waiting for him to answer, wanting to cross her fingers while waiting.

"I'm falling for you quickly, and this is new for me," he said softly. "You have become one of my favorite people. I missed you when I was in California, which is crazy because we barely knew each other. I look forward to seeing you every day. And even more so waking up next to you. And even more than that, I trust you and feel like you see the real me. That's hard to come by in Los Angeles."

"I missed you too," she whispered. "And I feel the same. I never knew it was possible to feel this safe and to look forward to seeing someone as much as I do."

"I want you to trust me too," he urged. "Talk to me when things are bothering you and ask me questions. You may not have noticed, but I can be pretty spoiled. People don't like to complain to me, they like to keep my world looking perfect and happy. But with you, I want the real stuff. Not fantasy world."

"Will you keep Whiskey?" The question burst from her lips before she had a chance to process it. "No matter what happens with us, will you keep her safe here?"

"Yes, I already told the rescue she was going to live here," he told her. "There was no way I could make her have to move again, when she's finally feeling settled. I know she means a lot to you, and I can easily promise that Whiskey will spend the rest of her time here. She's young, and once she gets comfortable, she will make a great trail horse. But even if she doesn't, she will have a place here."

"Thank you," she said, feeling the relief course through her. Never would she have imagined the life of an animal would hold such weight for her, but she felt a connection to the horse like no other. Their sad paths seemed to be the same, both cast offs searching for safety, and knowing the horse had found a home healed a broken piece of her heart.

Chapter 25

Patrick spent the morning answering emails and speaking to people on his management team, all trying to find a way to get him out of Vermont and into the spotlight. Plans were being made for the fall premiere of the newest movie, and everyone wanted him to start scheduling appearances. Normally after a few weeks at home he was somewhat ready to get back into the job, the role he presented to the world. Somehow this time it was different.

He knew a big part was Emma, but it was more than that. Having his own house now, and not sleeping in his childhood bedroom, made him even happier in Vermont. His circle had grown larger here, moving beyond just his trusted family. Normal time at home would be spent with his dad and Stella, hanging out with Charlie, and his brothers when they could come home at the same time. Suddenly he had new friends in Mike and JJ, two sisters, a niece who could wrap him around her finger, and a stable full of horses all competing for his time. And Emma.

Thinking of her as he added dates to his calendar brought a smile to his face. He could see them on the red carpet together, her glowing in a gown. Her standing backstage while he joked with Jimmy Kimmel, or sitting in the front row as he hosted Saturday Night Live again. All the events that would lead up to his next movie release he could now only picture with her at his side, a thought that both terrified and thrilled him.

"Hey." Dan's voice called from the front door as he walked in. "What are you doing?"

"Putting some crap in my calendar that my manager just sent over," Patrick said as he put his phone down. "What's up?"

"I've got some paperwork for you to sign, figured it was easier to come by. Your manager has been busy this morning," Dan laughed.

"They better not sneak something in there that I just said no to," Patrick warned.

"We can look through it," Dan said. "Nothing looked unusual at first glance. Anything in particular you're worried about?"

"I'm just trying to stay here longer, and they have a million things they want to send me off to do."

"Like what?"

"All the usual. Some photoshoot for People, another commercial overseas."

"All the stuff you usually agree to, you mean?" Dan prodded, pulling papers out of his bag.

"I'm tired," he said. "I don't want to travel as much."

"Is that what we're calling it?" Dan grinned at him as he asked. "Or are you reluctant to leave someone behind?"

"Who are you? What did you do with my brother?" Patrick took a step back and pretended to be shocked. "The Dan I know would never come at me with mushy questions about my emotions."

"Hey, I'm in love and happy. I'm all mush," Dan said. "Kendra is a good influence. Plus, I'm your big brother, I should be giving you words of wisdom."

"Maybe save that," Patrick laughed. "Let's get this stuff dealt with before Mike and Jake get here to work out."

"You guys work out mid-day without me?" Dan threw a pen at him and glared. "I can't believe I'm the one left out."

"Just today," he laughed. "Mike is busy later, and Kendra said you had a date night planned anyway. I offered to have Calle come here, and I was turned down for a sleepover with Charlie."

"Better luck next time," Dan said. "If I had known having a six-year-old in your life would keep you humble I would have had kids way earlier."

Patrick laughed and got to signing the documents in front of him, barely seeing the words in front of him. For years, he had blindly agreed to anything his team had put in front of him. It felt good to say no for a change and settle on a compromise between what the world wanted from him and what he needed.

***

When his workout was done and Jake and Mike had headed out, he retrieved his phone from the island. Scrolling through the messages from his team, still intent on convincing him to do half the things he had turned down, he frowned at a message from his assistant. It explained that an email had come into his website that they weren't sure was real or fake, and they wanted to send it to him. He scrolled down to the forwarded message, a feeling of dread in his stomach.

Hey, I'm trying to get in touch with you to discuss something important. I tried calling but couldn't get you. I'm in room 412 at the Inn. It's about Emma. This is Hoyt, her father. Keep this between us.

He dropped the phone again and groaned. He wished he had never opened the email, or that his assistant had never thought to forward it to begin with. Now he had to decide if he shared the message with Emma or go to talk to Hoyt behind her back. Neither felt like a great option, and ignoring it entirely felt even worse.

He grabbed a sweatshirt out of the closet and headed to the one person who he always trusted with the right answer. Ten minutes later, he was knocking on the door to the small cottage behind the house he had grown up in. His father's voice called out to come in, so he let himself in, immediately comforted by the smell of baking bread and the fire in the stove.

His father was sitting in his recliner with a book on his lap, Stella behind the small kitchen island smiling over at him. "Hey, honey, what a nice surprise." She waved him over. "Come keep me company."

"He might be here to visit me," Ben grumbled, then smiled at his wife. "But I would probably pick you over me too."

"Nonsense, you can hear us from there," she clucked. "But if my boy is here unexpectedly, it means he needs some advice."

"Maybe I was just hoping for some of your cinnamon bread," Patrick teased as he pulled off the sweatshirt and moved closer.

"You're in luck, it will be out in just a minute," she answered, checking the oven. "What do you want to drink?"

Patrick let her fuss over him for a minute, enjoying the feeling of being a young kid being cared for again. Stella always brought that out in him, she was such a nurturer and put everyone around her at ease.

"What's on your mind," she asked finally, sliding a piece of the bread toward him. She dropped her hands into the sink full of soapy water and started washing bowls, giving him time to think.

"I got a strange message," he started. "It was from Emma's father."

"That's unusual," Stella murmured. "He left town, didn't he?"

"I thought so. But now he's asking me to come to his room at the Inn to discuss something important," he said. "Either he left and came back, or he never left."

"What do you think he wants?" Ben asked from his chair, clearly listening in on the conversation.

"I have no idea," he admitted. "I limited my interaction with him all along, because I had a bad feeling. I know he asked Emma to let him move into my house, and that's when she told him to leave. As far as I know, she hasn't had any contact with him since then."

"Did you ask her what she thinks it could be," Stella asked.

"No," he shook his head. "That's another thing. Hoyt told me to keep it between us, not to tell her."

Stella pursed her lips and studied him, silencing Ben with a look when he started to speak. "What do you make of that?"

"I don't know," Patrick admitted. "It makes me feel weird to not tell her. But I also feel weird asking her about it. I don't know what to do."

"You've gotten pretty involved with her," Stella commented. "Your dad and I were talking just last night about how happy you seem."

"That's true," he said.

"You trust her," Stella said, making it sound more like a statement than a question.

"I do."

"Then why are you here wondering about this? Tell her about the message and figure it out together," Stella advised. "You aren't the type to keep secrets from people you care about, unless it's something good."

He watched as she carefully dried a glass bowl and set it on the towel that she had laid on the counter. She dried her hands carefully before circling to sit next to him and take his hand. "Not everyone in this world will care about your fame or money," she said. "There are people who genuinely like you for who you are, and that goes beyond just your family."

"I know that," he said, not sounding terribly convincing even to his own ears.

"Do you? Do you have friends outside of Windsor Peak that you have let see the soft side of you? Or are they all Hollywood types who are entertaining for a bit, but you can leave them in the rearview mirror when a shoot ends?" Her gaze stayed steady on his as she pushed. "You don't open up to a lot of people, Patrick. You do good deeds and keep them secret, so you don't have to be exposed to more people."

"That's not why," he argued. "I just know if it gets out, then more people will come asking. Like this guy."

"That will always happen," Stella said. "There will always be people who can't see past your money, or what you can do for them. But that sweet part of your heart doesn't have to be hidden from the world, Patrick. You can love, and trust, and be generous, and not think people will respond badly."

"It makes people feel weird," he admitted. "Especially when it's a money thing. But that has nothing to do with this situation."

"First of all, money always makes people feel weird," she said. "Either they have it and are weird about it, or they don't have it and feel weird about it. It's not unique to you. Secondly, no one in this town only cares about you because of your money. And that includes Emma."

"You think I should tell her about this?"

"I do," Stella nodded. "I think you should be looking at this as a team. I don't know what he wants, but I suspect it's not going to be good. Emma should know that and be a part of the solution. Otherwise, this will stick between you two until it tears you apart. Secrets tend to do that in a relationship."

He sighed, knowing her words made sense. "What's holding me back is more her feelings about him. I know she was upset when she told him to leave, and she has been able to move past that now. I would guess he's here to ask me for money, and that's going to make her more uncomfortable. What if the thing that will tear us apart is the biggest difference between us?"

"Patrick, you have never once in your life judged someone for what they have or don't have," Ben's voice chimed in.

"I'm not judging her, Dad. I admire her so much, how she overcame all the obstacles in her life, and she's still so amazing.

But I can't help but think that if she really started thinking about what I have, or if her family started asking for handouts, that it won't make her hesitant to be with me."

"You are the only one who can decide what to do," Stella said. "I trust you'll make the right decision. Just remember that you can't predict how someone will react, and it's unfair to make a judgement based on what you think will happen."

"Thanks for the advice," he said as he stood up. He hugged Stella and kissed her on the cheek before grabbing his jacket off the back of his chair. "And the bread. I'll keep you updated on what happens."

He walked home slower than he normally would, the weight of the decision on his shoulders. Although everything Stella and Ben said had made sense, he couldn't help but worry that if Emma's father asked him for money, it would cause an irreparable rift.

Chapter 26

Emma flopped down on Zoe's bed, closing her eyes when her head hit the pillow. "Just let me take a ten-minute nap," she begged.

"Absolutely not," Zoe responded, pulling her back to a sitting position. "I haven't had a girl's night in one hundred years, and you are not falling asleep on me before we even go anywhere."

"We could just watch a movie here and have wine," Emma suggested. "Then I won't have to get dressed up and put makeup on."

"That's the whole point of a girl's night," Zoe said. "You spend ninety percent of your time in leggings and sweaters, and don't tell me I'm wrong. Putting on a nice outfit just makes you feel good."

"Putting on pajamas makes me feel good," Emma grumbled, laughing when Zoe pinched her. "Okay, fine, I'll get changed."

She slipped into the bathroom and found the outfit that her sister had chosen for her to wear. Jeans and a V-neck sweater, both clinging to her more than anything she would have chosen, and a pair of knee-high leather boots were her uniform for the night. She tugged on the sweater as she came out of the bedroom, frowning at her sister.

"Stop pulling on it," Zoe ordered. "You look amazing."

"It's too tight," she complained. "And too short. Can you see my belly button?"

"It's not that short, and it looks great. Leave it alone." Zoe stood, confident in her miniskirt and cropped t-shirt, covered partially by a leather jacket she pulled on. "Let's go."

"You look like you're going to a night club, and I look like a nun tagging along."

"Do you want to change?" Zoe turned, studying her sister. "I can get you a much hotter outfit, but I didn't want to push it."

"No, it's fine," she said. "I'm guessing most people in Windsor Peak will be dressed more like me, and I hate to stand out."

"Good luck with that," her sister laughed as she locked the door behind her. "Dating Patrick will have everyone staring at you, no matter what you're wearing."

"It's hard to get used to," she admitted. "Everywhere we go, it's like the whole room is just watching us. Or him, really."

"No, they're watching you too," her sister said. "The girl that he is dating is a hot topic online right now."

"What? Why didn't you tell me? Where are you seeing this?"

"Relax," Zoe laughed. They started walking down the sidewalk toward town, being only a few blocks from Main Street meant Zoe didn't have to worry about what she had to drink, since she could walk home. "Twitter, TikTok, Instagram, everywhere you can think of, really. Every picture has a million comments demanding answers about you."

"There can't be a lot of pictures of me," she objected.

"No, but even just a promo for his next movie, people are jumping all over it asking if he broke up with Natalie, and who you are." Zoe bumped her hip lightly. "Nothing to worry about, really. No one is answering them."

"It's still really weird, having all these strangers asking questions about you."

"True," Zoe agreed. "Speaking of that, and before we get to the girls, I wanted to ask if you had heard anything from Hoyt lately?"

"No," she shook her head. "Nothing since I told him to leave town and not come back. Well, the one text asking me to pay his bill at the Inn since I was 'rolling in it' now."

"You didn't." Zoe looked horrified.

"Absolutely not," she confirmed. "And I deleted the message quickly, so Patrick wouldn't see it by accident and try to deal with it."

"Good," Zoe said as she pulled the door open to Windsor Palace. "I'm glad he's out of our lives. Good riddance."

"I do wish he had come with better intentions," Emma said softly.

"As long as I have you back in my life, I don't care about any other family." Zoe said it so firmly before pushing into the crowd towards their friends, Emma couldn't question her any further. Putting the thoughts about her sister's relationship with her mother, and any thoughts about their shared father, to the back of her mind, she greeted their friends.

Kendra had reserved a small area in the back of the bar, far from the dartboard and TV's broadcasting sports games. Comfortable club chairs circled a large round table, perfect for having book club meetings, or for friends to catch up after a long week. Shea and Kendra were already sitting, along with friends Christine, Tina and Julie, when they arrived.

"Sorry to be late," Zoe chirped as she sat next to Christine. "I had to play dress up with my little sister."

"You look great," Shea said with a kind smile. "Have you met everyone?"

"Yes, thank you. Nice to see you all," she sat in the last empty seat, between Shea and Kendra. She had met all of the other women at the restaurant as she spent time with Zoe, although hadn't talked to them one on one at all. The rest of them had a comfortable camaraderie that showcased years of friendship, and even Zoe seemed to fit right in. It felt as though everyone was watching her as she crossed her legs, and she felt a blush start to creep up her face. "Thanks for inviting me."

"Of course," Kendra said easily. "We try to get together at least once a month, more if we can. Our husbands seem to have no issues finding time to golf together, or come out to watch a game, but it's harder for us somehow."

"Children, work, pets," Tina counted on her fingers as she smiled. "Not to mention I love being in my pajamas by seven, so this is a rare occasion."

"Amen to that," Christine smiled. "Anyone who's not pregnant, order a drink so we can live vicariously."

"I did get us some non-alcoholic champagne, if you want that," Kendra laughed.

The women all ordered their drinks, and Kendra asked for some appetizers to be brought out. Zoe and Christine settled into a quiet conversation, as did Julie and Tina, leaving Emma to squirm between Patrick's two sisters-in-law.

"Relax," Kendra laughed, reaching over to squeeze her hand. "We don't bite."

"I'm so glad to have a chance to get to know you better," Shea said. "When we are all together, it can be a little chaotic. But Patrick seems happier than I've ever seen him. Although I haven't known him nearly as long as you, Kendra. What do you think?"

"Oh, that's easy. He's never been this happy. Or brought a woman around the family, that has never happened. Even when Dan lived with him in California, he said he rarely ever saw the women Patrick was dating," she said. "It's always been like he wants to keep the two parts of his life separate."

"What was he like as a kid?" Emma couldn't help but ask, wanting to know everything about him she could.

"He has always been so sweet, so thoughtful. Even Dan and Jake couldn't ever really pick on him, they just fought with each other," Kendra said, causing her and Shea to laugh. "Much like now, I guess. But Patrick was off limits to them, and they wouldn't tolerate anyone else picking on him. Dan and I were never in school with him, since we're older, but he was Mr. Popular."

"Of course he was," Shea said with a smile.

"All the girls in town had a crush on him," Kendra said. "He was the best athlete of the three of them, but if you tell Dan I said that, I'll deny it. He would have been Prom king if he had stayed here in high school, but by mid-way through junior year, he was living in California."

"Remember when that show started? As soon as he came on screen, all of my friends were in love," Shea said. "It was a little weird, since we all knew him from high school, and he was younger than us. Did you watch it?"

Emma shook her head. "No, I didn't. I'm a little younger, and I didn't have much access to TV around then."

"Patrick mentioned to us that you grew up in foster care," Shea said softly. "I have some students who are in that program, although the local families who foster sound better than what you had."

"It wasn't terrible," she said quickly. "I wasn't abused or anything, like some kids I talked to. But there also wasn't a lot of nice things around, and we had to compete with each other for the little bit we had. I wouldn't recommend it."

"Compete for what?" Kendra asked.

"Clothes, food, bedding, towels. Anything, really," Emma said. "Foster parents don't want to spend a lot on their foster kids usually. They only get a certain amount of money for having us, so they spread it as far as they can. But it was hard when I was moved into a new house and didn't know the rules yet, if that makes sense."

"I'm sorry you went through that," Shea said. "Your mom didn't have any family or friends who could take you in?"

"No, she was an only child and her parents had already passed. They tried to find some random distant cousins, but finally gave up. My mom's friends were all in similar situations as us, living paycheck to paycheck and trying to provide for their own kids. It wouldn't have been fair to take me in."

"And Zoe's mom," Kendra asked quietly.

"Is horrible and not worth our time," Zoe's voice proclaimed loudly. "Simple as that."

"Sorry," Kendra said. "I know that's a touchy subject."

"To say the least," Zoe mumbled as she threw back the rest of her drink and waved for another. "Let's change the subject."

Christine jumped in, saving the moment by sharing stories of her husband's attempt to put together their nursery furniture. They were all laughing again within minutes, and Emma could see Zoe relax again as she sipped her second drink. At some point, she would need to get to the bottom of what had gotten so ugly between Zoe and her mother, but this was clearly not the time.

***

Hours passed in what felt like minutes, and when everyone switched from laughter to hiding yawns, they all started to make excuses to leave. As they started to stand, the door opened and JJ came in, followed by Jake, Dan and Ryan. Emma strained her neck to hopefully catch a glimpse of Patrick behind his brothers and friends, but the door closed.

"We came to bring our women home," Ryan declared, perching on the arm of Christine's chair.

"You spend three hours with these guys, and now you're a caveman?" Christine laughed as he wrapped an arm around her.

Emma watched as Jake urged Shea to sit up, only to take her seat and pull her down on his lap. Dan stood behind Kendra's chair, rubbing her shoulders lightly.

"Who's with Calle?" Kendra asked, looking up at him.

"Charlie, of course," Jake and Dan both responded.

"I hope she's asleep," Kendra said.

"She was," Jake assured her. "She forced Charlie to watch a Princess movie with him but fell asleep ten minutes in, so he was able to switch to something else. He texted me a little while ago asking if it was alright to carry her up to bed."

"He's so sweet," Kendra said, wiping a tear away.

"No," Dan said. "No crying. These hormones are out of control."

"You don't get to tell me if I can cry or not," she pointed out. "Let's go home so I can do it in private."

"I'll find a way to get you smiling," Dan said with a wink before pulling her to her feet.

"You ready?" Jake asked Shea, who looked half asleep.

"Yes, please."

"Need me to carry you?" He laughed as she struggled to get up.

"No, that would be embarrassing," Shea said. "Good night, everyone."

"You'll make sure everyone gets home safe?" Jake asked JJ, who was already settled into Kendra's seat.

"You know it," he said as the two fist bumped, ignoring the women's eye rolls.

"We're all set," Julie said, collecting her bag. "Thanks anyway, but we can make it from here."

The two friends said goodbye, followed by Christine and Ryan, so it was only JJ, Zoe and Emma left. "I'll just use the restroom," she said to Zoe, knowing her sister wasn't paying attention. Zoe and JJ seemed locked in some silent battle, and she wanted no part of it.

Locking herself in the stall in the bathroom, she checked her phone and was surprised to see no messages from Patrick. Assuming he just wanted her to enjoy the girl's night, she sent a quick text asking what he was up to before heading back in her sister's direction.

JJ had moved closer, leaning so close to Zoe that she was surprised they weren't kissing. Zoe still had her glare on, so Emma quickly changed directions, heading out the back door for the short walk to her sister's house. She texted Zoe when she got in the Jeep for the quick drive home, assuring her she had only had one drink and was fine.

Pulling up the driveway that led to Patrick's property, she felt a keen disappointment when his house stood big and dark in front of her. Her hopes to dash into his house and end the night with him were gone, between the lack of response to her text and the darkness of his house. It was unusual that his brothers were out without him, and she felt a pit start to grow in her stomach at the thought. What would have kept him away, other than to avoid her?

She stood silently outside the stable long enough to get cold, hoping a light would turn on or her phone would chime. When neither happened, she forced herself to walk into the small cottage and pull herself together. Up until that moment, she hadn't realized how heavily she had grown to depend on him. Or how quickly it could destroy her if he was out of her life, something she had promised herself she would never let happen.

Chapter 27

Hoyt answered the door to his room at the Inn almost instantly when Patrick knocked, looking too eager. It was like looking a fox in the eye, knowing they wanted to eat you, and it sent a chill down his spine. Coming had been a mistake, and he turned to leave before they had said a word.

"You can't be leaving so soon," Hoyt asked. "Without even hearing about the plan Emma and I made?"

Patrick turned slowly, watching as the older man sat in the chair by the small desk. The only word that could be used to describe him was oily, and he felt dirty even being around him. But the words had sunk in, and he couldn't shake them enough to take the extra steps to leave.

"I heard you were a soft one," Hoyt continued. "Always wanting to help some lost soul out there. Almost as if you have something you have to atone for, isn't it? I have to admit, you fell for it far easier than I would have ever guessed."

"What are you talking about?" Patrick demanded.

"It was my idea, of course. Emma is too dim to figure out a plan like this on her own. But that girl is pretty enough to catch any fish I put in the pond for her, you just happened to have been the biggest one yet."

"She didn't know who I was," Patrick insisted. "And you weren't here. What are you trying to claim?"

"Oh, she knew. She wasn't happy about having to sleep out in that stable of yours, I'll tell you that," Hoyt laughed. "Imagine my little princess having to get down and dirty. But she did it, because Daddy told her to. And she did everything else, didn't she?"

Patrick felt sick, visions of his time with Emma running through his head as Hoyt laughed.

"You didn't really fall for her, did you? That would be a shame. Man like you, there are a million women out there. You don't need some trailer trash like her bringing you down," Hoyt snickered. "Here's how it works. You'll give me a cashier's check, and I'll have the little tramp disappear. Then I'll delete everything she has been recording of you."

"What are you talking about?"

"Oh, she got your good side, don't worry about that. I can't say I enjoy watching these videos, given I'm her father. But I make myself watch just enough to make sure we have the goods," Hoyt grinned. "And we can sell it to the highest bidder, or you can pay up."

"There is no way she—"

Hoyt held up a flash drive. "It's all right here. Looks small, but it's worth a pretty penny, I know that. I already reached out to some folks who would love to fly out tomorrow and take it off my hands. But I thought I'd give you a chance first."

"How much do you want?"

"Good question," Hoyt spun the drive between his fingers. "Guess that depends how much it's worth to you, doesn't it?"

"I need some time," Patrick ground out, desperate to be out of the room.

"You have twenty-four hours. Then I sell it."

Patrick almost fell out of the room; he was so determined to get out quickly. His stomach was rolling, and he knew it was only a matter of minutes before the contents came up, so he rushed to the lobby and locked himself in the bathroom. After emptying his lunch into the toilet, he splashed cold water onto his face and tried to wrap his head around what Hoyt had said.

Emma had set him up. Jake and Dan had been right when they were suspicious of her, when they tried to warn him. Now he looked like the biggest fool, not just to his family but to the world if this got out. And the worst part of it was that he had believed everything she said. He had even fallen in love with her, and in a moment, his dreams for the future were gone.

When he finally got himself together, he drove around town for an hour before finally making his way back home. Of course, it only felt like a home because of the time he had spent in there with Emma, a truth that stabbed him all over again. He had spent most of the previous day pacing around the house, debating his actions, before hiding like a coward in his room when he knew Emma would be coming home. Every room he had stepped into had smelled like her, or he was forced to revisit the bond they had made in these rooms. The house that had been such a comfort to him all these weeks now held only reminders of her, which he couldn't bear right now. Veering at the last second, he turned and headed back to town instead.

Without thinking, he hit the speed dial on his car's screen to call Dan's cell phone. The phone rang twice before Dan greeted him, and Patrick was terse. "Meet me at the Palace, please. And call Jake."

"What's wrong?" His brother's voice sounded concerned.

"I'll tell you when I see you," he answered. "Don't call Dad."

"I'll be there in five," his brother promised.

He pulled into the alley to park behind the bar and was relieved when he opened the back door to the kitchen and didn't see Zoe. Although he didn't blame her for what had happened, any reminder of Emma right now would bring him to his knees.

Kendra was behind the bar when he came in, and he debated sitting at the bar versus a table in the corner. The bar would allow him to tell his brothers what had happened without having to look them in their eyes, he decided. He made his way to the end where Jake preferred to sit with his back against the wall, nodding at Kendra as he sat.

"Hey, you," Kendra greeted him, before frowning. "We aren't open yet. What's wrong?"

"Dan will tell you later," he said. "I can only get through it once. I'm sorry."

"Can I listen when you tell him?"

"Sure," he sighed.

"It can't be a problem too big to fix," she promised, reaching over to squeeze his hand. "Especially with Dan in your corner."

"Jake is on his way too," Patrick said as the door opened, and Dan walked in.

He watched numbly as his brother smiled at his wife and walked around to greet her with a long kiss. "This is the nice part of my brother having a crisis," Dan said to her. "I get a little mid-day check in with you."

"If you don't mind, I'm sitting right here," Patrick groaned.

"Jake is on his way," Dan responded without looking over. "Let me enjoy my wife for a minute."

Patrick dropped his head onto his crossed arms and waited until he heard the door open again, then Jake's heavy boots crossing the room to where he sat. He glanced over at his brothers, seeing the look they exchanged from either side of him where they had settled in, and took a deep breath.

"I just met with Hoyt," he said. Seeing the confused look on all three faces, he explained. "Emma and Zoe's father."

"I thought he left town?" Kendra asked, leaning her hip against the bar.

"I did too, but I got a message from him saying he had important information and that I should come to his room at the Inn," Patrick said. "I went there this morning, feeling badly that I was going behind Emma's back. But he had said it was between us, and I didn't want to worry her."

"What was it that he had to tell you," Jake asked. "And why the secrecy? I don't like this guy."

"Me neither," Patrick sighed. "He said that they were playing me. Emma was planted by him, and she recorded me. Or us. Everything, apparently. And if I don't hand him a big check tomorrow, he's going to sell the footage."

"What the—" Jake's stool screeched as he pushed it back. "I'm going to kill them both."

"Sit for a minute, Jake." Kendra said it calmly and quietly enough for Jake to pay attention. "I don't believe any of this, Patrick."

"That's what happened, Kendra. He told me himself."

"What did Emma say?"

"I haven't talked to her," he said. "I was so furious, and embarrassed. I didn't even want to tell you guys, but I had to. If I withdraw that kind of money, it will raise red flags and Dan would find out anyway."

"I always find out," Dan said ominously. "But that's not the important thing. Kendra is right about part of it, at least. Did you see the footage he claims to have?"

"No," Patrick said. "I don't want to sit there with him and watch that."

"Tough," Dan replied. "You aren't giving this guy a dime on an empty threat. For all you know, it's blank. That's the first thing we need to figure out."

"And then you need to talk to Emma," Kendra said gently. "Patrick, I've seen her with you. She's not faking anything."

He shook his head, refusing to let the thought of her innocence enter his brain. "I can't deal with that. How would I trust that what she's telling me is the truth?"

Kendra looked at Jake, then Dan, as if waiting for them to speak. When it seemed like they wouldn't, her mouth opened, but Jake beat her to it. "I'll talk to her," he offered. "Let me see what the truth is there. You guys deal with this jerk of a father she has."

"Maybe Shea and I should talk to her," Kendra offered.

"No," Jake shook his head. "I don't want you two within a mile of this. And I should be able to tell if she's telling the truth or not."

"I'm sorry," Kendra said softly to Patrick, her hand on his arm. "I hate this for you."

"I should be used to it," he responded without thinking. "I thought I was safe here, away from it. In California, every place I go there is some girl who wants to sleep with me so she can say she did, or thinking I'll get her a part. And I have to worry about stuff like this, so I'm so careful. I never get involved with women I don't know, I stick with people in my circle, or friends of friends. Even the women that I do trust enough to date, I make sure we're always at my house, that I'm always in control. That way I'm not looking like a fool if she drops me for someone else, or if she starts talking to the tabloids."

"They know better than to do that," Dan said, referring to the non-disclosure agreement that his assistant always had women sign. It had always made Patrick feel dirty but protecting his image had been important. And now that was all out the window, thanks to his own stupidity.

"I think we should get JJ involved," Jake said. "He should know what's going on. If this does turn out to be a lie, he can chase them out of town."

"I really don't want more people to know about this," Patrick groaned.

"He's your friend," Dan said. "Jake's right, let's get him and decide how to approach this."

"And I'll head out to talk to Emma," Jake said. "Do you want her gone no matter what?"

"I don't know," he said. "I feel like I should at least talk to her, but I don't know."

"Patrick," Kendra's voice chastised him. "You're assuming she's the bad guy here. She might have no idea what is going on. Don't assume it's over based on what a stranger is telling you, when your own experience is the opposite of what he's saying. I've never seen you so happy, and you just told us how hard it is for you to trust a woman. What if she's innocent and you throw her away?"

"What if she's not?" He challenged back. "How could I trust her if there was any possibility that even one percent of what Hoyt said was true? What if he planted her there but then she decided she liked me, or how she got there was true, but she recorded me for him. I don't know how to move past that."

"You're going off someone you don't know," she argued. "You know Emma. She isn't capable of this, and if she is, she fooled us all. But in my heart, I don't think that any of this is true. I think she loves you and would do anything to not hurt you. And I think you know that deep down inside too."

His mind flashed again through all their moments together. Quiet nights by the fire, talking about their favorite books or playing cards. Nights out with his brothers and their wives, laughing and feeling like she was the perfect addition to their family. Waking up before her and watching her sleep, thinking that he could never tire of her face.

"Maybe I'm meant to be alone," he responded, turning to walk from the bar.

"Or maybe you'll be brave enough to let her love you." Kendra's parting shot hit him right in the hole where his heart used to sit, as he let the door close behind him.

Chapter 28

Emma checked her phone the second she woke up, shocked to see no message from Patrick. They had made plans for her next day off over the weekend, looking forward to taking some of the tamer horses out on the trail. Since she had started learning to ride with him, it had become a favorite activity of hers, especially when he was by her side. A day off together had sounded like heaven, but now she felt the pit in her stomach that had landed the night before grow into something bigger. She knew something was wrong, but until she saw him and found out what, she would keep herself busy, starting with a visit to Whiskey.

"Hey sweet girl," she whispered, nuzzling the horse. "How's it going out here?"

"She's ready to go run around the paddock if you want to take her out," the stable manager said. "I can put a lead on her if you want to try and walk with her. We're still trying to get her to let us put a saddle on, but she's getting better being around people now."

"What do you think happened to her?"

"Honestly," he tilted his hat back and studied the horse. "I wish I knew. I think she was a mama, because she favors that little colt as if he were her own. Someone either ignored her or was mean to her, and from what I hear, she went through the ringer with the traders."

"I can't believe no one wanted her," she said.

"You'd be surprised," he responded. "She didn't look like this, she was underweight and dirty. Plus, she has that attitude to contend with. It's easier for the people at auctions to take the young ones, the ones who look like they can still do work."

"You really think they would have killed her if the rescue hadn't saved her?"

"Oh, yes. Her next stop from this auction was going to be Texas, and from there it's a short ride across the border to Mexico. For her, the hardest part would have been getting to Texas," he explained. "Crammed into a trailer not meant for horses, no access to food or water. It's no way to treat an animal, that's for sure."

"I'm glad she ended up here," Emma dropped a kiss on the horse's nose.

"Think she's mighty glad of that herself," he smiled as he clipped the lead on. "Here you go, bring her out nice and slow, make sure she knows you're in charge."

They walked to the paddock, Whiskey happy to trot alongside her for a few laps before she started tossing her head and looking like she wanted more speed. Unclipping the lead, she stepped back to the fence and watched as the horse raced around a few laps, before she caught sight of a car pulling into the driveway. Expecting Patrick, she felt a stir of disappointment when Jake stepped out of the truck and walked in her direction.

He hopped up on the fence to sit beside her and sat in silence for longer than she could bear. "Hi, Jake."

"How you doing," he asked without meeting her eyes.

"I'm good," she said. "Patrick's not here."

"I know, I just left him."

"You did?" She was surprised and trying to wrap her head around the last twenty-four hours of silence from Patrick. "Is everything alright?"

"Not really," he said, removing his sunglasses and tucking them into the front pocket of his flannel shirt before meeting her eyes finally. "He got quite the shock, as it happens."

"What do you mean?"

"Do you have anything you want to tell me before I start asking questions?" His eyes drilled into her, and it felt like he could see straight into her soul.

"Jake, I have no idea what you're talking about. Is Patrick okay?" Her hands were sweating, and she wished she were still holding onto Whiskey, or anything that could give her some support.

"He's okay," Jake responded, then paused and looked deep in thought. "I'm just going to lay it out, and you can tell me what's true and what's not."

"I appreciate that," she said softly.

"Your father reached out to Patrick, demanded they have a meeting," Jake said, the words cutting through her. "When Patrick showed up, he was confronted with the news that you had been playing him this whole time. Not just playing him, but also recording everything and giving it to your father. Which he is now using to get money from Patrick."

"What—"

"Before you say anything, I want you to think carefully," he warned. "I'm very protective of my family, and Patrick especially. I was starting to like you, and I was happy to see him falling for someone. Shea raves about you, and I can't quite figure out how becoming friends with my wife would have benefited you if this was all a game. But you and I, we're a little alike, aren't we?"

"How so?" she asked, feeling numb inside as she did.

"We've both seen the darker parts of the world," he explained. "And my family, they haven't seen much of it. They don't know what it feels like to have no options; to think you've run out of anything good that could happen to you. And I was starting to soften for you, because Shea kept pointing out how you seemed less skittish the more we got to know you. And she compared it to how I was when I came home, and didn't trust anything that resembled happiness, because I was sure it would be taken away. I started to relate to you, believe it or not, thinking that we had that in common. But maybe you're a good enough liar that everything you told us was bull, and you were just here to take advantage of my brother after all."

"That's not true," she whispered.

"Which part," he snapped. "The part where you screwed my brother to get a check for your dad? Or the part that you grew up alone and didn't know you had any family to plot with?"

"I didn't know him," she said, feeling hot tears on her cheeks. "That's the truth. Zoe knows that, and she wouldn't lie. I did grow up alone, I do have no one. Other than Zoe, but I hadn't seen her in a long time before I came here. I thought for a brief moment that things might finally be taking a turn in my direction, that maybe things would go well for me."

"Explain that, please." His voice was quieter, but it was a demand, not a question.

"I would never hurt Patrick. I certainly wouldn't hurt him for a man who walked out on my mom and never looked back when she was pregnant," she sobbed. "I don't know what he says he has, but it's a lie. I didn't give him anything. I haven't seen Hoyt since the day at the diner when I told him no to moving in here, that he was selfish and to leave me alone. I didn't want to take anything from Patrick as it was, never mind take something from him like this."

She jumped off the fence, feeling her knees buckle beneath her as if her whole body was ready to crumble. Turning, she faced Jake's boots, because she couldn't bring herself to meet his eyes. "I'm sorry you think that I would be capable of that. I'm not, but I don't have any way of proving that to you."

Jake hopped down and stood next to her, silently studying her face. "It's really all a lie?"

She nodded, feeling a lump in her throat so big she didn't know if she could speak around it. "It is."

"Okay then." Jake turned to leave, climbing over the fence in one swift move.

"Jake," she called, her voice barely a whisper, but enough to cause him to turn. "Why didn't he ask me himself?"

He turned, his face shaded by the hat and sunglasses he had put on, so she couldn't make out his expression. For a moment she was sure he wouldn't answer, but as Whiskey came up and nudged her shoulder, he finally did. "His first instinct is to trust and second is to watch out for himself. My first is to look for the danger, see the threats even when they look innocent. I hope this hasn't broken his trusting nature, but he was too shaken up to see any truth here."

She would have fallen to the ground if Whiskey wasn't there, pressing against her as if she was trying to give a hug. She pressed her face into the horses' neck, wrapping her arms around to feel the warmth and security offered. Before stepping away from the horse, she whispered into her ear for what she assumed would be the last time. "I'll miss you, beautiful girl. Go run and play with the other horses, you're safe here and don't have to worry."

She wished she could say the same about herself, but it was time to pack. She knew better than to stay where she wasn't welcome.

***

Hours later she was tucked into the couch at Zoe's, after having told her sister the whole story. Showing up at her house with just her small backpack of pre-Patrick belongings had almost broken her again. Only the relief that she had one person to turn to when things had gone wrong, one person who would take her in unconditionally, had gotten her through the afternoon. Zoe had called in to work, taking great care to make sure she spoke to the manager of the restaurant rather than Kendra.

"I'll have to find a new job," she raged after hanging up. "I can't work for them anymore if they think so little of my sister.

There's a restaurant up in Burlington that keeps trying to get me to move, maybe we can both live up there."

"You aren't moving for me, Zo. That's ridiculous," she said, wiping yet another tear from her face. "Give me a couple of days to make a plan, that's all I ask."

"I'm going to kill him, you know."

"You can't be mad at Patrick," she said. "He didn't do anything wrong, really."

"I'm not talking about him," she said ominously. "Hoyt is the one that will pay for this."

"You aren't killing anyone. He's not worth going to jail for."

"I bet I could get JJ to look the other way," Zoe said. "Besides, it would be worth it. What kind of person does this? Only appears in his daughter's life to try and make money off her? And destroys his kid in the process?"

"I don't know," Emma admitted. "I thought he was gone."

"Maybe I can tie him to train tracks," Zoe suggested. "Or throw him off a cliff."

"No," Emma shook her head. "We just need to get him out of our lives once and for all."

Zoe's phone dinged for the hundredth time that hour, and she swiped furiously to unlock it. "JJ wants you to file a restraining order, and he won't shut up about it."

"Do you think I should?"

"I don't know that it will do any good," Zoe said. "He's already done the damage, right? I don't think he's going to try and hurt you because he won't get his way."

"It hurts already," Emma said. "This was the worst way he could have hurt me."

"I know," Zoe dropped to the couch and pulled her in close. "We'll get through it. I think you and Patrick will work it out."

"How? He won't trust me, and I don't blame him."

"But you didn't do anything wrong," her sister said. "You left everything there, even the phone he had given you. You and your sad little backpack are giving him some space, and when he realizes what he's missing, he'll want to make it right."

"My backpack isn't sad," Emma sniffed. "It's durable."

"And so are you, so you're going to get through this. Let's watch some sad movies and drink too much wine, and then things will look better tomorrow." Zoe stood to leave the room, then turned back. "And for the record, he'd be a total fool to let you go based this. Especially someone he has no reason to trust, and when he's spent months getting to know you and who you are and should trust you. What Hoyt did is no reflection on you, or me, and we both need to recognize that. He's a scumbag who happened to donate some sperm to our moms, and that's it. You are not letting him ruin your life. You will always have a safe space here with me, and I do believe that Patrick will come around."

"What if he doesn't?"

"Then he's not the man I thought he was," Zoe said. "And none of the Burrows are the people I thought they were. They know you. They like you. They have to recognize this as what it is, a shameless gamble by a loser to get a fat payout."

"I wish I could talk to him," Emma admitted.

"Hoyt?" Her sister sounded and looked horrified at the thought.

"No," she shook her head, feeling more tears threaten. "Patrick. It's horrible, I miss him so much already, but I know I can't go to him. If he trusted me at all, he would have come to me immediately when Hoyt confronted him. I have to let him go, even though I feel like it's going to kill me."

Chapter 29

"What's the plan?" JJ walked into Dan and Kendra's apartment looking ready to go fight someone, with Mike at his heels.

"Hey guys," Dan greeted them. "We're waiting for Jake and then we can figure this out. My suggestion is to lure Hoyt into demanding money from him while you're in earshot, so you can arrest him. But Patrick is worried that arresting him just keeps him in town longer."

"That's true," JJ nodded. "He would have to appear in court, so it could keep him here."

"I can take care of him," Mike offered.

"Thanks," Patrick said. "I appreciate that, but this is my mess."

The door opened and Jake entered, tossing his hat and jacket on the rack by the door before joining them in the kitchen. He grabbed a bottle of water from the refrigerator and drank half in one gulp, while Patrick waited anxiously for his brother's report.

"What happened?" He finally demanded, needing to know.

"I talked to Emma," Jake said. "I don't think she knew anything about this."

"Really," Dan asked, doubt in his voice. "Then how does he have a flash drive full of videos of Patrick?"

"Does he?" Jake's gaze never left Patrick's face. "Did he show you them?"

"No," Patrick said slowly. "Just held it up."

"It could be blank," Jake said. "Or maybe some photos and videos of you from a distance. Did he ever set foot in this house?"

"No," Patrick shook his head with certainty. "I always made sure the doors were locked and the alarm on, even if I just went out back to the cottage or stable. I only leave it unlocked when I'm waiting for you guys to come over, or if I know Emma will be back soon. Plus, I have cameras all around the outside of the house and stable that records any movement. I have heard too many horror stories about finding fans naked in bed, I never wanted to deal with that."

"If you're sure," Jake said. "Worst case is some unclear videos through windows. But I doubt he even has that, so the first thing you need to do is demand to see what is on the drive."

"No, the first thing I need is for you to tell me about your conversation with Emma," Patrick countered. "What did she say?"

"She said she knows nothing about this," Jake said. "She was shocked and said she hasn't seen or heard from Hoyt since she told him to leave town."

"And you believe her," Dan speculated.

"I do." Jake placed both hands on the countertop and looked at Patrick. "I've seen enough bad liars and a lot of good ones to know when someone is lying to me. I gave her a hard time when you first introduced us, and I was just starting to soften towards her, because Shea was so sure she was a good person. And that she was the one that you would settle down with, be happy with. I've been selfish in my life, and I've hurt a lot of people, including those that I love. I know what that looks like in someone. Emma didn't know anything about this."

Patrick sank into the chair behind him, the relief giving him one second of happiness before awareness of what he had done hit him. He hadn't trusted her and had been ready to throw everything away. And while the majority of him wanted to run to her now, beg her forgiveness, a small voice in his head warned him not to. That this hurt he had been feeling could be ten times worse if he let himself fall further for her, build a life and a family. What if this time was wrong, but something terrible happened down the road?

"I need to be alone," he said quietly. "I think maybe I should go back to California for a while."

"First we need to fix this issue with Hoyt," Dan demanded. "Then you can be alone to spiral. Here's what we're going to do…"

***

Patrick settled himself at the bar at Windsor Peak, grateful that the early afternoon hour had the place almost completely empty. Kendra gave him a wide berth after handing him a cold beer, having been alerted to the plan. He kept his head down until the stool next to him scraped back, and Hoyt settled into it.

"Glad you came around so quickly," Hoyt grinned. "Let's take care of business and I can get out of your way."

"First," Patrick said, holding up a finger. "I need a few things, starting with a guarantee that once you have the money this never happens again."

"Unless you decide to start sleeping with one of my other daughters," Hoyt laughed. "This is the only copy, and I'm going to give it to you."

"In exchange for what?"

"What do you mean? For the money you're going to give me."

"Speaking of that, you never gave me an amount."

"No, but you're a smart man. You know this is worth at least a couple mil."

"That's what you think you'd get for selling this?" Patrick forced himself to meet the man's eyes before taking a long drink of his beer.

"Oh, more than that," Hoyt bragged. "Some of the people are offering more than ten. But I want to protect my little girl, of course."

"The same one you used to get the footage?"

"Hey, she was a willing participant," Hoyt said. "Don't worry about her."

Patrick felt his blood boiling but forced himself to stay in character. Thinking of this as a role was the only way he could stomach sitting next to this scumbag. "Second thing I need," he said, reaching into the bag next to him and pulling out a laptop. "Is to see what's on there."

Hoyt blanched, his eyes darting around the bar as he thought. "No freebies," he said feebly.

"You want a couple million dollars," Patrick said drolly. "Just based on your word that the drive has what you said it does?"

"Yes," Hoyt insisted.

"What is on there, exactly?"

"Like I said before, she recorded everything. Nudes, intimacy, everything."

"Here's how this is going to go," Dan's voice on the other side caused Hoyt's head to snap around. "We are going to see what's on that drive. And if it is what you say it is, we're going to have you arrested. And if it isn't what you say it is, we're also going to have your arrested."

"Hey, man," Hoyt threw his hands up. "I don't know what you think you heard, but you must have misunderstood."

"I heard plenty," Dan said. "Give him the USB."

Hoyt attempted to put the drive back into his pocket, but was stopped by Jake, who had stepped behind the barstool. "I'll take that," he said, pulling it from the man's fingers.

"Hey," Hoyt argued, arms held behind him by Jake. "This is harassment. You can't do this."

"Oh, but we are," Jake replied. "Sit quietly and I won't hurt you."

"You just threatened me," Hoyt sputtered.

Patrick stuck the drive into the side of the laptop and opened the file explorer. Nothing showed on the screen, so he closed it and tried again. "There's nothing on here," he said. The reality of what happened hit him again, and he stood so fast the chair fell behind him. "I'm going to kill you for doing this to her."

"No one will kill anyone," JJ said calmly, as Mike stepped between them. "I'm going to take Hoyt for a little walk, explain his options. Both of which end with him leaving Windsor Peak and never coming back, but one will be a little easier than the other."

Patrick watched as JJ, followed by Mike, marched the older man out of the bar, confident that they would never see him again. The fear that he would also never see Emma again, and the worry that he should never see her again, ran through him at the same time. Before he could decide which was stronger, Kendra crossed the bar and pointed at him.

"You, upstairs." She turned and kissed Dan quickly. "Only him, sorry, boys. You can all have drinks on the house, including JJ and Mike when they come back."

He followed her up the stairs, surprised to see Shea and Stella sitting in the living room of the apartment. His head was still spinning, trying to wrap around what had happened and how to move forward.

"Where's Calle?" he asked, looking around for his niece.

"Charlie took her for ice cream," Shea explained. "We needed you to focus."

"On what?"

"On your heart, honey," Stella said softly. "How are you feeling?"

"Miserable," he admitted. "And conflicted."

"Of course you're miserable," Kendra said. "You're a big idiot."

"Hey," he tried to object, knowing it was true.

"Let me start, girls," Stella instructed them. "Patrick, of the three of you, I always felt like you were the hardest nut to crack. Sure, you would tell me stories and share parts of your life, but you have always kept a part of you locked away. I thought it was because we were so far apart physically all these years, but it's more than that."

"I talk to you all the time," he protested.

"You do," she said. "You tell me about what other people are doing, or funny things that happened. But we don't talk about your feelings, and maybe I let you get away with that for too long."

"Have you ever been in love before?" Kendra asked.

He paused, looking from face to face, thinking about the question. It didn't escape him that they all knew he was in love with Emma, even without asking. "No," he finally said. "I don't think I have. I thought I was once or twice, but now I know that was wrong."

"Do you feel like you've opened up to her, really let her in?" Shea asked gently.

"I do," he nodded. "More than anyone."

"That must be scary," Stella said. "Knowing that someone has seen what you keep locked away from the rest of the world so well. Even from us."

"I really don't think that's true," he argued again. "I feel like I'm very involved and open with everyone, especially this last year. Look at what we all went through with Jake, and then with Calle."

"Yes," Kendra nodded. "You were a rock when Calle was missing, and I don't honestly know if we would have gotten her back without you. That scares me to this day. But at the end of it, when Jake broke down and Dan was a mess, you still had to be the one to hold it together."

"You're always looking for how you can help," Shea said.

"And never looking for anyone to help you," Stella added.

He stood and started pacing around the small room, unable to sit still for one more second. "I get what you're saying, you want me to fix things with Emma."

"If it's not right with Emma, we don't want you to force it," Stella said. "But we've all seen you with her, and we think it's real. What we want is for you to be open to the possibility of someone loving you, someone putting you first. I don't think you know how to do that."

"Dad did it," he protested, hating that he sounded like a kid. "And Dan. They both moved to Los Angeles for my sake."

"They did," Stella nodded. "And neither of them would trade that for anything. Even though it changed you."

"What do you mean?" His head whipped around to stare at the woman he had always thought of as his mother.

She stood and crossed to where he stood, placing her hands on his arms. "You came home always looking over your shoulder. Unable to relax fully, not really sharing a lot of what your experience had been. You were such an open, fun kid, and now it's like the weight of the world is on your shoulders. You don't have to solve everyone's problems. And not everyone is out to get something from you."

"Emma isn't," Shea said confidently. "And neither am I, or Kendra. Or JJ and Mike."

"The one thing I wish you hadn't learned in Hollywood is that everything is superficial," Stella said. "There are good people there, people who have been friends to you. Not just your own team, who have to, but people who consider you a friend. Like Liam, Zane and Natalie. But you keep them at arm's length, too afraid to let anyone close to you."

"I was so green when I went there," he said slowly. "I learned quickly what it will do to you if you're open to every sad story, every person trying to glom on to you. It's easier to just avoid it all, or it has been all these years."

"But what have you missed out on during those years," Kendra challenged. "Look at how stubborn Dan and I were, refusing to be open to the possibility of a future together."

"And how sure Jake was that happiness wasn't in his future," Shea added. "Thinking that Charlie was better off without him. That's not true, and it's not true that you have to be alone."

"We love you, and want you to be happy," Stella said. "It's time for you to do some hard thinking about how you can help yourself, instead of just everyone around you. People who love you want more than what you can give them, or what problems you can solve. Make sure you can give that to Emma if you decide to go beg for forgiveness."

Shea reached over to squeeze his hand. "I know I'm the newest to the family, but you've been wonderful to me. As much as I appreciate all you did for the wedding, what I love the most is when you're sitting with us. When I see you fully relaxed and enjoying your family, that's when I think I see the real you."

"She's right." Stella reached over and squeezed his hand. "You are more than the good deed you do for people."

"Like paying off my mortgage," Kendra said, tears on her face.

"I didn't—"

"Oh, shut it, you big liar. I know it was you, it finally clicked for me." Kendra laughed and swiped at the tears. "Thank you, by the way."

"You're welcome," he said gruffly. "I really didn't want you to know."

"I appreciate it, but like Shea said, I'm just glad to have you as part of my family," Kendra said, eyes shining with tears. "Now go let yourself be in love and be happy like the rest of us, would you?"

He sighed, knowing it was true. He loved Emma, and he had never experienced this kind of love before. He had also never experienced this kind of pain before and wasn't sure which was greater. "I really appreciate all three of you, and I love you. But this whole thing has kicked me hard, and I don't know what to do."

"You do, deep down inside," Stella answered. "And it's not run off and hide. Go, talk to Emma. Give yourself a chance to love without worrying about what might happen."

Chapter 30

There was some relief in seeing the sun rise over the mountains surrounding the small town, after a long sleepless night. Emma was bundled in a blanket and sitting on the porch of her sister's house when Zoe came out with a steaming mug of coffee.

"Thanks," she said, accepting the hot drink.

"How long have you been out here," Zoe asked, shivering slightly.

"Just a little bit, I wanted to clear my head."

"How are you feeling? Did you sleep at all?" Zoe sat next to her and pulled part of the blanket over herself.

"No," Emma shook her head. "Every time I started to fall asleep, I thought maybe I heard your phone ring, or a knock on the door. But nothing."

"You don't know that he knows where you are," Zoe pointed out. "And you left your phone behind."

"It wouldn't be hard to figure it out," Emma sighed. "I'm sure you told JJ that I'm here."

"True," Zoe said. "But give it some time. Don't give up."

"I don't know what to do," Emma admitted. "I should leave town, this is his space. But I have barely started rebuilding my savings account, so I can't afford to go far."

"You aren't leaving me," Zoe said. "If you decided to leave, I'm going with you. We will figure it out, I promise."

"I'm not pulling you away from here. You've built a life, and it was a good life until I came to town."

"That's not true," Zoe said. "I was existing. Working nonstop and keeping everyone at arm's length. Since you came to town, I've been to girls' nights and even let JJ get to me. I belong now, because of you."

The two sisters sat side by side, silently watching the small town come to life around them. "I should go to work," Emma said suddenly. "It's not fair to Piper that I don't show up."

"You should," Zoe agreed. "Keep your mind off this."

"There's no way my mind can escape this," Emma said, thinking that her heart was too heavy for that. "But I'll try."

***

Emma spent the morning dodging questions from Piper and the locals who came into the bakery to pick up orders or grab a treat. Everyone had a smile on their face and greeted her by name, making her feel worse as the minutes ticked by. She really had become a part of this town, and the only thing worse than saying goodbye to Windsor Peak would be losing Patrick.

The bell over the door rang as the door opened and Patrick stepped in, as if conjured by the thought of him. The sight of him took her breath away, even though it had barely been two days since they had seen each other. Dark circles appeared under his eyes, and his clothes looked as though they had been hastily thrown on. Normally careful to make sure his clothes looked neat and matched, seeing him out in the sweatpants and hoodie he wore around the hou

se was a shock.

Piper's head popped out of the kitchen door before she slowly backed away and pulled it shut behind her. Though out of sight, Emma wouldn't be surprised to find out her boss had her ear pressed to the door, trying to figure out what was happening.

"Hi," Patrick said so softly she barely heard it.

"I can't do this here," she warned him, feeling the tears form.

"I know," he said. He looked as miserable as she felt, but she refused to let that little nugget of hope take form. "But you left your phone, and I didn't want to involve Zoe in this. Will you meet me when you finish?"

"Where?"

"I can come to Zoe's house if you would rather," he offered. "I assume you're staying with her."

"That's fine," she heard herself agreeing without giving herself a chance to think. Her brain was too tired, it couldn't overcome the strong urge to see him at least once more. "I'm leaving here at two."

"I'll be there," he said. He looked so sad, it was all she could do to not throw her arms around him. Reminding herself that he was likely going to break up with her officially in just a few hours, she gripped onto the counter in front of her to stay put. Watching him close the door behind him brought the tears back, but she forced herself to take a deep breath and stop them from flowing.

"Are you okay?" Piper's soft voice came from behind her, where she had come through the kitchen door.

"Yes," she said, swiping at her cheeks. "Sorry."

"Don't be sorry," Piper said. "Do you want to leave?"

"No, it's just a few hours. I need to keep busy."

"If you change your mind, just let me know. I'm finishing these cakes, but they can wait until the afternoon crew come in if you need me to man the front."

"Thanks, Piper. I appreciate that."

Her boss grabbed her in a quick, fierce hug before disappearing again into the kitchen. Glancing at her watch, she realized time was going to move very slowly until she was able to see Patrick again.

***

He was sitting on the porch when she arrived home, a vision to her sore and tired eyes. He stood as she came down the sidewalk, hanging his head and keeping his hands plunged into the pockets of his sweatshirt.

"Let's go inside," she suggested, not wanting Zoe's neighbors to be watching them. At the relieved look on his face, she could tell he was happy with the suggestion. "Do you want a drink or anything?"

"No, thanks," he said. He started to sit, then stood back up and paced the length of the small house. "I wanted to explain what happened."

"Please." She sat, pulling a pillow onto her lap as if it would shield her from the hurt to come.

"I got a message from your dad," he started. "Hoyt. Asking me to come see him and not to tell you. I didn't know what to do. My first instinct was to call you and ask you about it, but for some reason, I just couldn't."

"When was this?"

"Two days ago."

"The same day I went out with the girls?" At his nod, she frowned, thinking back to his unusual silence. "That's why you avoided me?"

"I didn't know what to do," he answered. "I figured he was going to ask me for money, and I didn't want to put you in that position. To have to think about what that meant, or just our differences."

"Because I have nothing," she said slowly. "I'm not entitled to the truth? I didn't realize that the lack of money in my account was a part of our relationship."

"It's not," he said quickly. "But mine kind of is. It's the third party, in a lot of ways. I have to think about things you don't have to worry about, and people will always be asking me for favors or handouts. It's uncomfortable for me, and it would have put you in an even more uncomfortable situation."

"No, it wouldn't have," she responded. "I would have told him to get lost. Just like I did the first time he tried."

"You think that now," he argued. "But if he had come and claimed some health issue, or if he played the good dad card, and I had to turn him away, you would have looked at me differently."

"Because you know me so well?" She felt anger start to brew. At herself, at him, at the universe for putting her in such a position to start with.

"I think I do," he said, meeting her eyes. "You close off when I try to talk about your past, or if I even make a suggestion about the future. This part of me, the fame and the money, is something we haven't really had to deal with yet. But it's there, and it will continue to be there. And based on your reluctance to talk about things that are big like this, I was afraid it would end us."

"Do you have any idea how hard my life has been?" Emma angrily swiped a tear from her cheek. "I lost my mother before I turned thirteen. Before I got my period for the first time, before I had my first kiss. I went to bed most nights not sure if I would still be in that house the next day, and even worse, some nights worried I wasn't safe. If I told you how many times I hid a knife under my pillow, would that help?"

"That's not—"

She cut him off with a wave of her hand as she stood up. "I grieve for my mother in an unhealthy way. Sometimes, inside, I'm still a scared twelve-year-old girl sitting in the social services office. That little girl is still inside me, and she wants her mom. I want her to hold me, tell me that it will be okay. I want her to brush my hair, teach me how to put lipstick on, or shop for a dress with me. And I can never have that again."

He stepped closer, holding his hands out as if he were going to touch her. The emotions she had been holding inside for over thirteen years were coming out, and if he touched her, it would only get worse. She stepped out of the way, seeing the hurt look on his face and not allowing it to soften her.

"You have no idea what it's like. To have no one. Not one single person that you can count on; that will always show up for you. You have your whole big, amazing family, and you take them for granted. You could pick up your phone and have a hundred people ready to make your problems go away. I have Zoe, and I'm so glad I found her again so that I can say that. But, yeah, I'm closed off. And it has nothing to do with you, Patrick," she said, her voice hitching on a sob. "I don't know how to be normal."

"I'm sorry," he whispered. "I didn't know—"

"And that's on me," she sobbed. "I was so struck by how perfect everything was, how perfect you are, that I didn't want to ruin it with the ugliness that's inside me. But it's there, Patrick. And you not trusting me, not wanting to let me be half of this relationship, that's not something I can do."

"This is not at all how I thought this would go," he said. "Please, let me fix this."

"Is that really why you came? To apologize and make this right? Or are you saying that now because you can see that I'm broken, and you feel like you need to fix me." She felt as if there wasn't enough oxygen in the room as she asked, and realized she was breathing in short pants, her chest feeling tight.

His inability to respond instantly was all the answer she needed, so she walked to the door and opened it for him. He stood silently staring at her for a long moment before crossing the room and starting to walk out. Just as she was about to close it, he stuck his hand in to stop the door.

"I came here because I'm broken too, and I don't know how to fix it. And if I'm being honest, I didn't know until this moment what I wanted to happen here. But now I know that I love you. And I don't want to give up on you, on us." He let go of the door and stepped back, his eyes meeting hers once more. "If I could go back in time, I would have told you about that message instantly. But I'm not sorry that we had this conversation, or that we have to face our ugly truths right now. If it's causing you more pain to have me here and you want me to leave, I will, but I would rather stay so we can work this out."

"Please leave," she heard herself say, barely able to breathe as she did. She slumped to the floor, pulling her knees in and making herself as small as possible, trying to keep the hurt tucked inside where it belonged.

Chapter 31

Patrick stumbled to his car, needing to take several deep breaths before he could even see straight enough to open the door. Once he was settled in the driver's seat, he pulled out his phone and managed to open a text to JJ. Shooting off a quick message asking his friend to rush Zoe home to be with Emma, he threw his phone down and put his head against the steering wheel.

How had this gone so wrong? All of his fears and worries were nothing in comparison to what she had gone through, and he had just made her pain so much worse. It had been selfish and self-centered of him to think that she wasn't worth risking a relationship on, that she would turn on him once the reality of his life hit her. The reality of who she was had hit him full force as the door closed on him, and it was all he could do not to go rip it down.

She had fought through life, looking for a safe place to land. And thought she had it with him, until he let his fears get in the way. Now he had ripped apart their relationship and torn her to pieces in the process. She was the type of woman who would have stayed by his side no matter what, and the realization was like getting hit by a bus.

He was jerked back to reality when someone banged on his window, and he turned to see an angry Zoe standing with her hands on her hips. Slowly emerging from the car, he leaned back on it for support and turned to face her.

"What did you do to her?" Zoe snarled, looking ready to hurt him.

"I screwed up," he admitted. "And I want to make it right. But staying there right now didn't see like the best thing to do, I think she needs you now."

"How did you screw up?"

"I didn't trust her," he said. "First, I thought your dad was going to hit me up for money, and I didn't tell her because I thought it would make her uncomfortable. Then, I thought maybe Hoyt was telling the truth, and that she had fooled me. And even after I was that dumb twice, I came here thinking it maybe wasn't a good idea between us. That maybe everything I have would be too much, and the reality of a life with me would be bad for her. And if I'm being totally honest, I thought that it would destroy me if I kept falling for her and lost her, so I came here thinking it was best to end it."

"You are such an idiot," Zoe raged. "She is so amazing and sweet, and she loves you. She trusted you completely."

"I know, and that kills me," he said, feeling miserable. "I told her that I'm not giving up on her, I just didn't want to be there causing her more pain."

"You should leave. I'll get her through this." Zoe turned and started towards the house.

"Will you let me know how she is?" He called to Zoe's back. "And tell her that I want to talk to her again when she's ready?"

"No, and no."

"Please, Zoe."

She turned and studied him for a minute, turning the door handle as she finally answered him. "I'll think about it."

***

The drive home was a blur, and he found himself heading to the stable rather than his house. Here, he could feel Emma's presence everywhere he looked. Whiskey seemed to glare at him before walking closer to nudge his shoulder, as if telling him to go get Emma. He stroked the horse's face until she turned away, then slowly walked from stall to stall, giving each horse some attention.

"What are you doing out here," Dan's voice demanded from the door to the stables. "We're inside waiting for you."

"I'm not in the mood, Dan."

"Yeah, me neither. I have better things to do than to listen to you cry about your love life, but I'm here. Let's go." Dan turned and walked back inside, slamming the door to the kitchen behind him.

Patrick walked slowly, as if the gallows were ahead. The glass on the kitchen door revealed his two brothers and his dad sitting at his kitchen island, each scowling into their own glass of what was likely his expensive whiskey. Pushing the door open, he stalked to a cabinet and pulled out a glass, downing a shot before pouring a second glass to sip as his family lectured him.

"What's happening, Patty?" His dad's gentle voice almost broke him, and he had to lean heavily on the granite countertop to stay on his feet.

"I wish I knew, Dad," he sighed. "Two days ago, everything was great. I was happy, you know? And then it all blew up."

"Sounds like you blew it up," Jake said in a mild voice. "Completely ignored the advice you asked dad and Stella for, and you didn't talk to us."

"I'm a grown-up," he snapped. "I don't run every decision I make past my older, wiser brothers."

"Never said I was wiser," Jake started before Dan cut him off with a snort.

"I am," Dan said when everyone looked at him.

"Thanks for the help, Danny," Jake rolled his eyes. "As I was saying, I don't think of it that way at all. If you have a problem, you can come to us. That's what brothers do."

"That's what family does," his dad corrected.

"That's what best friends do," Dan insisted, not one to be left out.

"I didn't think this was going to be such a big deal," he said. "At least at first. Or maybe I did, and that's why I hid it from Emma. Not hid, really, just that I didn't tell her. And then when her dad said all that, I believed it. I hate myself for that."

"You're being too hard on yourself," Ben said. "Your experience has been that people use you as a means to an end, and it's been that way since you were sixteen years old."

"Of course you're jaded," Dan added. "Anyone would be."

"But I should have known her well enough to know that what he was saying couldn't possibly be true. It was just enough details that he had, it made me question her."

"Details that half the town probably knows," Ben said. "It's a small town and people talk, especially about you. I don't know what he told you, but I would guess unless it was something very personal between you two, he just heard the gossip."

"You're right," he groaned. "I should have realized that. I have no excuse. I made it a thousand times worse by believing him and not going straight to her, and then again now by pouring salt in the wounds."

"Boys, give me a minute alone with your brother," Ben asked. Neither Jake or Dan moved a muscle, other than to sip their drinks. "I asked you two for some privacy."

"No offense, Dad, but we are well past that point in our lives. We're just going to listen from the other room, and we don't keep things from each other," Jake said. "They saw me through the worst days of my life and made sure I was okay. I can do the same for them."

"Same," Dan said. "When Calle went missing, neither of you hesitated, you were by my side the entire time. Even when there was gunfire, and you were in danger. And you both wouldn't leave me alone until I fixed things with Kendra."

"Fine," Ben sighed. "Patty, Stella said something the other night that had me thinking. Somehow this bubble you've been living in has kept you safely at arm's length from everyone. Fame has made it so you can have anyone do anything for you, and you don't have to emotionally connect. Even your closest friends out in Hollywood, you don't invite them here. They aren't people you let close, you just pass time with them."

"Maybe I just don't fit in out there," he shrugged. "A lot of people are like that, only go there for shoots and live elsewhere."

"It's not about where you live, it's about how you live. Your life has been so glamorous and looks perfect from the outside, but now I see how lonely it must be for you." Ben stood and crossed to where Patrick was leaning against the kitchen and put his hands on his shoulders. "You're going to get hurt in life. That's all there is to it. There is no way to avoid it, there is nothing you can do to make it easier. But what you can do is revel in the happy moments, soak in the love that's around you. That will get you through the bad times; that will be the light at the end of a dark tunnel."

His dad hugged him, a short, fierce hug that he felt straight through to his heart. "You are going to lose people you love, Patty. And no amount of money or fame will stop that from happening. Let yourself enjoy the time you have with them and not worry about the rest."

"He's right," Jake said softly. "I lost Jenna so young, and I walked away from all of you, and from Charlie. I thought it would be easier, save me from the pain of heartbreak ever again. Instead, it hurt more, and it only stopped when I came home and let myself live. And now I finally have happiness, and some peace, that I never would have found if I hadn't given myself the chance."

"I have nothing to compare this to," Dan said loftily. "Because I'm perfect. But I feel for you all."

"Yeah, leaving Kendra was brilliant," Jake said with an eye roll, grabbing an orange from the fruit bowl and throwing it at his brother.

The two of them started wrestling and calling each other names, laughing when Dan yelped in pain. "You are too old for that," Ben stated. "I'm leaving before anyone gets hurt."

"Thanks, Dad." Patrick walked his father to the door, ignoring the antics of his brothers behind him. Once the door closed behind him, he turned to find his brothers staring at him. "Are we getting drunk now?"

"We already called Mike and JJ to come up," Jake responded. "Danny-boy will try an Irish exit soon, so keep an eye on him."

"I will not," Dan sounded outraged, then looked at his watch. "Actually, I probably will. I need to help Calle with her homework. But you know where to find me."

Patrick poured more into his glass and passed the bottle to Jake, happy to dull the pain. He knew his father was right, and he hadn't really been living until now. Feeling this pain was a reminder that he could love, and now he just had to figure out how to make things right again. Losing Emma wasn't an option, at least not if he had anything to say about it.

***

Rolling over the next morning and reaching for Emma only to find an empty pillow made his already rolling stomach drop. His head raged, his stomach rolled, and he groaned as he pulled himself out of bed. A cold shower helped clear his head, and the smell of brewing coffee inspired him to throw on sweats and head downstairs rather than crawl back into bed.

Mike was at his island, head in his hands, while JJ stood sipping coffee with a smug smile on his face. "I told you to slow down," he was saying to Mike when Patrick appeared. "I can't believe you're out of bed."

"You were drinking with us," Patrick groaned. "Why are you so chipper?"

"I know my limits," JJ responded. "Eggs?"

"Absolutely not," Mike mumbled. "I will kill you if you even think of making something that smells like that."

"I would love to see you try, especially in your condition," JJ laughed. He passed Patrick a mug of black coffee and studied him. "You look rough too."

"Thanks," Patrick mumbled, taking the seat next to Mike. The door banged open behind them, and both groaned at the noise.

"Morning, boys," Jake's voice was even louder than usual through the quiet house. "Dan and I brought breakfast."

"Thank you, these two wouldn't let me make anything. What did you get?" JJ beckoned for them to come closer with the tray of coffees and bags of food.

"A little of everything," Dan said. "I assumed at least one person would need carbs this morning."

"Carbs and only carbs," Mike agreed. "Pass them all here."

"I need that too," Patrick reached for a muffin, ignoring Mike swatting at his hand.

"The real men can have breakfast sandwiches," Jake said, passing one to JJ.

"I think the real man was the one who stayed and drank with their friend last night, instead of running home or sneaking water," Mike countered. "Although I really don't want to talk about that."

"Before we have a test of our manliness," Jake said dryly. "We need to make a plan. According to Shea, Emma is miserable. Our Patty is miserable. We need to stop this before it brings us all down."

"How could it possibly impact you," Patrick asked before realizing what he said. "Did Shea see Emma?"

Jake nodded. "The girls showed up at Zoe's last night with margarita fixings. It wasn't pretty for Emma and Zoe, apparently. They might be worse off than you two."

"I told Zoe to let Emma know I wanted to talk when she was ready," Patrick told the room. "I can't show up there and upset her all over again."

"Trust me when I say this," Dan said. "But you have to keep showing up. Especially when you're the one who screwed up. She can tell you to leave, or say she doesn't want to see you again, but you keep trying."

"He is the king of the grovel," Jake said around a bite of his egg sandwich.

"You call it groveling, I call it romantic gestures." Dan grabbed a wrapped sandwich before JJ could take a second.

"You'll need flowers," JJ said, glaring at Dan. "Maybe some chocolate? What does she like."

"Whiskey," Patrick said.

"Please, no." Mike dropped his head again. "I can't even think about it."

"Not the drink," Patrick explained. "The horse."

"How are you going to bring a horse to her?" Dan asked, staring at him like he had lost his mind. "That horse can't be ridden, and you can't walk her all the way to town. It would freak her out, and it's just dangerous."

"No," Patrick shook his head before standing. "I need to think about it. She loves that horse."

"Don't make up some crisis just to get her here," Jake warned. "That won't end well."

"No, I'm not that dumb," he said. "I'll figure it out. Thanks for breakfast. And for last night. I'm lucky to have you all in my life." He headed for the back door, happy at least to have a growing idea about how to win Emma back.

Chapter 32

Emma was sipping coffee when her sister rolled out of the bedroom, hair sticking everywhere and still in her clothes from the night before. She tripped over her shoes on the way to the kitchen and waved off Emma's concern as she beelined to the coffee pot.

"How are you awake," Zoe groaned as she sank to the chair across from her.

"I didn't sleep great," Emma admitted. "I've been up for a bit."

"And you aren't hungover?"

"I was," she admitted. "But I think it's mostly passed now. How are you feeling?"

"Like I got hit by a train. I need to go back to bed. Are you okay?"

"I am, thanks to you and your friends."

"They're your friends too," Zoe said. "Don't forget that. They didn't come last night because I asked them to, they just showed up on their own."

"They are all so nice," Emma said. "I appreciate their support. Even though Patrick is their family, they still had my back."

"Their husbands put them through it," Zoe said. "They know what it's like to deal with the Burrows boys."

"They gave me some good advice, and I'm going to spend some time today thinking about what they said."

"While you do that, will you be terribly upset if I go back to put my head under my pillow?"

"No, go rest," Emma laughed. "I'm glad we have the day off, there is no way either of us could work today."

"No kidding," Zoe groaned. "And Kendra assured me that she would kick Patrick out before she would accept my resignation."

"That was nice of her," Emma smiled.

"It was," Zoe agreed as she started down the hall to her bedroom, turning just before she disappeared. "But for the record, I hope you two work it out. I saw you happy for months, and I think you can get it back."

"Thanks, Zo." She smiled at her sister before she walked away, then let the smile fall. Shockingly she still had more tears to cry, even as she tried to fight them off. She woke up missing Patrick and had spent hours trying to determine if she was brave enough to face him. Brave enough to fight for what she wanted.

She showered and dressed slowly, carefully choosing her outfit from her small wardrobe. The night before, Kendra and Shea had shown their support for her while also quietly encouraging her to talk to Patrick. She knew their efforts were genuine, they wanted both of them to be happy, and as she had stared at the ceiling all night, she realized they were right. Punishing him for one mistake wasn't fair, and it was hurting her as much as it was him.

The biggest risk she could take was giving him her whole heart, and she had done that without even realizing it. Turning her back on him now might close off her chances of ever having a happy life, as dramatic as it sounded. But they were right, she was afraid to open up to him and be a part of his life fully, and she either had to fully commit or let him go.

She left a note for Zoe and grabbed a water bottle for her walk up to his house. The day was getting warmer, and soon summer would fully arrive in Windsor Peak. She hoped she was there to see it, to splash in the lake with her friends, and see the town square come alive with festivals and movie nights. Piper had been regaling her with tales of summer activities for weeks, explaining that after a winter spent bundled inside, residents didn't waste a moment of the warm weather.

A truck was pulling down the long driveway of Patrick's house as she approached, and she forced herself to stay put on the road and not hide behind a tree. Jake's face became visible through the windshield as he slowed, and then stopped next to her. He rolled down the window and pushed sunglasses to the top of his head as he studied her.

"Hey," he said. "I'm glad to see you here."

"You are?" She couldn't hide the surprise from her voice as she asked.

He nodded, drumming his fingers on the steering wheel. "I know I was hard on you. Even yesterday, when I came to ask you questions, I was tough. I hope you'll forgive me, and know it was just out of concern for Patrick."

"Already forgiven," she said softly. Shea had appealed to her on her husband's behalf the night before, and Emma admitted that although she was intimidated by Jake, she wasn't angry with him.

"I was the last to leave, so he's alone now. If that's where you're headed."

"Is there anything else up this way?" She smiled slightly as she responded to him, appreciating him making it a little easier for her.

"A nice walk in the woods? But I wouldn't suggest that; the bears and moose are all out in full swing this time of year. And Patrick is far less scary than anything out there," he said. "I think he'll be happy to see you."

She huffed out a breath, surprised that he shared that. "Thanks." She watched as he rolled away down the mountain, leaving her to face Patrick alone. She started walking again, her pace slightly faster now that she knew she would see him in just a matter of minutes.

As she approached the house, she detoured from the front door. The only time she had ever gone in that way was the first night, when she helped him get inside. She thought of those first few hours, caring for him and unsure whether he would awaken and throw her out. Staying on the driveway, she headed toward the kitchen door, which was the one she always used. As she turned that way, her eye caught movement in the stables, and she ran in that direction.

"What are you doing," she cried, seeing Patrick in Whiskey's stall. The horse was pawing the ground and seemed agitated at his presence but turned toward her voice and hurried in her direction. She snatched a bridle off the wall next to the door and slipped it over the horse's head before grabbing a lead and clipping it on. Once she had them secured, she opened the door to the stall and started walking with the horse toward the paddock.

Patrick hurried behind her, but she ignored him as she took Whiskey into the open area and walked her slowly a few times around. "She could have killed you," she called over to where he now sat on the fence.

"I wouldn't have let that happen."

"Why were you in there? You know better, she's still afraid."

"Is she? She wasn't upset at first, only when I ran out of sugar. She let me brush her, and I was going to try and saddle her today if she seemed up to it."

"Why would you do that?" She turned to look at him, stunned at his thoughts. "The horse trainer has a plan for getting her ready to ride."

"I know, but I've been around horses my entire life. I thought I could help."

"That wasn't smart." She unclipped the lead and patted the horse on the side, signaling she could run. Whiskey took off at a fast clip, running off her demons. Emma watched for a moment before starting to make her way towards Patrick. "Why did you really do it?"

He jumped off the fence rail to stand in front of her, and she could see his hands shaking just before he stuck them in the back pocket of his jeans. "Honestly? I think of Whiskey as an extension of you. I know how much you love her. I thought if I could make this big gesture with her, you wouldn't be able to resist."

"What was the big gesture going to be?"

"I honestly hadn't thought that far ahead," he admitted. "In one, I could see myself riding her into town, and making a big speech about how the three of us are the same and belong together."

"That would be quite a spectacle," she said. "And one sure to land you on the front of all the magazine covers."

"I wouldn't be doing it for publicity." He looked insulted, and she reached over and touched his arm.

"I know that," she said softly. "I just meant that you want your privacy more than you want to make a public plea. And I don't need anything to be public. Just between us is perfect."

"I'm so sorry," he said in a rushed breath. "I should have told you right away when I got that message. And I certainly should have asked you if he was telling the truth, and not assumed he was. I've been alone for so long, it's just me against the world, really. I have a whole team of people who look after me, tell me what to do and where to go, but no one who ever really takes care of me. No one who would sit next to me all night, forcing me to take medicine and making sure I was alright."

"That's not true, you have your entire family," she said. "Look how quickly they came running when you came home, and how they rallied around both of us last night."

"They did," he nodded. "And they stopped me from running away, from just closing my eyes and letting all of this go away. That's been easy to do the last few years, just let someone else fix a problem for me. Even just facing Hoyt was a bigger thing for me than I realized, because I would never do that in my normal life. This whole thing had me questioning if I could handle losing you if I got in deeper."

"I get that," she said. "I feel the same way. It's scary, but I think you're worth it. I think we're worth it."

"You said I take my family for granted, and I think you're right. I let them take care of the hard stuff for me, just like I let my team do in California. And for a few years, I didn't see them as much as I should have, because I was so busy being newly famous. When Jenna died, it really kicked something off inside of me, though. I made sure to come here all the time, see Charlie, make sure my dad and Stella were okay," he said. "I've done everything I can to make their lives easier, more comfortable."

"I'm sorry I said that," she said. "That wasn't fair, and it was my jealousy of them that had me even think it."

"No, you were partly right. I had been keeping them all at bay a little, and now they've come crashing into all parts of my life, like it or not." They both laughed softly before he met her eyes again and reached for her hand. "The years since I went to Hollywood, I haven't had to deal with anything bad. I can hand off anything to my team, and they'll deal with it. My family helped me to see that's sheltered me so much, that now it's hard to let anyone in. I feel like a hypocrite that I said you were closed off, when I was too."

"I didn't see you as closed off at all," Emma argued. "You have been so generous and good to me, and you shared a lot about your family and life here."

"That's the easy stuff, problems I can solve with money or sharing this part of my life. But I held on to the fear that when you see my real life, you'll run the other way. I'm not here all the time," he said. "I'm on sets and running around the world, or in Los Angeles to be seen. This has been like a dream come true, being home for all these months and being with you, but it's not my real life. I didn't share a lot of that world with you, because I worried that my reality will scare you away."

"All I care about is being with you," she said through tears. "I've been so lonely, and these months with you have made me feel like I was safe for the first time ever. Wherever you are is where I want to be."

He grabbed her tightly, his nose pressed into her neck. "I love you, Emma. I'm sorry I didn't say it before, that I waited until we were in a crisis."

"I love you too." She was barely able to say the words before his lips crashed down onto hers. And she would have happily stayed locked in his arms there for days, if Whiskey hadn't objected to it by pushing at his arm until he laughed and stepped back.

"I guess she wants her time with you too," he said.

"Let me bring her back to her stall," she said. "Give her a quick brush and then I'm all yours." They had a lot to talk about, but the world felt right-side up again.

Chapter 33

"Hello," Patrick answered his cell phone without looking at the screen, something he rarely did. Hearing his publicist's voice on the other end had him realizing why he usually screened.

"Patrick," she gushed, making his name sound like six syllables in the process. "I'm so glad I caught you. We have some decisions to make, and you've been avoiding me. I went ahead and agreed to the Kimmel interview, because I know you wouldn't want to let your friend down."

"When is that?" He pulled a pen out and started jotting down the dates she rattled off. "That's going to keep me in Los Angeles for weeks."

"And New York. I know you hate it, but it's time to feed the beast. You can't stay hidden for this long and not come out in your glory to promote this new movie," she pointed out. "Plus, it's in your contract. Grin and bear it, sweetheart."

"I'll be there," he promised.

"I'm taking your word for it that your body is as perfect as ever," she said. "But if you need to get some sessions in with a trainer before this, let me know."

"I'm good," he said.

"Want me to have my assistant arrange your travel?" she offered before they hung up.

"No, thanks. I'll have mine take care of it," he answered, already lost in thought. He put the phone back and looked out the window to where Emma was in the paddock with Whiskey.

Things had been good between them over the last two weeks. They had talked for a long time about both of their insecurities, and how to overcome them. In addition, they had spent a significant amount of time with his family, dragging Zoe along with them.

The only thing she hadn't done was spend the night at his house or consider moving back into the cottage. She wouldn't discuss it, just kept telling him that they were having a fresh start and she wanted to make sure they weren't going too fast. Moving before he could change his mind, he crossed the kitchen and went to lean on the fence until she saw him and came closer.

"Hi," she smiled and kissed him. "Guess what? We got a saddle on Whiskey today."

"You did? That's amazing," he said, glancing over at the horse. "You didn't try to ride her, though?"

"No," she shook her head. "I know better than that. I just helped to keep her calm, and she did so good."

"Seems like she's finally settling down."

"Yes, the trainer said she's been doing good with him. I think she's going to be a great horse for you."

"Oh, she's your horse," he said. "No question about that. We just need to make sure she's safe, and that your skills are up for it."

"Patrick, you can't give me a horse," she rolled her eyes. "I can't afford it, and I can't accept a gift that big."

"Let's shelve that for a minute," he suggested, knowing he would eventually get his way. "I just had a call from my publicist, and it gave me an idea. How would you feel about coming to California with me for a few weeks?"

"Seriously?" Her eyes were wide, shock on her face.

"Yes, seriously. I want you to see that house, meet some of my friends. Get a taste of that life, in case you like me enough to make this long term. I do have to spend a lot of time there," he said.

"I know, I just—"

"Don't say no," he said in a rush. "Think about it. I know it seems like a long time, and if you get sick of me or California, you can come back. We can even invite Zoe and JJ out to visit, my brothers and their wives won't travel because of the babies coming soon, but I'm sure everyone else would."

"Patrick, if I'm with you, I'm going to be fine," she said softly. "It's just my job, and yes, I'd miss Zoe. And I don't want to miss summer here."

"We'll be back before summer kicks into gear, I promise. I don't want to say that money won't be an object, because I know it's important to you that you have your own money," he said slowly. "But for this one period of time, could you let me take care of everything? It's really important to me that you come, and that you have fun."

"What if I discover an incurable shopping addiction?" she teased, smiling up at him.

"Rodeo Drive would be happy to shut down for us," he laughed. "Is that a yes?"

"You know my only hesitation is my job, because I would follow you anywhere. And I don't want you to give me money or solve that problem. But I also don't want your money and my lack thereof to be an issue in our relationship," she said. "For that reason, yes, of course I'll go with you. There is no better way to figure out if we can survive our differences than to jump headfirst into them."

"And if you spend all my money on one shopping trip, we have nothing to worry about." He slung an arm around her as they walked to the stable, Whiskey following behind. If he had to leave Windsor Peak behind for a little while, at least he'd be taking a big piece of it with him.

***

A few days later, he enjoyed seeing the look on her face as they boarded a private plane bound for Los Angeles. As they buckled into their reclining seats, she leaned closer to him. "Is this really just for us?"

"It is," he nodded. "I wanted to take you home with me in style the first time. I do try to fly commercial as much as I can, but this is a nice perk of my job."

"This is my first time on a plane, and it's private," she whispered.

He laughed, grabbing her hand and happy that he could do this for her. He made a mental note to talk to his assistant about some other luxury trips, the idea of traveling held more appeal now that he knew she would be with him.

Hours later, they walked into his Malibu mansion and Emma stopped and stared. "This is not what I expected at all."

"No, I can see that." He studied it through his new perspective, the one of a man in love and who loved his home in

Vermont. This house was the opposite, with none of the warmth of the old farmhouse. White walls, glass everywhere, the beach visible from almost any spot you stood. "I bought this when I was in my early twenties, wanting to be in the trendy spot. Maybe it's time to sell this and find something else."

"Don't be silly," she swatted his arm. "I say one word and you're going to sell a house? We'll have fun and be comfortable here. I've never stayed anywhere right on the ocean like this, so I'm excited. Show me around, please."

He showed her the first floor, including the doors that slid all the way open to walk out to the deck, and beyond that, the beach. He hesitated before leading her up the stairs, unsure of what she would want to do. At the top of the landing, he opened the door to the master suite and waved her in.

"You can have this, and I can sleep down the hall, if you want," he said, suddenly feeling shy.

"No," she shook her head, then crossed to him. "I think we've been apart long enough, and I don't sleep nearly as well alone."

"Is that so?"

"You're so warm," she laughed before meeting his eyes with a sober gaze. "And I feel safe with you next to me."

He kissed her lightly, then pulled back and pointed at a door on the opposite side of the room. "Go check out the bathroom and the closet, then I'll meet you on the balcony."

A screech came from the closet before she ran across the room and stopped in front of him. "Whose clothes are those?"

"Mainly mine," he said, teasing her.

"The women's clothes," she ground out.

"Oh, those. I called a designer friend and told her about you, and she delivered them yesterday. Zoe helped me with sizing, so you can blame her if anything is too big or too small," he cautioned her. "Maria will come out tomorrow to help with the gowns you'll be needing."

"Gowns?" She stared at him, mouth agape.

"Yes," he nodded. "For the premieres, and the parties."

"I don't think I thought this through all the way—"

He grinned at her and pulled her close. "Don't worry, I'm here. I'll get you through. This is a weird land called Hollywood, where nothing makes sense, and everything is a party. You'll be fine."

"Promise me one thing," she challenged him.

"Anything."

"We have at least one night a week where we can wear pajamas and watch a crappy TV show while we eat junk food."

"Deal." He stuck out his hand and she shook it hard before turning to take in the view.

"This is really beautiful."

"It is," he said, studying her profile. She looked ethereal in the sparkling sunlight, like a dream come to life. She turned and saw him staring and bumped his hip.

"The view, you bozo."

"That too," he laughed. "But I think we should go look at some other houses while we're here. I hear great things about Pacific Palisades, maybe we can check it out."

"Sure, let me count my millions—" She screeched as he tossed her over his shoulder and carried her back into the bedroom, hitting a button on the way that would close the blinds automatically.

"I think we're done with the talking part of the evening," he said as he dropped her on the bed, landing next to her. "Unless you'd rather discuss real estate."

"As tempting as that sounds—" she dissolved into laughter as he tickled her, and all thoughts of California and his wild lifestyle flew out of both of their heads.

***

He sat on his couch mid-morning, sipping a vegetable smoothie his housekeeper had handed him, watching as Maria pinned dress after dress on Emma. "You couldn't have found a girl who wouldn't need alterations?"

"Maria, I know how you love a challenge."

"This one," Maria gestured up and down Emma's body. "She's perfect. But she's too skinny. No more dieting for you."

"I don't diet," Emma protested. "I work in a bakery, and I almost entirely exist on cereal."

"Don't tell anyone in Hollywood that," Maria ordered. "They'll hate you instantly. Next dress."

Maria's assistant swooped in and unzipped what she wore, dropping it to the floor. The first time it had happened, Emma had tried to cover herself and blushed. By the fourth time, she seemed almost accustomed to standing in front of everyone in her undergarments.

"Emma, I just got a text from JJ," he called to her. "He wants to go to some concert in Vegas in a few weeks when we're there for the fundraiser. I invited them to come here first, and then we can all go out together, if that's okay with you?"

"Sure," she said, looking puzzled. "That's odd, I never realized JJ was really into music."

"I know," he shrugged. "He just asked if I could get good seats for us, and that won't be an issue. I'll have someone book a hotel suite for all of us. Maybe we can time it so that we can fly back home with them."

"Back home," she said, grinning at him. "I am so happy that you consider Vermont to be home. Not that this isn't lovely, but Windsor Peak is more my speed. And Kendra said they are moving into your dad's house, so I can rent their apartment from them."

"What?" He frowned at her, and Maria had the good sense to excuse herself and run to the kitchen.

"She said Jake's house if finally done, and your dad and Stella asked her and Dan to move in," she explained. "So that apartment upstairs will be empty. As much as I love having the time with Zoe, her couch is not comfortable."

He stood and walked to her, taking her hands in his. Even with her standing on the small platform Maria had brought in, he was taller than her. He took in the powder blue, shimmery dress that was hugging her hips and making her eyes glow. The soft lips that he lived to make smile.

"I want you to live with me," he explained. "I thought I would be able to ask you when we got back from here, but of course my brothers have to mess that up. Please, say you'll think about it."

"I don't have to think about it, Patrick. Of course I want to live with you," she smiled at him and cupped his cheek with her hand. "As long as you'll still have me, even if I trip on a red carpet."

"No matter what, although I kind of hope that happens."

He kissed her and went to sit back down, Maria and her helpers rushing back in to continue. He watched her transition from country girl to glamour and couldn't wait to see what else would unfold during their lives together.

***

The next night, she fiddled with the small purse on her lap as they rode in the back of a limousine as she watched the streets of Los Angeles roll by. He reached over and took her hand, able to feel the nerves coming off her. "It's going to be fine."

"Fine? I'm about to walk a red carpet with my super famous boyfriend for the first time. I don't think there's any way you can call this fine."

He laughed, then sobered when she shot him a look. "I promise, it will be easier than you think. Just smile, and don't react to anything. My publicist will be right there to help, and if she takes you inside, I'll be right behind you. She's a pro, she knows when it's gotten to be too much."

"Okay," she said, taking a deep breath as the car came to a stop. The waiting photographers all swung to see who was in the car, and he climbed out first before reaching a hand in for her.

The cameras went crazy as she stepped out, a vision in a champagne-colored dress. He smiled with pride before tucking her hand into his arm and starting toward the press line. "It will be over before you know it, I promise."

They stopped and smiled for pictures before another car pulled up, and Natalie emerged. She caught sight of them and smiled, quickly walking toward him and kissing him on the cheek before doing the same to Emma.

"I'm glad we could time this out," she whispered. "Put an end to my jealous rage. I'm glad to meet you, Emma. I'll see you inside."

"Nice to meet you," Emma replied, looking stunned.

The reporters went crazy, all shouting for them to come closer to answer questions. Nat simply smiled and walked inside, leaving them alone to face the press.

"All of these people want a piece of you," Emma said to him. "Now I kind of get what your life is like."

"Oh, this is just the start," he laughed. "And it's not me they want, it's you. The mystery woman who stole my heart."

Heart content, loneliness abated, he smiled at her and reveled in the thought that she was everything he wanted. His happiness, his love, his home, all wrapped up in one person. The picture of them beaming at each other graced all the magazine covers the next week, and this time, he asked for a framed copy of the shot.

Acknowledgments

I have met so many amazing people since I started on this writing journey. This was a lifelong dream that I kept putting off, because I was scared. And every person who messages me, or comes to meet me at a signing event, helps ease the fear that such a big piece of me is out in the universe. I appreciate each and every one of you and want you to know how much your words mean to me.

BookTok, Bookstagram and my Facebook groups – especially my favorite, PMBC – have been so instrumental in keeping my motivation up. On days when I feel down, or that I just won't get it done, all I need to do is go and see how excited readers are about a book. It doesn't have to be my book, just the idea that we have our own little world where reading is celebrated keeps me on track.

Somehow when surfing Instagram one night, I came across a post from a charity called "All Seated in a Barn". It's run by a woman name Tahlia and her sister, and they rescue horses. It's brutal, heartbreaking work, and something I had never heard of before. These women attend auctions in Texas to save the lives of horses who have been surrendered or sold for cheap money. Horses that have worked on farms, or were a prized pet until the owner passed, are suddenly doomed to an awful fate in Mexico. Even purebred horses that trained to race are fighting for their lives, hoping that some kind soul will purchase them and give them a home. That's where the idea of Patrick finding Emma in his stable came from, and why I wanted to incorporate Whiskey into the story. Tahlia, thank you for all you do, and for sharing your hard work with us.

As always, my parents were the first readers of this book, and their unwavering support is so appreciated. Thank you for everything you do for me and our family, from proofreading to showing up at a rink for a freezing cold hockey game, we love you.

Jeff and Danielle, who are always in my corner and willing to lend an ear. I always know where to turn when I need support or honesty, a shoulder to cry on or a good laugh. Timmy, Tessa and Emmy, I can't wait until you're old enough to read all these books! You'll keep me writing forever, just with your excitement every time you see a new book. Now that this book is finally finished, I owe my two princesses a pedicure and Sephora day – now it's in writing, so it's official! Timmy, you and I will work on our project together all summer. I love you all!

Brendan and Conor, I love you both, and know you'll likely never read this. But I'm so proud of the men that you are becoming. You amaze me with your resilience and strength every day.

My friends who have helped me in this are too long a list to type out, just know I love you and appreciate you! From text messages to talking about name choices, trivia nights to cheering on our kids at games together – I appreciate you all and am so lucky to have such a circle.

Finally, to my husband Tom and our two boys, Camden and Calum. Who all have gotten used to me hunched over a computer at the dining room table, ignoring the chaos around me. They forgive me for the things I forget because my brain is in Windsor Peak, and they listen as I try to work out a problem that exists only in my imagination. I love you all.

And to answer questions in advance – yes, I will be returning to Windsor Peak! How could I ever leave this town and these people in the rearview mirror? Connect with me from one of the options on the next page to stay up to date on the next book in the series!

If you enjoyed this book, please remember to leave a review and share with friends and family! The more people who read it, the faster the next one will come out!

About the Author

Denise Latham lives in southeastern Massachusetts with her husband, two sons and two dogs. She obtained her BA in English Literature from Saint Michael's College many, many years ago, before shelving the idea of being a writer out of fear. After years of working in the "fun side" of academic publishing (aka marketing and trade shows) she obtained her nursing license and currently works on a dementia unit, where every day is a bright new day.

Connect with Denise by signing up for her newsletter at www.deniselatham.com, or finding her on Instagram or Facebook under @deniselathamwrites.

Made in United States
Orlando, FL
14 June 2024